Falsification and Assumption:

Jewish and Europeans Assassinated African Characters

by

Aheu Majok Lat

DORRANCE
PUBLISHING CO
EST. 1920
PITTSBURGH, PENNSYLVANIA 15238

Dorrance Publishing Co
585 Alpha Drive
Pittsburgh, PA 15238
Visit our website at *www.dorrancebookstore.com*

ISBN: 978-1-6386-7103-9
eISBN: 978-1-6386-7920-2

Tabel of Contents

ACKNOWLEDGMENTS

I owe many thanks to my wife, Anip Majok Nhier, and our children, who had encouraged me to make this piece of information to be possible. My daughter Yom, who devoted her time to edit this project, has thousands of appreciations from us to her, and may God bless her understanding more. Also, my friend John Thompson and his wife Lynn, Honorable Joseph Malwal Dong, who provided the book who wrote the Bible, the Sudanese community who encouraged me to prepare weekly Sermon notes, and Grace Community Church Pastors who provided free space for my preaching; otherwise, I wouldn't have concentrated on reading the Bible if challenges of preaching were not available. This book aims to let the theology and social anthropology experts find more information about Africans in the Bible. That idea was before I read a book by Nana Banchie Darkwah, Ph.D. I have narrated the history of seven nations which might be a clue leading to the facts of the Promised Land; to also answer? Why we are related socially to the Israelites, and why the Bible says we were given to the enemy as a ransom for the sake of Israelites. Secondly, this book will teach both our leader's spiritual leaders and African dictators how they should work together side by side—in other words, listening to the advice of spiritual leaders rather than their immediate families, relatives, and lobbyist. Should those families be destructive to the leaders, they focus on their stomachs and create disunity among the communities. Finally, using an oath is not funny to the leaders; you must have severe people, as I stated clearly. It will also give the guidelines on why they should not mishandle orphans and widows, especially those who emerged as guerrillas. Church leaders should not misappropriate church funds under the pretext that African believers do not pay much. They pocket the blessings and do not help vulnerable citizens, hoping they will get assistance. Thirdly, it may reflect the clear structure of human beings and where they were lodging before their sins. Egypt, Sudan, and Ethiopia were centered Movement of human beings for centuries before Christ's surface on earth physically, should you verify it in the reading of the Bible. Thousands of thanks go to South Sudan Nation website editors for allowing me to use valuable quotations from our leaders.

When Europeans and Jewish say Amen after praises and prayers, the word AMEN was coined up from the word "Aram Nhialic" in the Dinka language. Aram Nhialic means "we deny the occurrence of something bad" and that no one except God (Nhialic wende Madhol) will rescue us. HAL-LELUJAH, which translates in Dinka to mean "koc aa luui yai" literally means people praise and glorify God for any purpose of well-being. Calling Him to Rain was an apparent phenomenon before Christianity praises.

Aheu Majok Lat was born approximately 1963 in Maleng-Agok Rumbek East County, currently Lakes State-Rumbek in the Republic of South Sudan and went to primary school in the same village in 1972. He went to Rumbek Intermediate in 1978 and attended Juba Commercial Secondary School in 1981 before the cancer of "Kokora" of 1983. Later, he completed secondary school in Wau commercial in 1986. He worked in various places in Rumbek and Bahr El Ghazal University as a bookkeeper from 1994-1998. Then, he later came to the United States of America during the deadly civil war in Sudan in 1999. He obtained an associate degree in arts and accounting from Strayer University in North Carolina State in 2012. He also attended multiple Bible studies in Egypt; Bible Victory Institute (BVI), where he got Diploma and Global Leadership Training Center (GTCL) in Winston Salem in North Carolina State in 2008.

Preamble

PART ONE

"And you will know the truth, and the truth will make you free (Gospel of John 8:32 NIV)". I'm not an archaeologist, anthropologist, historian, nor a student of theology. However, I am an ordinary citizen devoted to the readings of the Bible with doubtfulness of it being a Jewish or European text since I began to involve myself to know precisely what the Bible means and how they spoke with God as they claimed. However, Dr. Nana Banchie Dark-wah reinforced my suspicions of where the text originated and who wrote it. As a linguistics scholar, he specifically mentioned where these Jewish tribes originated from during ancient Egyptian time and where they are found today in Africa. These tribes are found in present-day Niger, Nigeria, Ghana, and Ivory Coast, and I added South Sudan. Though I'm not a linguist, I have observed chapters containing suspicious verses and names, as I detail in many subtitles. The wisdom of Africans who imagined or prophesied the existence of living a God has been switched off by ancient Egyptian exciters before they became Jewish and Europeans, later assassinating Africans and humiliating us, for example, calling us evil, demonic, satanic, and involved in witchcraft. All those descriptions were given to us because of European Christian doctrine. Indigenous Africans had their own way of worshiping "Nhialic Wende Madhol" God before encountering European Christianity.

Europeans switched it around and deceived the world community by claiming to be called by Almighty God. Though evangelist Europeans fooled indigenous Africans who joined their school of writing and reading during colonialism and slavery, our native senior elders remained vigilant, questioning what type of God besides "Nhialic Wende Madhol" existed before you. Our native elders often told us, "Do you think we didn't know God before you sons and daughters?". We were fooled by evangelists Europeans, yet our native senior elders remained vigilant questioning what type of God besides" Nhailic Wende Madhol?" It is true; they were right, and I personally believed they were intelligent more than our assumption of undermining them. This retaliation against black communities worldwide ultimately suggests that the pretension and assumption of white people's superior thinking has no evidence of tangible things they created more than modifying what was already existing like biblical doctrine. The people who made a mass departure from Ancient Egyptian came back and translated the Bible with bad wishes for indigenous Africans after their skin assimilated to be white to conceal tracing their originality.

Also, our physical blindness and misinterpretation of the Bible made Europeans to deceive African tribe owners, and the whole world not to figure out some details like after Abraham rescued his nephew Lot. He came back with war material equipment, and he was blessed by Melchizedek, a priest of God Most High in Genesis 14: 18&19. Does this not support Nana Banchie Darkwah Ph.D. theory that they learned of the existence of God from Ancient Egyptians before they emigrated to Europe. If we accept that Jewish people spoke with God, how could Abraham get the blessing in Genesis, and how did the wisdom of Egyptian instruct Moses if they were not African? In other words, Africans worshipping God existed before they were Jewish and spoke with God as they claimed. How could Abraham get a blessing from the priest of God of Most High, and subsequently, he became the father of nations and a blessing from another human being before? Was it not an indication that the chosen people, including those who changed their names after the exodus, were Ancient Egyptian or African peoples for sure? Another point is the description of Cush: (Kuc in Agar Dinka in the Republic of South Sudan) that we are a "tall, smooth-skinned, Mighty and Aggressive Nation!" Could you believe such descriptions were about Jewish and Israelites who were white Europeans? Even if they spoke with God and wrote the Bible, they wouldn't describe us wonderfully like that, and therefore, I am extremely supported by Nana Banchie Darkwah truths because white people who enslaved black communities couldn't describe us like that. My thanks go to our Ancestors of Ancient Egyptian Africans who wrote the Bible; however, it was plagiarized by those who were denying themselves that they were not originated from indigenous African tribes before they exited to Europe and came back to compile, translate, edit, and own our Ancestors' ideas, documents, doctrines, and philosophy.

6

Still, they had left signals behind during the translations from Ancient Egyptian African names. The attempt of Charles R. Darwin of evolutionist was evidence of denying or erasing what African black people who wrote the Bible have done. It was a network lies that never held water of the reality of his attempt; in other words, it was a distorting attempt to deny black Africans who wrote the Bible. Another attempt was the introduction of the so-called New Testament, in which they were trying to dismiss the African invention. They were switching some words from the Old Testament. "Nhialic" or God has no Old and New; it is the same God. Nevertheless, in Hebrews, His word says, "I'm like yesterday, today, and forever" however, I was wondering how they coin the new God apart from what they called Old Testament. If Jewish scholars and Europeans have had accepted that those who wrote the Bible were not of Jewish or European origin, they would have saved their dignity and be honest about plagiarizing important documents and references rather than being humiliated by the legitimate sons of Africa. Another important story I heard, Jewish and European never had a clue connection too, was honey's story in the Bible. Honey is holy, and that is why it is mentioned in the Bible. According to the story, honey is holy no one may steal it. A piece of liquid will be dipping down, and the stealer may not notice; they will try to steal it in your own house. My parents told me that honey is "Nhialic" (God) and an important product to Him, and you can't steal it. I emphasized five similarities later in chapter five. If Jewish Israelites deny that they did not originate from African tribes or were not black, why are there social similarities in the faith book they claimed while they are white? How did such close cultural and linguistic connections occur between people who were not living in the same place? How were Africans simultaneously practicing the same customs in the Bible if Jewish people or Europeans wrote the Bible? One question I had was how others with white skins color have- certain similarities rooted in African tribes. Once I read "The Africans Who Wrote the Bible: Ancient Secrets Africa and Christianity have never told," all my hesitations were supported. Reading the Bible was like somebody drowning who left nothing when they were swimming to help. Still, all my predications and consciousness prevailed that African names were corrupted, and that's why information about the socio-economic, political, and spiritual similarities was always left out. Dr. Nana revealed many things about Christianity that I was personally struggling with. An important observation confirmed was the imagination of Christian faith were Black African ideas and are still black! Even now, many paintings or imaginations of Angels by European creators contain Black angels. Is this not an indication that they also secretly knew that the God and angels they were worshipping were black? White people's superiority was based on skins color, which they failed to indicate in the claim book of faith how their skins color came to be during creation. They just reached the dead-end of lying that being black is cursed, and the same white scholars confirmed biblical stories' existing before they plagiarized from the places inhabited by Ancient Egyptian Black communities. If the Bible, which everyone worldwide accepts to be something communicated by God who selected Jewish people as His chosen people, and Jewish people are descendants of Ancient Egyptians who were black African. Then why were they hiding these facts for so long? Thankfully, the text written by Dr. Nana exposes these lies that African people do not know the roots and authors who wrote the text of the Bible. There is the parable of Dinka Agar which says, "Adopting someone's child may not fit in your womb." That's what happened to the white Europeans and Jewish. Being a Black person has made African women feel inadequate to the point they devalue the same skin Solomon was proud of on his lover, but African women should remember before they bleach themselves that their skins is the skin of their ancestors who invented the book of faith to the world. Whatever the Bible attributed, as negative traits affecting us as Black Africans came from the compiling, translating, and editing by those who called themselves Jewish and Europeans today. Isaiah 43:3&4 speaks on how God will punish Sudan and that Sudanese were paid as ransom for the Israelites. I believe the interpretation of this verse is distorted because the original ideas of the Bible originated from African tribes. If we were paid as a ransom, then who bailed us out from captivity? As a result, it was unacceptable to believe the two verses above. Dinka Agar were participants in inventing the imagination faith or the so-called Pagan, which African tribes created before they became Europeans and, twisting the famous faith of the world. "According to the Bible, the Jewish peoples supposedly went to Ancient Egypt because of hunger. If these hungry people have survived up to today, what would have made the people that feed these hungry people to disappeared from the face of the earth? P.11." Ph.D. Nana Banchie Darkwah. Reinventing and enslaving our understanding to the point of denying the validity of our "paganistic" celebrations was their victory over Africans, and therefore, they may assume that the capacity of our understanding disappeared. When our abilities of understanding and analogy of questioning similarities were perverting, consequently, we remained vulnerable to any point of no choice not to accept any point of lies. I stated clearly that the Biblical truths of God's imagination were sources where we will be able to build an open society of multi-coexistence worldwide, should God's truths never been distorted to create human classes of superiority and inferiority. This book is not meant to be used to ignite explosive outrageous between color communities and their opponents of the world, but it is correcting and ironing out wrong ideas toward people of color. In other words, I elaborated clearly how human beings contracted white skins, which made others arrogant toward people of color, which had nothing to do with being special to the Creator because of your skins, however, the imagination of faith, which was and is accepted worldwide, was an idea of Ancient Egyptians text, not Israelites nor European as we have believed for tow thousands of years back. If this Bible text proves beyond doubt, indigenous Africans wrote the popular faith book accepted wherever human being exists, what else would the white communities have as powerful more than the Book of Faith? If white European scholars and Jewish scholars were aware that Jewish did not write the Bible, would they still have the wealth and military power that they currently hold in the world? Readers should understand me; I'm not claiming wealth; I'm indicating the superiority thinking and origination of Jewish people. If the Bible, being the first book on earth after the creation of human beings, was written by Africans, or based on African ideas, what else would whites supremacists today have above the Bible? Being evil is not having black skin as others believe, however; it is about your attitudes and actions of assassinating leaders of other countries. That is an evil act among the individual colonialist.

Secondly, I'm addressing ignorant African tribal or clan leaders who treat their community so inhumanely that they must flee their homelands and be hated immigrants around the globe.   They made the African continent known as a continent of diseases, starvation, and suffering of civil wars because of their greediness, stubbornness, and stupidity Leadership. They abuse power and don't become tired of being president for too long. Thirdly, according to the Bible, I narrated the subsequent roots of white skin and where it came about, which disputes that they were not made especially because of their skins. In addition, I address social closeness between Dinka groups of the Nilotic people and Jewish people. Dinkas were governing themselves before the emergence of Christianity or Judaism because Biblical facts show that the people who inhabited the Middle East and African were brothers and sisters based on the Bible.

By then, the Exodusters of Ancient Egypt was using sacrifices for well-being, atonement, the scapegoat (Machar Anyuon Ater Dut in Dinka Agar), for blessings as well as removing any misfortune. These traditions are the same with Nilotic peoples in Africa before those who called themselves Jewish stole these traditions and beliefs and revealed different stages of worshipping of today. These traditions were photocopied from Ancient Egyptians and African tribes, including the Dinka before they were pushed further south to Sudan by following the Nile River for their survival. The word "Christianity" or "Christians" was introduced for the first time in Acts chapter eleven during apostles. Many scholars may disagree with me because of today's skins and religious affiliation, nevertheless; the historical background may justify the reality before I read a book by Dr. Nana Banchie Darkwah. Most of scholars favored skins and religious differences, whereas roots of existences identified my claim. As I explained, Christianity doctrine forgery created confusion by creating a caste system in Christianity and Islam globally where color communities were subjected to brutality, suffering, misrepresentation, and misinterpretation of what indigenous Africans originally wrote in the Bible. This philosophy is like a mirror. Suppose African Christians were reading and worshipping Gods and do not see the reflection of the previous life of our ancestors and generations of today. In that case, our mindset, misinterpretation, and observational verses are dead. I quoted in every chapter by studying the Bible with critical analysis and closely questioning verses where you see yourself in those verses. The differences between global communities are not deeply rooted in blood, however; the controversial behaviors from colonialist supremacist attitudes toward people of color are the real concern of our differences. Also, it examines the usefulness of same-sex marriages and the sinned of polygamists according to westerners, which ones is based on Biblical principles of gay marriages and polygamists if the Bible was theirs? Finally, people of color should not rely on physical power to resist their opponents. The essential power of the twenty-first century remains in economic power, which brings more world alliances regardless of their races and religions.

Suppose the Black community strengthens itself by forging the best financial structure globally and avoiding excessive corruption in Africa. In that case, the military strength factor will emerge through a strong economy of no doubtfulness. You could see now how Jewish communities are respected though they knew their roots in Africa secretly, yet the same wisdom they stole from many tribal Africans made them the wealthiest of the world. I explained clearly; the consequences of political violence, whorings, and corruption in all forms from an ancient people from their time and down the road all way to us in multiple chapters. Furthermore, please read Leviticus from chapter one to the end to understand the activities of changing skins due to a leprous disease that changed the skin from black to white or brown, and Numbers 12: 10 and 2 Kings 5: 27 respectively. I'm aware many tribes in South Sudan may misunderstood me because of mentioning Dinka, however; the Bible is a world book if you don't see verses revealing your tribes! That is your ethnic problem not my pride as a Dinka. If other African tribes, or South Sudanese are not encountering similarities in the Bible, do not question us, may be fall of your ancestors' and you were reading the Bible and worshipping the God you do not know to please Europeans, and Jewish not questioning similarities because you were so much concerned of seeing Heaven.

CHAPTER ONE

The idea of Creation in the Beginning:

"God hath made the universe, and he hath created all that therein is He is Creator of what is in this world, of what was, of what is, what shall be. He is the Creator of the world, and it was He who fashioned it with His hands before there was any beginning, and he established it with that which went forth from him. He is the Creator of the heaven, and the earth, and the deep, and waters, and mountains, God had stretched out the heavens and founded the earth. What His heart conceived came to pass straightway, and when He had spoken His words came to pass, and it shall endure forever" (from the Africans who wrote the Bible Ancient secret Africa and Christianity Have Never Told page, 294),2000). That was how an idea that Ancient Egyptians and African tribes had before the text was plagiarized by those who were black Africans after the exodus from Egypt to Europe.

Visualizing the above quotation properly, you would figure out exactly the text of Faith book called Bible existed before five thousand years as purely African Tribes idea not Jewish, Israelites, nor Europeans.

In 2013, I was in my country South Sudan enjoying the third Anniversary of our independence. Governor of Lakes State, general Matur Chut Dhuol, allowed Derr Makuer Gol, who is a traditional Dinka spiritual leader, to lead the prayers! Native spiritual leaders led anniversary prayers first before the bishops. When this happened, groups of ignorant pastors left the event thinking that paganism had blessed the occasion. Hence, the Governor was conscious of affirmative feelings that we knew "Nhialic Wende Madhol" or "God" by the imagination of the Ancient Egyptians, the Akan in Ghana, and the Dinka Agar in present-day South Sudan. The angry pastors do not even have basic principles of interpretation nor visualize the close connection of what they called paganism to what was plagiarized to become the doctrine of modern Christianity and Judaism. The author of "Who Wrote the Bible?" emphasized that George Smith of the British Department of Oriental Antiquities found clay tablets with stories of Creation and the fall of man as narrated in the Bible. Smith and his colleagues also found the myths of Paradise, the Flood, and the Tower of Babylon in the folklore of Ancient Egypt and several other places (p.295). That was paramount where Jieng or Dinka Tribes have known the story of Noah who was left on earth after the flood, in other words "Thou nyieg Noi Nhial" which means Death left Noah alone in Dinka. Such emphasizing points above are what western scholars called oral stories, however; Western scholars depended on black Africans' information they stole in the previous stories and pretended to legitimatize them. Suppose Ancient Egyptians were black Africans that were creative and intelligent. What do you think would prevent they Exodusters whom became Israelites and Europeans from forging Ancient Egyptians ideas into stories of Biblical documents to the whole world for thousands of years? What I illustrated in the introduction and above are new clues of where the documents of the Bible originated and whose authors and ideas overwhelmingly globally become essential. Also, I question why polygamy became a sinned to those who are practicing Christianity today. Why has polygamy been given a negative connotation when the Bible said: "go and multiple yourself." The practice of polygamy was an indication that those who composed Biblical documents were indigenous Africans.

Whatever the readers will be encountering within this chapter and others are false to those who legitimized it and valuable to the Akan and Dinka Agar. They imagined the stories that Exodusters of Ancient Egyptians compiled, edited, and translated into the Greek Language to be Biblical documents of today, not the Jewish and Europeans. Before those indigenous Africans left Egypt for Europe, there was nothing called "Israelites" or "Jewish" people. However, the idea of an untouchable God was already in existence for worshipping from Ancient Egyptians. When Leprosy erupted in another part of Egypt, those indigenous Akan and other African tribes were chased way heading to Europe under the name called "Afrim People", and that's where they acquired white skins. I mentioned somewhere before I read the work of Nana Banchie Darkwah, Ph.D. Leprosy was the cause of having white skin, and Moses was educated according to Egyptian wisdom! If they were white, why they are claiming superiority today while the wisdom of indigenous Africans instructed their famous leader, whom they asserted he spoke with God? That word instruction by the wisdom of Egyptians proved the existence of indigenous Africans worshipping before Moses claimed that he had spoken with God. Again, you can see below and the rest of the chapters how they flipped up the biblical stories for thousands of years, as they were called by "untouchable" God.

In 1998 when I was attending the Bible studies course in Egypt, one instructor from America was lecturing something in (Exodus Chapter 12:7,8& 22,23) relevant to a Jieng Agar performance ritual. I told the instructor that we do the same things in our tribe at present. I was almost suspended because I was comparing "pagan" rituals with Almighty God. Thus, Nana Banchie Darkwah Ph. D asserted what I knew something was being covered up. Other evidence was the repetition of the words "I was there before FOUNDATION of the world," which attributed to Jesus Christ who said that he was in existence before the foundation of the world (see Proverbs 8:22-35; Revelation 17:8) and many times in Gospel of John from the beginning to the end). These words "I was there before the foundation of the world" were evidence of plagiarism and already transposing existential information. There were no Israelite nations or evidence to support the baseless claim that Jewish people have special status with God. A D.N.A study confirmed my verification of similarities between Jewish people and Africans, proving that Israelites or Jewish originated from many African tribes. Therefore, the information they compiled and translated into many languages was purely from Africans who were the inventors. All the information in the Bible is genuine except that attribution of being Jewish and Europeans, which is not true and that's what I'm clarifying here. Almighty God did not call them "special" people. The idea that indigenous Africans were subordinate to the Almighty God is a lie. God spoke to the Akan, who are in Ghana, and Jieng Agar, in Sudan and South Sudan, because of transposing their names into Israelites and Jewish who are predominately Israelites today. All Biblical stories existed before those who called themselves Jewish existed; they had tribal African names, worshipping African Gods and exited Africa with the information they knew already and changed their names. Christians could verify below the two rivers passing through Sudan, Ethiopia, and other rivers in present-day Iraq; if Jewish Europeans wrote the Bible, they wouldn't mention rivers in Africa.

All things were visible when their eyes opened and, they knew they were naked and even heard the voice of the Lord. Sins come from three things: choice of the eyes, choice of the flesh, and choice of the pride life. When these three things overtake human desires, there will be consequences. "When the woman saw that the fruit of the tree was good for food and pleasing to the eye, and also desirable for gaining wisdom, she took some and ate it. She also gave some to her husband, who was with her, and he ate it.

Then their eyes were open, and they realized their nakedness, and they had to hide themselves, as far as God created human beings according to His image; he was following them closely in the Garden. There were intermarriages between human beings and sons of the Lord (Genesis 6:2, 4). As a result of that interaction, God limited the life of human beings to a hundred and twenty years. These Giants were on the earth in those days, and after that, when the sons of God came in unto the daughters of man and they bear children to them, the same became mighty men which were of old, men of renown. Interestingly, these Giants were mentioned in (Numbers 13: 32 and 33) and (Luke 17; 27). Some of the Giants were wiped out during the Great Flood; however, some remnants remained at large, and many Scholars say they are categories among the tallest people in the Bible. Indigenous Jewish are still worshipping the concepts they knew before they left Egypt and that is why they do not believe in Jesus Christ though they are white.

MAP SHOWING THE TWO RIVERS WATERING THE GARDEN OF EDEN IN SUDAN (LAND OF CUSH OR ETHIOPIA) OTHER TOW RIVERS ARE FOUND IN IRAQ.

As I mentioned earlier, Adam and Eve were living supernaturally in Eden. "And a river went out of Eden to water the garden, and from there it was divided and became into four branches. The name of the first is Pishon: it is the one that flows around the whole land of Havilah, where there's gold, and the gold of that land is good: there is bdellium and the onyx stone" (Genesis 2:10). Havilah was one of Cush's sons (check Genesis chapter ten, because of that description, the first river was the Blue Nile of today. This is where the word Nilotic came about). The gold mentioned during the Creation still exists in the Blue Nile, the land of Havilah connects the Funj kingdom of Sudan and Ethiopia, as you can see on the map above. These gold and other resources have brought many sufferings to the people living in that area for long centuries of humankind. It's the cause of slavery that provided the manpower for many colonists like Mohammed Ali Pasha, because fighting over resources started thousands of years before us. The amazing point I will leave to the experts is the name of Ethiopians and Havilah, which were mentioned earlier before the beginning of Creation. Scholars, theologians, archaeologists, and anthropologists ask yourself how God predicted these two names before creating Adam.

Anyway, we may consider these two names might be the origin of human beings. The Ethiopian name was at the beginning of Creation, although another name later appeared called Abash. The name of the Second River is Gi-hon; it is the one that flows around the whole land of Cush. In other translation, that river is the White Nile of our present time. (Genesis 2:13) The Ham descendants completed those ancient people: they created an agricultural way of survival, legal codes of behavior, systems of government, and religious beliefs. According to Humanity Book 101, The Origins of Western Culture by Cunningham I. Reich, the basic advances that made possible the growth of western civilization were first achieved by the earlier civilization of the ancient Middle East. (Egyptians are not a part of the Middle East). That is an assumption made by Arabs. Geographically, Egypt is part of the African Continent; therefore, those ancient people were Africans. Those ancient peoples were the first who systematically produced food, mined and processed metals, organized themselves into cities, devised legal and moral codes of behavior, together with systems of government and religion). Arabs are generally related to Abraham and Lot's uncles' son, who occupied present-day Jordan, where he settled.

When Abraham had Hagar, ancient people existing in Egypt according to Genesis 16:1— Abraham had a slave-girl named Hagar. The descendants of Ham after the Flood are the following: Cush, and Miz-ram, (Egypt), and put, and Canaan. Africans came out from Cush, Miz-ram became the Egyptians of today, Puts are found in Somalia and Djibouti, and Canaan is the Philistines. The Arabians' origin was from Ham; Westerners tried to amend historical facts simply because they do not have the proper picture. For example, they say Africans have oral history, which means unwritten documents, and at the same time, they have stated that civilization started in Africa.

How do people have a civilization if they were not writing and documenting events? How did they trace the civilized way of life if it was not written? That's a contradiction to the Western Historians and Scholars. I mentioned the two rivers previously, what they were called at that time, and their present names. These rivers also passed through a place called Sudan (Land of Cush). Only four rivers are mentioned in the Bible. The Creation of many rivers' division came one day when Eber bore two sons: "The name of one was Peleg; for his days was the earth divided; and his brother's name was Joktan" (Genesis 10: 25). God did not create all rivers, oceans, and gulf without any reason; the first four rivers were watering the Garden of Eden where Adam and Eve were living. The second were expansions of oceans, gulfs, and small rivers because of Peleg. So that tells the readers when seas and the other gulfs were created and the reasons.

Whenever the Creator mentioned something in the Bible, it didn't happen day after day. He created each one in different periods of times because the Bible says: "But, beloved, be not ignorant of this one thing, that one day is with the lord as a thousand years, and a thousand years as one day" (2 Peter 3:8 KJV). That's exactly how things were created. As we imagined, God couldn't make things randomly—He is not a reckless De Ciek (Creator).

The beginning of nailing Jesus spiritually started in Genesis Chapter-three Verses fifteen. Its meaning was confirmed in Romans Chapter Sixteen Verses twenty and Hebrews Chapter Nine Verse twenty-six. Here is what

Bible says with regards to what I mentioned above: "For then must he often have suffered since the foundation of the world: but now once in the end of the world hath he appeared to put away sins the sacrifice of himself" (Hebrews 9:26 KJV). "And the God of peace shall bruise Satan under your feet shortly. The grace of our Lord Jesus Christ is with you Amen" (Roman 16:20 and in Proverbs 8:22-31). Therefore, Jesus' existence before the foundation as the spirit of God was not in a physical body.

When God said, "Let us make man in our image, after our likeness; and let them have dominion over the fish of the sea, and over the fowl of the air, and over the cattle, and over the all the earth, and over every creeping thing that crept upon the earth," He meant three things: Himself, the Holy Spirit, and physical body of the dust. Adam was also given authority in advance. After Adam and his wife sinned, they began to have a sexual relationship. Before they sinned, they did not have sexual activities, indicating that they lived like Angels in the Garden of Eden. They were clothed by the glory of God before they ate from the Tree of Good and Evil. As the Bible mentioned, immediately after they sinned, they were chased away from supernatural Eden into natural Eden or into the ground. (Genesis 3:23- 24). God predicted that human beings who were in his mind would sin, and that's why His Son was nailed spiritually before being physically nailed to the cross. Two important things that must be questioned here are:

How did the children of Adam get married? Did the brothers and sisters marry amongst themselves? If not, then they had marriages with the Angels of the Lord. Also, after Cain killed his brother Abel, God instructed people not to harm him for his guilt, and before that. He gave him a mark. Then Cain walked away from the presence of the Lord, and dwelt in the land of Nod, on the east of Eden. And from there he knew his wife; and she conceived and bore Enoch: and he built a city, after the name of his son Enoch. Who was Nod living in the east of Eden? Is he one of the Giants? Is this mark related to being in Asia? This is because these groups of human beings live in the eastern part of the world, and their eyes are different from others. God said to them, be fruitful, multiply, replenish the earth, and subdue it: and have dominion over the fish of the sea, and over the fowl of the air, and over every living thing that moved upon the earth. The meaning of the word replenish is to fill something again or make something complete again. Furthermore, the other word is subduing, which means to control someone, especially by using force. Before I make many claims about how this might be correct information, let's look at Jeremiah 4:23-29 KJV (or Jeremiah 4: 23-29 NIV).

In KJV, "I beheld the earth, and lo, it was without form, and void; and the heavens, and they had no light. I beheld the mountains and moved lightly. I beheld, and, lo, there was no man, and all the birds of the heavens fled. I beheld, and lo, the fruitful place was a wilderness, and all the cities thereof were broken down at the presence of the Lord, and by his fierce anger. For thus hath the Lord said, 'The whole land shall be desolate; yet will I not make a full end. For this shall the earth be black: because I have spoken it, I have purposed it, and will not repent; neither will I turn back from it. The whole city shall flee for the noise of the horsemen and bowmen; they shall go into thickets and climb up upon the rocks: every city shall be forsaken, and not a man dwell therein'" (Jeremiah 4:23-29 KJV).

"I looked on the earth, and lo, it was waste and void; and to the heavens, and lo, they had no light. I looked on the mountains, and lo, they are quaking, and all hills moved to and from I looked, and lo, there was no one at all, and all the birds of the air had fled. I looked, and lo, the fruitful land was a desert, and its cities were laid in ruins before his fierce anger. For thus says the Lord: 'The whole land shall be a desolation, yet I will not make a full end. Because of this earth shall mourn, and the heavens above grow black; for I have spoken, I have purposed; I have not relented nor, will I turn back. At the noise of horseman and archer every town takes to flight; they enter thickets; they climb among rocks; all the towns are forsaken, and no one lives in them" (Jeremiah 4:23-29 NRSV). These two translations were not predicting what would happen in the future to humankind. No, it's an explanation of the past event. We shouldn't be emotional, not considering what 'replenish' means. Verses Twenty-four and Twenty-five clearly explain what happened already—he looks at mountains, hills, and cities...were ruins, in other words, destroyed totally. The fact of the matter is that there were no cities without human beings, but because of mankind, cities were destroyed. That's where replenish comes about. There are no words in the Bible put there for fun or to entertain readers without reflecting on past events or the future to come. The other important information we should pay close attention to is the words "birds of heavens," which supports my point: after Adam was created, he lived in the supernatural Eden. The birds of that time were birds living in the heavens, not the natural Eden of today. Being arrogant to deny the facts simply because there is no scientific proof should not blind others because God is not a product of science. The opposite is this: God created scientists, lawyers, economists, and the rest of the specialists. Evolutionists say that human beings have developed from different forms of life not created by God. However, the funny thing that they did not elaborate very much on is who named them according to how we know each of them today? The attitude of evolutionists had made considerable damage to the faith of God's existence. Apostle Paul says these statements in Romans Chapter-three Verse four: "By no means although everyone is a liar, let God be proved true, as it is written, so that way be justified in your words, and prevail in your judging." God demonstrated His capacity during Creation and what He does when He gets angry at human beings. These are signs of the father's responsibility, like what we carry out in our capacity as parents. God disciplines His people, whereas evolutionists do not have directives on how we should conduct our daily businesses if their findings were correct. God has commanded Adam to be responsible for everything, in other words, an authority (dominion). "God brought all things He created to let Adam name them, and it is how we knew each category today" (Genesis 2:19). The Evolutionists' idea was to have human beings discuss the fallacies of their thinking. Desolate is the state of being desolated or laid, waste; ruin; solitariness; destitution, gloominess.

2)   A place or country wasted and forsaken.

3)   The act of desolation or lying waste; destruction of inhabitants; depopulation.

According to these definitions, it means destruction took place before Adam because when God was looking down, he saw the earth was empty (void), and there was no light. The mountains and hills were trembling or had moved slightly, and there was no man, and all birds of heavens fled. All the cities were broken down in the presence of the Lord, which is Jesus as spirit. The power of God made even the heavens so black because He had spoken. But the interesting point is that God never repented for what He had done. Although the Bible doesn't tell us whether there was the first Creation,

21

these words 'never repent' give you a clue something had been destroyed before Adam was made. Let me illustrate the difference between never repenting and repenting. Repent, neither a formal word, means to be sorry for something that you have done. Therefore, those who existed were destroyed by God without repenting or changing His mind about what he had done because they were wicked and evil. Repentance is a change of mind that involves turning away from the evil heart and making a complete change of direction toward God. Again, repentance means abundant grieving over our sin, which God hates, and coming to the sobering realization that our sins were wiped out by Jesus' dying on the cross.

CHAPTER TWO

Isaiah and Zephaniah

The definition of Falsification is forging, fabrication, and distortion of information to lead people to believe that they spoke with God! Falsification also is the act of deliberately lying about, misrepresenting, or hiding facts. Whereas assumption is an attempt to deny the other races in the biblical principles and assume the Bible represents particularly Jewish people, it was disinformation. The original Jews being white people was questionable because they described purely black Africans in the two books above: Isaiah 18:1&2 and Zephaniah 3: 9&10, and other books within the Bible. Were they describing indigenous Africans of today or previous African ancestors? Was it after they evangelized them or before they photocopied the idea of existing documents of worshipping and their tithings and offerings? These are questions Jewish scholars and Europeans should be ready to answer for indigenous Africans. The tall and aggressive Nation brought in tithes and offerings to their God, "Nhialic Wende Madhol," before the African tribes' Exodus from Egypt to Europe, and that's where they knew their tithes and offerings to "Tor" (not Torah).

Nevertheless, what the Jewish call "Torah" Judaism Law of Moses was plagiarized from "Agar- Girl," whom they called "Hagar," Abraham's concubine, the spelling changed from "Agar" to "Hagar." It's that faith we are still worshipping today and beyond which they called us Spear- Master or Rainmakers. "Tor" are likes stairs blinking's at daytime and night in circles found inside "Luk" (which is like a Church Building), but in a special corner where a "spear-master" masters them, not anyone else. A "Spear-master" in Dinka-Agar's culture is like a senior pastor; he is the one to officiate many important ceremonies. Even though we are still encouraging worshippers without telling them the truths surrounding the Bible, yet they were worshipping what they called Pagans. We were told these "Tors" had been moving with Spear-masters or Rains-Makers from ancient Egyptians until today in Rumbek, lakes state and Tonjdit in warrap state. Moses was one who introduced this God called "Tor" Torah to the people of exodus before the went to Europe. There is possibility of many God's which there combined the people of exodus to be one God according African tribes.

Moreover, another impressive remark in three books, (Genesis 29:23&26), (Deuteronomy 25:5-8, and) (1 Samuel 19:9&10) were also identifying those who were practicing such was not Jewish or Europeans. Such social practices exist today among the Jieng Dinka's in South Sudan and other African tribes. Consequently, those who wrote the Biblical documents of worshipping were Africans. If they were Jewish and Europeans, why mentioned such essential issues while they are not practicing at present, while other black African tribes are still practicing Jewish and European social norms if they belonged to both? "I know Christian Europe would not want it to be revealed that for over two thousand years Europeans have been worshipping a God that was imagined, created, personified, and worshipped by black people for thousands of years before Europeans were introduced to this God. I did not set to write a popular book because I also know that Christians Europe would not want to know that person, they have called Jesus and worshipped for thousands of years, was a black man called Ayesu." Nana Banchie Darkwah Ph.D. pg. 35."

It's true that Bible was and is a non-negotiable document, and the reason behind it was that; Jewish deceived the world that they were and are special people who spoke with God. As a result, God's word is non-negotiable. Furthermore, Europeans and Jewish felt guilty after they were worshipping what they called "African beliefs" or "traditional pagans." At the same time, they switched "Tor" be" Torah" in Hebrew.

Ph.D. Nana and I are not nullifying the worshipping of God "Nhialic" nor the process of practices. However, he who made the delicious food must be known as who came up with the delicious recipe. Consequently, photocopying black African ideas and never acknowledging them for thousands of years has reduced the integrity of Jewish scholars and Europeans. Nevertheless, I have the same feelings as Dr. Nana. Other African Pastors may disagree with Dr. Nana and me because of enslaved mentality and mindset, always prepared to believe what people with white skin say.

Beyond Christianity, the other major world religion that also directly sprung out of Ancient Egyptian descendancy and theosophical ideas was the Muslim religion. The Bible tells us that there is an Ancient Egyptian connection in creation of Muslim religion among the Arabs. This biblical narrative suggests that Arabs descended from the child of Abraham and his Ancient Egyptian maidservants who supposedly given to him when he traveled Ancient Egypt (see Genesis 16 Ph.D. P 86)"

She was not an Arab girl during Ancient Egyptian, Arabs were not there by that time. Those Ancient Egyptian were purely Black peoples'. It was distorted claimed as I explained above that her actual name is called Agar.

Based on page 96 which says other (Afrim peoples) returned to Ancient Egypt as early as 6th century B.C. Hagar was not an Arab girl because it was same corruption's spelling. Also, examine the word Rameses in Exodus 12:13, that word was corrupted from Dinka " Ramthei" which means "Youths."

Previously, and even at our, we were told Hagar was an Egyptian slave-girl given to Abraham as his concubine. Despite that, she was a biblical person in the Book of Genesis Chapter (16:1& Genesis 21:9&10) Hagar also, spelled in Latin "Agar." Agar is both a male and female name from that time and now. However, who may claim that name Worldwide today? Which ethnic group besides the Agar who are found in present-day South Sudan? This name is also found in Funj Sultan Kingdom of Sennar where Malik Agar Ayeru is waging war against the Sudan Government. Those who copied the Bible humiliated Agar Girl, who gave a gift to millions of believers worldwide, calling her a concubine when she brought blessings from her tribe Agar to Abraham.

Who was Cush or "Kuc" in Dinka Agar? "Kuc" means a child born in unexpected circumstances. When a couple is married and does not bear a child for more than fifteen years, when that woman becomes pregnant, that child will be called "Kuc." The meaning of "Cush" in Hebrew is defined as black, which does not make sense at all because naming is not given according to your skin color. I have never come across where Shem and Japheth were named so because of their white colors if they were white. In Genesis, we know that Hagar was an Egyptian concubine to Abraham.

Her name was corrupted to be Hagar instead of Agar; this was the beginning of corrupting African tribal names! For instance, Kuc was flipped-up to be Cush, Chawul was written Shaul, Riel was transposed into Ariel Sharon, and Benny Gur corrupted into David Ben Gurion, who raised the Israelites flag on May 14, 1948, in Tel Aviv. Agar to be Hagar and Agar tribes and other Jieng were pushed by different circumstances from Canaan Land to Sudan till they settled in Rumbek Land for centuries and they were part of Ancient Egyptians. After all, Agar was part of an Ancient Egyptian people, so Cush or Kuc definition makes sense to the readers.

Being African is not a problem. Stealing black African ideas of God's existence and imagination and crediting yourself as white people is ridiculous. Before the spirit of compassion possessed Sarah to instruct her husband Abraham to have sexual intercourse with Hagar or "Agar," Abraham was not a blessed man by then; he was an ordinary human being! His blessings came when Hagar and her son "Ismail" were experiencing suffering in the wilderness, and Angels of God appeared and rescued them from the wilderness. Sara's compassion and love for her husband became their blessing, though human being interpretation was totally different human being's interpretation was different from God's interpretation because Hagar was the source of opening Sara's womb to have multiple children as positive sides. Today's intellectual girls felt upset to Sara; why she allowed her husband's to had sexual intercourse with a "concubine was negative at present." As long, as human beings are living, our movements are not fully positive and negative until we leave this world, we will be entitled to blame. What Abraham was practicing above was normal for indigenous Africans from that time and today if you can financially manage many wives and children.

Don't tell me Sara was primitive! Primitively, is when you live between the fundamental principles of Almighty God and adapt to being Gay and Lesbian, which was attempted in Genesis chapter nineteen and resulted in punishable consequences. The time indigenous Africans lived in Northeast Africa, God was so quick to punish evil, that's the God Africans should be searching for, not God of Aid and political punishment. This God of Aid made us vulnerable to the point we abundant cultivating food for ourselves, praying for five hours to the God of Aid, when we would not provide all necessities of daily life, except working hard to eliminate Aid verified (2Thessalonians 3:6-12) to those who are depending on Aid. Today, less developed countries are subjected to punishment because of rejecting same-sex marriages, which is contrary with plagiarized Bible doctrine they claimed belongs to them. We had been deceived for so long by white people that they are evangelizing Africans, in other words the Jewish spoke with God and that was false. If you are aware of Jieng Dinka cultures properly, you may not accept the deception of evangelism they were doing. Apparently, what I'm expressing here to devoted and dedicated Christians may not sound comfortable because they received the wrong information of praying too much, Christians will receive blessing abundantly. That's not true, my friends in Christianity, if we are neither dedicated to working hard nothing may God answer our prayers just by praying thousands are poor more than the none-prayers. Prove me wrong by reading Deuteronomy (28:12,13&14). These blessings and obedience don't mean praying for five hours to receive; we must discipline ourselves with a time of prayers and reserve another time for working different things for earning necessities of life.

"And God saw that wickedness of man was great in the earth and that every imagination of the thoughts of his heart was only evil continually. And the Lord said, I will destroy man whom I fowl of the air; for it repented me that I have made them. The earth also was corrupt before God, and the earth was filled with violence. And God looked upon the earth, behold, it was corrupt; for all flesh had corrupted his way upon the earth (Genesis 6:5, 7,11, and 12 KJV)."

Viewing the above quotation properly and thinking logically value the research of Ph.D. Nana Banchie Darkwah and George Smith of British Department of Oriental Antiquities, sound mind will agree with both that the ideas was plagiarized. Dr. Nana said indigenous Africans or Ancient Egyptians made an imaginative should the word "imagination thoughts" above had confirmed that those who said they had spoken with God copied the African's God before they became Jewish or Israelites. Viewers or Christians, the important Book of references, which is the Bible, was written by Ancient Egyptians, specifically Akan and Jieng Agar, because their names and Israelites God name, which is called Torah, and Yahweh were transposed from them. Readers should understand my points properly! I'm not changing the contexts of the Bible; however, I'm clearly giving you missing information were millions of people believed that Israelites had spoken with God was white lies based on serious research and confirmed by Nana Banchie Darkwah Ph.D. from Gahanna African Son. If Moses was educated in all the wisdom of the Egyptians and was powerful in speech and action- Acts 7:22. Was white Jewish parents were borrowing wisdom from black Egyptians or Moses' Parents were black themselves.

Another fascinating point many African Christians never questioned was why Moses, Son of the Jewish who got wisdom from black Egyptians, became superior to the point that he spoke with God? Indigenous African were all intelligent! Those who exited fooled Europeans that they spoke with God and therefore, worshiped our God. The exciters deceived those who remained in Africa to accept their own God in different forms.

Nevertheless, descendants of the inventors doubted the validity of Biblical principles. Some names within the Bible are even closely connected to our present names. Subsequently, the Bible was written not by the Jewish, and we are claiming the ownership of the Bible. Don't assault me before you understand the contexts of the Bible thoroughly to challenge me. Jewish were targets because they were originally African. They were subjected to the brutal killing, called the holocaust, because of the introduction of African religion.

Why was the single white race Jewish subjected to maximum killing if they were not originally black? We both paid an unimaginable price because of this God called Christianity! Those who smuggled out the ideas of African worshipping paid the ultimate price. As a result, denying us and denied themselves of being African from the very beginning. We who lost civilization and our pretenders who came back with their friends to enslave us thinking that other generations may not track down their roots.

As a result, they paid a proportion price in 1939-1945. Nana Banchie Darkwah Ph.D. does not direct followers of Christianity to abandon worshipping of Almighty God, but they are given the facts surrounding biblical stories where Ancient Egyptians who were inhabitants in Egypt and created the stories existing of God. The analog of Christianity and so-called African traditional beliefs were used as social-psychological controls behaviors because analyzing and contrasting each; you would conclude they were the same methodology concepts.

In the second destruction during the time of Noah, God repented for what he had done; He was grieving why He had created human beings. This means He had changed his mind. As a result, destruction took place where all people were wiped off. There are certain things God hated from the very beginning and even during our time. The cause of the second and third was particularly on two issues: one was violent, whether social-economic and political, and second was corruption, whether administratively or economically, either social corruption or political corruption of injustices among mankind. Biblical principles are guidelines for us if the people and leaders respect them to avoid using violent and excessive corruption against their citizens, specifically in less developed countries and countries inhabited by Ham. This land of Ham and his descendants were the Son of living God turned water into wine.

This land of Ham and his descendants was where Adam and Eve were multiplying the whole world of today's people. This land of Ham and his descendants where civilization, science, arts, architecture, and alphabetical order of writing were discovered. Yet, our African leaders are not proud of all these and live in peace. Instead, they are killing each other, which causes more poverty and diseases.

The Nilotic revolution of agriculture and small manufacturing was the turning point of survival, and it connected us with "Purr" and "Yip," which means Hoe and Axe. Those two have a significant effect on a Dinka's life. Should an old father almost pass away, he will call his boys and tell them what he will inherit. This inheritance is cultivated by a Hoe and Axe for the survival of the siblings.

Today we are being fed by those who learned cultivation from our Ancestors, and it is sad to Africans generally. Let the so-called white Supremacists develop what their Ancestors created besides what they copied from our Neolithic Ancestors.

When Noah was instructed to build the Ark (Genesis 6:14-16 in any translation KJV and NRSV), many readers believed those before us knew how to write and calculate the width and length of The Ark.

If the Scholars, Scientists, and Philosophers were very sincere, they should accept that they were teaching mathematics before the flood. Noah was singled out because of his righteousness in the eyes of the Almighty God. Noah himself was a mathematician, according to the description of the Ark. Otherwise, he couldn't have built the Ark according to the directives. Somebody must carry out what he/she knows appropriately, and that's what Noah did. What we have done is modify the existing one from the Creator Madhol. If you read Old Testament, you would find out something called chariots, (this has wheels like cars of our present time) they were using it for wars like tanks and armor. Moses wrote the Bible according to God's directives. He showed Moses how to write, not Moses by himself.

Let us have a look at Biblical facts: "When God finished speaking with Moses on Mount Sinai, He gave him the two tablets of the covenant, tablets of stone, written with the finger of God." Who wrote this? Was it Moses or God? It is God who wrote on tablets; some individuals may deny that fact. Instead of praising Him if we have discovered tangible information, we begin to be so arrogant about our achievements to the point of dismissing the visible facts created by Him, and we think that we are superior to God. Moses was just given information to air out like a microphone. He didn't write a single sentence in the Bible. "Then Moses turned and went down from the mountain, carrying the two tablets of the covenant in his hands, tablets that were written on both sides, written on the front and back. The tablets were the work of God, and the writing was the writing of God, engraved upon the tablets" (Exodus 32:15, 16). In our lifetime, we are increasing what He gave to his spirit who is living inside us.

This spirit is the source of our success in discovering any new information. "You, yourselves are our letter, written on our hearts to be known and read by all; and you show that you are a letter of Christ, prepared by us written not with ink but with the spirit of the living God, not on tablets of stone but on tablets of human hearts" (2 Corinthians 3:2, 3). Again, it is clear now that we are not competent as scientists alone without the help of the spirit of the living God inside us. He is the source of discovering things, like making planes for flight, cars to drive, computers, and ships for navigating the oceans. Those achievements are the works of the living spirit within us; otherwise, we will end up with nothing to prevail. Denying His great help and insisting on our abilities will never yield the right direction in our lives.

Why do we feel ashamed to accept God as being superior? How do we become superior on our own while we cannot put our breath somewhere and restore it on our own accord? "I will lead the blind by a road they do not know; by paths, they have not known I will guide them. I will turn the darkness before them into light, the rough places into level ground. These are things I will do, and I will not forsake them" (Isaiah 42:16). This passage is for the pilots because we will lose our way by mapping alone with no guidance from the living God spirit inside us. We are part of Him, and He is a part of us, but the only difference between Him and us is the continuous sins we make now and then, whereas He is perfect in His actions.

Hebrew word appeared in the Book of Genesis six times on different occasions. It first appeared when Lot, nephew of Abram, was in captivity. Abram was informed as Hebrew. The second time was a scandal made by the Pharaoh's wife; she was trying to complicate sexual attitudes with Joseph when he refused to do so. The readers may complete the story in Genesis chapters Thirty-nine and Forty-one. After Joseph interpreted Pharaoh's dream, the Egyptian Pharaoh gave him all powers except enthronement powers will Pharaoh's be more significant than him. Joseph married among the Egyptians; the First-born name was Manasseh. He forgets all life's hardships and what his brothers did to him when he was sold to Ishmaelite Egyptian. The second child's name was Ephraim because God made him be fruitful in the land of his misfortunate. That's what the two names mean; they have nothing to do with the assumption of Western Evangelists.

The survival of Jacob and his kinship was because Joseph's brother sold him to Egyptians, which (Madhol) God turned to be their welfare during the Great Famine in the Land of Canaanites. The recapitulating of this chapter consisted of survival after the Great Flood and Creation, and how the sin of human beings become visible, the Great Flood, and the story of Joseph are what the Genesis focuses. "According to the Book of Jubilees, Hebrew is the language of heaven, and was originally spoken by all creatures in the Garden of Eden, animals and human beings; however, all animals lost their power of speech when Adam and Eve were expelled out after they committed sins."

I agree with these statements because even my natives, who do not know the alphabetical order, knew the story that animals were speaking before. In my opinion, other information in Jubilees Book is misleading because it repeats the same illustration in the Bible, and therefore there are no credentials distinctions between both. Also, it is unclear whether the Jubilees Book was written before the Bible or after the Bible. Readers of the Bible always get confused because the Bible is not written in systematic sequences where you follow information from Book to Book.

CHAPTER THREE

Pretension and Claim

When missionaries came to Africa and Sudan with news Gospels, they found Dinka's were worshipping the Old God who doesn't change, according to the Malachi 3:6, doing offerings to our spiritual leaders. They were called rainmaker from that time up to the present moments "Beeny Bith" in other words "spear Master". For example, Macot Awut, all away to Derr Makuer Gol up to today as my writing our offering to our "spiritual leader" are still continuous up today.

Look at what Zephaniah had said before, "Instead of asking us how do we knew this, they begin to discourage our spiritual way of life, God knows Cush children in Sudan and other places in Africa before millions of years ago. We were the only people knowns to tithes to our spiritual Leaders.

How do they know God more than us while they divided Him into tow being Old and New? Before missionaries came with the new claims that they knew Nhialic more than us, we tithe everything produced from lands, cattle, goats, sheep, and all first born. This is according to what is written in Leviticus tithes of everything from the land, whether grain from soil, or fruits from the trees that belong to the Lord; it is holy to the Lord. If a man redeems any of his tithes, he must add a fifth of the value to It" (Leviticus 27:30 and 31).

"You are to give over to the Lord the first offspring of every womb. All the first-born males of your livestock belong to the Lord. Redeems with a lamb every firstborn donkey, but if you do not redeem it break its neck" (Exodus13:12 and 13). The tithe of our grandfather's was not meant to the magicians as others believed; it was to God check Zephaniah again. Praise the Lord we pay arrears of last year of the tithes, plus the current year if somebody fails not to pay last year's to spiritual leaders, and that is still up to today. Dr. Francis Mading Deng made wonderful remarks in his book. The Dinka of the Sudan written thus: Cucumber may be invoked, cut into halves, and thrown into the air. The half that turns upside down is believed to contain the evil spell and is thrown away; the other half or both, if they fall the right way, are rubber on the head and chest of the ill person and kept near him or her. Despite the continued association between the dead and the living, they are paradoxically by a ritual known as "Cuol," performed three or four days after death depending on the sex of the dead person (Mading Deng Majok, The Dinka of the Sudan page 129). These final activities mentioned by author has no difference with today's Christianity or Islamic symbol of the last funerals of 21st centuries. The question is who adopted who's performances? Of course, an ancient performances funeral, in my views, was translated into Christianity by Nilotic and photocopied by westerners. These performances symbolize spiritual Cross if you visualize it properly because the elder put its forehead perpendicular and, on the chest, where spirit reside, and that's what Baptism stand for today. Dinka believed all people are children of God regardless of their colors and languages, and no races qualified to illustrate the same God to them.

Another interesting point is this: Did Christian know the existence of the Cross before Christ was nailed physically? Let me give a clue in this is what the Lord said to Moses and Aaron during the Passover.

"Take care of them until the fourteenth day of the month, when all the people of the community must slaughter them at twilight. Then they are to take some of the blood and put it on the sides and top of the door frames of the house where they eat the Lamb."(verse twelve;)

"On that same night I will pass through Egypt and strike down every first born, both men and animal and I will bring judgment on all gods of Egypt. I'm the Lord. The blood will be a sign for you on the houses where you are; and when I see the blood, I will pass over you. No destructive plaque will touch you when I plaque I pass Egypt. When the Lord goes through the land to strike down the Egyptian, he will see the blood on top and sides of the door frames and will pass over that doorway, and he will not permit the destroyer to enter your houses and strike you down" (Exodus 12:7,12,13,23).

This blood was representing the Crossing of Jesus Christ, pay close attention or looks on your door frames; in other words, just put blood on the door frame on the top and looks at it attentively; it will give you an idea.

Children of the descendant warrior Cush (Kuc in Dinka) recognized that sign before the know alphabets. Although they do not know the meaning of it, they have been practicing that sign which saved the Israelites from that time for many years. Yet Western people do not appreciate they became jealous because of why the Cush descendants knew this before us which of course they exodus were leaning from us.

We must not indulge in sexual immorality as some of them did and twenty-three thousand fell in single day. We must not put Christ to the test, as some of them did, and were destroyed by serpents. And do not complain as some of them did and were destroyed by the destroyer (Corinthian's 10:8,9, and 10). These three verses are explaining the disobedient to God; He will permit the destroyer to punish His people severely. Westerners' evangelist wrote many books about Christianity in Africa, and especially in Sudan, they mentioned indigenous were not believers', but what Isaiah and Zephaniah had said is not worshipping of today, it was a long time ago, and we were worshipping Him. Nobody has the right to present false teaching to the people according to what he/she thinks because our existence is not by mistake; God himself knows who have accepted him and who did not.

Another reality which was well-known to the Cush descendants in Sudan is the Day of Atonement.

"But the goat chosen by Lot as the scapegoat shall be presented alive before the Lord to be used for making atonement by sending it into desert as scapegoat. He is to lay both hands on the head of the live goat and confess over it all the wickedness and rebellion of the Israelites- all their sins- and put them on the goat's head. He shall send the goat away into desert in the care of a man appointed for the task. The goat will carry on itself all their sins to solitary place; and the man shall release it in the desert" (Leviticus 16:10, 12, and 22). Atonement in Hebrews scriptures means reconciliation with God after having an injury during the fighting or any kind of misunderstanding between the parties where the blood was spilled. Slaughtering a bull or white sheep without defect is atonement in our traditional way of life before Christianity spread out to Africa and especially Sudan where Dinka's and the rest of Cush descendants live in Sudan who already knew atonement before the missionaries came with the message of Christianity. The Nilotic's were living the basic principles of GOD, even before civilization. For example, a "scapegoat" is another thing well-known to Nilotic in Sudan before the Christ. Scapegoat in Hebrews scriptures is to take away bad things from the Israelites community and the same way Dinka's knew scapegoat as (Maar Anyoun taking out epidemic diseases). "Despite the great threat of Ancient

Egyptian civilization, the greatest problem of the catholic Church was its own internal corruption in which people were asked, for example, to pay money for the to forgive their sins. This foundation of corruption in Christianity can still be found among Christian capitalists that seek to make their money through the Christian religion around the world" (Pg 151). What are also fascinating differences of western tithing and offering and our spiritual leaders was the facts that our spiritual leaders don't accumulate tithes and offerings for their benefit like the case of Christianity. They used them for sacrifices to praise Nhialic, who is to make His people to prosperous in the next season whereas in Christianity tithes and offerings were meant for Bishops to enriched themselves by accumulating tithes and offerings for theirs owned used, even laymen in churches are left suffering. That corruption was precisely transferred to Africa where most pastors do not preach prosperity in the churches; except sow seeds by tithing heavily not showing prosperity like Ancient Egyptians (Deuteronomy 28 12, 13 and 14).

"Then Israel entered Egypt; Jacob lived as an alien in the land of Ham. They performed his miraculous signs among them, his wonders in the land of Ham" (Psalms 105:23 and 27). In fact, they were observing how ancient Egyptians were performing worshipping and other miraculous signs, which they transformed to be their owned after they exodus to Greek. This means Ham, Cush's father, was in Egypt before the Israelite's, they had welcomed them as an alien to their land; the Cush descendants have had history ever since.

"If brothers are living together, and one of them dies and without a son, his widow must not marry outside the family. Her husband's brother shall take her and marry her and fulfil the duty of a brother in-law to her. The first son she bears shall carry on the name of the dead brother so that his name will not be blotted out from Israel."

However, if a man does not want to marry his brother's wife, she shall go to the elders at the town gate and say, "My husband's brother refuses to carry on his brother's name in Israel. He will not fulfil the duty of a brother in-law to me". Then the elders of his town shall summon him and talk to him.

If he persists in saying, I do not want to marry her," his brother's widow shall go up to him in the presence of the elders, take off one of his sandals, spit in his face and say, "this is what is done to the man who will not build up his brother's family line. That man's line shall be known in Israel as The

Family of the Unsaddled" (Deuteronomy 25:5-10). Ham was living in Egypt before the Israelites came; he welcomed them under his supreme authority power during the ancient times. To me this might be where we interacted culturally with one another because today those who are still having tribes and clans are Israelites and Africans, although Israelites might have abounded this practice of performing deceased duties, yet Dinka's and Nilotic are still performing duties of deceased brothers in South Sudan. I'm a product of such performed after a deceased brother. My mother was married after her husband became deceased. I'm not a product of the deceased, but I proud to have his name among our community. I'm not encouraging it, but it is not a sin as alleged by Western countries to compare it with gay marriages. God never changed his ways of blessings things; my point is not practicing as matter of having sex or enjoyment of that matter. Make sure of the capability you had to support tow families rather than being a burned to others, in other words, putting yourself in a jeopardizing life because of a lack of resources. Having children or not is the same in Western culture's because there is no reward at all from kids to their parents, and as such, they encouraged divorce, so that to have another opportunity to marry rather than to maintain the same woman and kids. The concept of the soul has strong links with the notion of an afterlife, but much opinion may vary widely, even within a given religion, as to what may happen to the soul after the death of the body. In theology the soul is further defined as that part of the individual, which partakes of divinity and often is considered to survived after the death of the body. Spirit come the Latin, meaning "breathe," soul is searching, penetrating, examining one's motives, conviction, and emotional attitudes. Dinka know heaven, they call it "Wei Pan-Nhialic" because that concept of living spirit is still there, that is why Dinka's and Nilotic's marry a deceased person, so they can keep his or her spirit alive and name among the family. To the Dinka's, death doesn't mean that they have totally departed, where they brothers and sisters will not meet anymore. Their souls will meet in heaven whereas living children will still helping one another. In fact, Jesus does not dismiss or nullify sacrifices for ceremonies as of much debate among the believers.

This is what Jesus said after he has healed a man with leprosy in Mark, (Ch.1:44) saying to him, "See that you don't tell this to anyone. But go, show yourself to the priest and offer the sacrifices that Moses commanded for your cleansing, as testimony to them." What sacrifices was he talking about? It was the sacrifices of goats' sheep, or cows. Although Jesus Christ has made a second covenant by His own blood, I doubt it will not bailout those who are addicted to alcohol, drugs, pornography, homosexuality, gay marriages, legalization of abortion, and legalization of prostitution. Setting us free is not an automatic as others do believe individuals must himself or herself why Jesus died for our sins.

In Genesis (10) Ham, the father of Cush, has become a mighty warrior. "When they found a rich, good pasture and the land was very broad, quiet, and peaceful; for the former inhabitants there belonged to Ham. These, registered by name, came in the days of King Hezekiah of Judah, and attacked their tents and the Meuim who were found there, and exterminated them to this day, and settled in their place, because there was a pasture there for their flocks"(1Cronicles 4:40 and 41).Traditionally , it is known that Ham was one of the sons of Noah who moved to Southwest Africa and part of the near North East Africa and was the forefather of the nation there. Isaiah also illustrated how we are tall and smooth-skinned, to a people feared far and wide, an aggressive nation of strange speech whose land is divided by rivers. Commenting on these tow words, "warrior" appeared first in Genesis (10), and it was used to described Nimrods, the son of Cush. "Aggressive nation" also was mentioned in Isaiah, with some descriptions related to our present-time, and so the Bible has confirmed our behaviors, and existence in the land called Sudan. Now if looked back of how the previous leaders have behaved. For example, Kwame Nkrumah, Patrice Lumumba, Nelson Mandela, Robert Mugabe, Gaml Abdel Nasser, and recently the late Dr. John Garang.

They had the same attitude described above, some of them did not at last because anybody who speaks about Africans should stand on their own feet will not accomplish the dreams, but you know what God will give us our rational empowerment. Power is not permanent in one hand. It started with us in Africa, and after we mishandled it, the European empire got an opportunity to maintain it and had moved to America and is now in a dilemma. Our power will come if we accept repentance and forgiveness to ourselves, so that all professional Africans hanging around western countries could go back. Could poverty be reduced by the rich nations in Africa? No, any other human being cannot solve our burdens; we had to recognize begging is a big of our failures. We have our resources, but the problem is that we do not listen to ourselves to solve our differences. The Party which brought people to the Promise Land will disintegrate because of misbehaviors of other leaders against each other and competition over the resources and blind loyalty.

CHAPTER FOUR

The Reality of the Black Race Existing

Reading Biblical stories shouldn't be based on worshipping only. It reflects cultural and traditional ways of life of the past and present. Evangelists and their followers in Africa didn't pay close attention to the biblical stories. These stories are close to the stories we heard before we came to school. Stories from the Bible were plagiarized by exiting indigenous Africans, re-packed, and brought back with Evangelists and Colonialists to deceive the owners of the stories. If you read the Bible and have nothing relevant to your grandfather's previous life before Christianity, you are nobody in the history of the Biblical facts. However, Africans of the Twentieth century have discovered various information connecting them with their grandfather's past life. They were practicing before Christianity and are the same as the Biblical principles of today. In this case, we identify with Biblical principles, even though westerners assumed otherwise. They have nothing relevant to previous life except Israelites, who have similar identities as Africans; see Genesis Chapter Thirty-eight of how to persevere family links or genealogies. Biblically, social similarities between Israelites and Dinka's within the groups of Nilotic are how marriages occur systematically. For example, the younger girl shouldn't be married before the eldest was another common denominator (Genesis. 29: 23&26). Viewing these values and cultures will give you an opinion that western nations have no links with Biblical principles, which they claimed as their legitimate text. The story of the serpent ("Keror" in Dinka) and how he deceived Eve in the Garden of Eden, the story of left Ribs where God took some from Adam and made Eve, and Noah were familiar to Dinka's before we encountered "Evangelists." After The Great Flood, God made a covenant with Noah and his three descendants that there would be no other disaster between human beings and God. However, within this context, the perception of human existence with different colors got distorted. This distortion was based on racial segregation. In other words, human races' differences of having colors, whereas white colors seem to be the best race. But they did not root their assumption self- glorification Biblically. In the actual Biblical facts, the reality looked different since the first human being mentioned in the Bible to have a kingdom was the grandson of Ham. All people of today were under his authority. Consequently, the Bible did not explain what types of races were under his kingdom, whether black or white. (Genesis10:6,8, 9&10). Scholars have different perceptions, definitions, or overlooked historical background and Biblical realities; they tried to preach the wrong events and hide significant positives. The fact that black skin plays a significant role in human history was ignorant to some Western scholars. What was rolling in their minds were statements that stated that Ham descendants would be slaves to Shem and Japheth, which means that they were white race according to them, and that was why Noah said that. In their assumption, they believed that Ham Descendants were black. However, according to the Bible, Abraham's father was born in the land of Chaldeans inhabited by the black. (Joshua 24:2&3) and (Genesis11:31). The people God selected first were the grandsons of Ham to make a covenant with them based on Biblical stories. "I passed by you again and looked on you; you were at the age for love. I spread the edge of my cloak over you and covered your nakedness; I pledged myself to you and entered a covenant with you, says the lord God, and you became mine." (Ezekiel 16:8) This illustrates Jerusalem's birth in Canaanites, and therefore, the chosen people were the grandchildren of Ham, not the Israelites. Why did we lose our Gifts from God? We lost our gifts because Nimrod, the son of Cush, was so arrogant and prideful after he became Lord of Babylon. He introduced his own Gods to the worshippers, which is called "Baal." On the other hand, his nephew, Jerusalem in the land of Canaanites, was practicing whorings.

Meanwhile, Nimrod was killing those who did not listen to his leadership as King of the earth. In this connection, "The LORD has poured into them a spirit of confusion; and they have made Egypt stagger in its entire doings as a drunkard stagger around in vomit. "These spirits of confusion are still going on among Blacks and Arabs where they don't come together for their common goal. Pouring confusing spirits has significant impacts on black communities. For example, the athletics industry; National Basket Association (NBA), and National Football League (NFL) in the United States where 98% of players who are African American.

Meanwhile, the owners are whites, which means the players get small portions of money rather than themselves as owners of the league. The power of money will be circularizing among them, and automatically they will be respected like Jewish in America. Jewish communities have special consideration in America, not because they are whites, but the power of money made them decision-makers in American policies. They organize themselves to protect their identity of being Jewish, which is lacking among Black communities worldwide. Organizing ourselves worldwide under the strong umbrella of Black Organization should be our way of survival; otherwise, we are endangering the generations not to know the dangers of events that consist of past, present, and future to come. For black communities to strengthen themselves, we need to pool ourselves and resources together; in other words, challenge future generations to lead in different professional fields, i.e., lawyers, medical doctors, and police officers. These categories are the keys for minority survival to exist in every complex society. Black teenagers being out in the above professional jobs made blacks vulnerable to injustices, killings, and arrests or imprisonments. On the other hand, black teenagers must dress professionally and appropriately because physical appearances reflect the inside and behaviors. This is the central core of our kids being targeted because physical appearances justify or subject them to criminality. Both parents cultivate positive attitudes toward their kids, not in the projects houses that Teenagers Black Girls find, as a haven for their reckless pregnancies. Also, Blacks are very aggressive to each other or feel that they are warriors or mightiest. Being arrogant, shedding innocent blood, whorings are unacceptable from that time and up to our present moment. Westerners ignore that reality today because of legitimizing whoring, legalizing abortion, and gay marriages in the name of freedom; the western empire will fall like Babylon. "He called out with a mighty voice fall, fall, is Babylon the great city! It has become a dwelling place of demons, for all the nations have drunk of the wine of the wrath of her fornication, and the kings of the earth have committed fornication with her, and merchants of the earth have grown rich from the power of her luxury." When fornication becomes the order of the day, it will damage the integrity of government officials and the nations at large because the society becomes bankrupt morally. Also, it causes social corruption, violence, and eventually the breakdown of the kingdom of God. The western empire is on the brink of social and financial collapse. Norms and values are collapsing because of Western arrogance, where everything is ignored for the sake of freedom. (Read Revelation Chapter 1-22 to ignore it or confirm my claim). When human beings deny the importance of social values, we are at war with the Creator. After Adam and Eve ate the fruits of wisdom, they realized first their nakedness, which awakes by itself to us, was marking our privacy so important to God and us. We descendants of Ham must make complete repentance to God, so that Almighty will reveres our gifts to us again.

Otherwise, following their styles, we will perish again like centuries ago in Babylon.

"For I the LORD do not change therefore you O children of Jacob, have not perished." God has never changed ever since; He still has the wisdom and power to destroy if moral values are taking a different direction like now in westerner's world where they worship their technology. When God chose Israelites and made grandson of Ham be the ransom of Israelites, it was because our superiority, pride, and wicked morality toward others were painful to God (see Isaiah 43:3&4 and Proverbs 21:18, proverbs 11:8). Therefore, he gave Israelites directives to follow like this: "If you do not oppress the alien, the orphans, and the widows, or shed innocent blood in this place, and if you do not go after other gods to your own hurt, then I will dwell with you in this place, in the land that I gave of old to your ancestors forever and ever." (Jermiah7:6,7&8). Our observances of the above will tell you how Israelites handle themselves with Arabs prisoners of war. One will agree that they are obeying what God told them. "By your great wisdom in trade, you have increased your wealth, and your heart has become proud in your wealth."

"A sword shall come upon Egypt, and anguish shall be in Ethiopia when the slain falls in Egypt, its wealth is carried away, and foundations are torn down. Ethiopia, and Put, Lud, and all Arabia, and Libya, and the people of the allied land shall fall with them by the sword (check Ezekiel chapters 28 &30)." Are all remarks above gone, or are they still to come among these nations?

The existing history will tell you that those nations have already paid the ultimate price because of their behaviors. Therefore, they need to kneel and repent so God will restore their fortune like before. Ham descendants have lost their wisdom foundation after they became haughtiest. After they created essential information of today, the girls practiced promiscuity, violence, and making their images for worship, denying God's existence, which backfired on them. The triangle, which consists of Egypt, Sudan, and Ethio-

44

pia, was the backbone of world civilization rather than the Roman Empire. Still, violence, corruption of all forms, arrogances, and pride erased them almost out of the history of humanity. When I observe Jerry Springer's show and Maury's show, the Holy Spirit of living God tells me the westerners' arrogance has reached the last corner. It was precisely how Jerusalem exposed herself in glorious Holy Land like girls that show their private places in public in Jerry Springer and Maury show, respectively (Read Isaiah Chapter Nineteen through the end of Chapter to confirm pouring spirit of confusion).

CHAPTER FIVE

Visibility of Nilotes in History

The roots of seven nations originated from Canaan's brother of Cush, Egypt, and Put in other translations (Somalia). Therefore, inhabitants of the Promised Land were the grandson of Ham, where King Sihon and King OG fought with Moses. But Moses could not finish conquering the whole Promised Land. Moses' successor began to send two spies to Jericho, where they met a prostitute, whose name was Rahaba. This prostitute hid them in her house, so rumors spread out to the King of Jericho that Israelites have sent out to spy on the land inhabited by seven nations (Joshua 3:10), comprising seven nations to match (Genesis 10:15). When people are at war, prostitutes collaborate with the enemy either for the welfare of their people or the benefit of the enemy. Joshua Nun and his soldiers surrounded Jericho city according to God's instructions, after that the Lord gave an okay to let them destruct the whole town with all people and any living things except the prostitute's family and relatives because she had hidden the spies (Joshua 6:17, 22-25). There must be prisoners of war in any war situation. After the tension had calmed down, this guy Salmon married Rahab (the prostitute); her genealogy had interconnection with King David, where Jesus Christ had originated from (Matthew 1:5 and Psalm 87:4). These seven nations' land had been given to the Israelites by perception God. If my readers are not lazy, you will frequently be going back and forth to confirm my claim in Genesis Chapter Ten Verses six and fifteen. But before I dig into details, I will explore some analogies between Nilotic and "Pan- Afrim" before the Exodus. Later, they became Jewish, Hebrews in Europe, meaning Israelites at present. Nilotic have five things in common with African Israelites, based on the Bible, because those who fought have some remnants on both sides.

The Cross symbol: had saved Israelites in Egypt when God instructed Moses to let Israelites slaughter goats or bulls and put the blood on the door frame and top. This sign represents the nailing of Christ spiritually to the Nilotic. This was how God distinguished houses of Israelites at night when He came to destroy the Egyptians. This symbol also represents when relatives living far away came back; such performances are done for peace and blessings. He would see the signs on both sides of the doorframe and at the top.

Two: The practice is done when a person who was married dies. The deceased person's wife will not marry outside the family. The brother or nephew will perform the duties of the deceased person to preserve his name in the family. The children belong to the deceased.

According to the Bible, the Israelites' families were following this tradition from those days, although I'm not sure what they do at present. Visit Deuteronomy Chapter Twenty-five to the end. "Then an evil spirit from the Lord came upon Saul, as he sat in his house with his spear in his hand, while David was playing music. Saul sought to pin David to the wall with the spear, but he eluded Saul so that he struck the spear into the wall, David fled and escaped that night" (1 Samuel 19:9-10). These statements of an evil spirit from God may disturb young believers or those who think that Christ has erased curses. The masters manipulated my thinking, but those statements matched God's words in Numbers (14:17-18).

Third: the spiritual leader or spear master, Saul, has been stated several times in the Bible. He had intended to kill David, and the reason might be that David was seeking to be the spiritual leader before Saul died. Saul spoke with his son Jonathan and with all his servants about killing David. An ignorant believer may say God does not have evil spirits, but this statement matched what He said in Numbers (14:17-18).

The fourth: marrying sisters-in-law if your wife has died and both families agree to let her sister take care of her sister's children is also a common denominator between the Israelites and the Dinkas. Ariel Sharon, the former Prime minister of Israel, was living testimony in his book, An Autobiography Warrior, but I'm not quite sure about the other Nilotic. Finally, the division of tribes after Israelites came out from Egypt; Almighty God instructed Moses to account for each descendant of Jacob. Their tribes are twelve, and that is how Dinka's exist in South Sudan; they are twelve in number. Though they are twenty-four in number, if you divide twenty-four by two, the result is twelve, and the vital part in the twelfth number is faith and blessings. That is the meaning of the twelfth number in the Bible. Dispute over who will be the leaders among them Israelites spiritually was a natural phenomenon since the beginning of human history. The interesting point which motivates me to mention was the type of weapon Saul had intended to use to kill David, which was a spear. This is relevant to what our spiritual leaders have in my area and is what Israelites had in those days (1 Samuel 18 and 19 read in different translations). All those five above similarities happened while they were still indigenous African; their African Ancestors learned them before they emigrated to Europe. Those who were practicing were Jieng tribes which are found in Sudan and South Sudan at present. If they were not Jieng, why did these things appear during the translation process of the Bible from Ancient Egyptian to Greek? The names of African tribes were corrupted here, like Saul instead of Chawual in Jieng, Hagar known as Abraham concubine; the spelling is Agar which could be male and female. They were a tribe of Ancient Egyptians who are found today in Sudan and South Sudan. It is accepted worldwide that Israelites wrote the Bible. Before these people became Israelites, they learned elements of their faith from Indigenous Ancient Egyptians who were African. They emigrated to Europe and compiled ideas into Greek, thinking that adapting the ideas may fit into their culture and linguistic translations.

I want to elaborate on the meaning of animist or animism as both a noun and a verb. Animism- as a noun- (from the Latin anima, meaning soul, life) is a philosophical, religious, or spiritual belief that souls or spirits exist not only in humans but also in animals, plants, rocks, and natural phenomena such as thunder, geographic features such as mountains or rivers, or other entities of the natural environment. Animism may further attribute souls to abstract concepts such as words, true names, or metaphors in mythology. Animism is mainly widely found in religions of indigenous peoples, although it is also found in Shinto, and some forms of Hinduism, Sikhism, pantheism, Neopaganism (Wikipedia founder Jimmy Wales). Animist as a verb (Free Merriam- Webster Dictionary) has the following definitions. (1) A doctrine that the vital principle of organic development is immaterial spirit. (2) Attribution of conscious life to objects and phenomena of nature or inanimate objects. (3) Belief in the existence of spirits separable from bodies.

Another definition of animist by the free online Dictionary states: (1) the belief in the existence of individual spirits that inhabit natural objects and phenomena. (2) The belief in the existence of spiritual beings that is separable or separate from bodies. (3) The hypothesis holds that an immaterial animates the universe.

All definitions stated above have nothing to do with worshipping idols, as alleged by Western evangelists. In that sense, the so-called animists do not worship the living God is not true because they cannot believe the existence of spirit after death while they worshipped an idol. This is a fabrication of Western evangelists in those days, and they continue describing people, especially the South-Sudanese in Africa. What our grandfathers were performing or worshipping thousands of years ago was the living God. Spiritual leaders (Benny Bith) or Spear masters called God to rain while some intellectuals in the Western world are protesting or demonstrating, demanding legal abortion, same-sex marriages, and much more. Are these people worshipping God to approve abortion, gay marriages, and prostitution in Christianity? Or are they defaming the image of the Creator? Nilotic believe in the living God (Wei pan-Nhialic), the living spirit in heaven. Because of that conception of life after death, we marry the deceased person's wife to preserve his name in the family genealogy should his spirit be still alive in heaven.

Have you asked yourself while reading the Bible why the name of Cush was mentioned before Adam's name? Do you think that God did it by accident to put Cush's name first? The Almighty God does not make anything by accident, He carried His word by purpose, and that's what we need to visualize why. God called the Israelites His people. If that argument is the point of qualifying them to be People of God, then God called Cush's people also in Zephaniah (3:10) and in (Isaiah 18:1, 2, 7). Also, check 2 Chronicles (7:13-17) on the universal address to all mankind. This address will be answered by those who acknowledge Him. In Dinka Societies, during periods of droughts, "spiritual leaders in the community come together and pray for rain. When this happens, it rains, and the drought ends. We have been doing this for thousands of years. If these people are worshipping "idols," who is providing rain to these people? God cannot permit the living water to those who do not believe in Him. Luckily, the time of fooling Africans about Christianity has passed. More and more Africans are becoming aware of the original African origins of Christianity.

Pretenders are abusing the right way under the pretense of practicing freedom. This arrogant attitude will never bring salvation to white societies should

God's salvation not be based on race. They are in churches saying Hallelujah while permitting marriage certificates to the gays; they are saying hallelujah, whereas demonstrators are demanding legalizing the killing of infants.

Pointing the fingers into the eyes of others while they are doing the worst things will never light the reality should God judge our attitudes, not by race, as others may have assumed to be so. The spirit of the living God exists in any human being, and the nailing of His Son to save people from day one to the present moment is not based on certain races which might assume that the way to heaven is here in the West. God saves individual soul and spirit who does the right to please Him, not by race. The ignorant majority—who follow the footstep attitudes of Western behaviors and do not read the Bible for themselves, thinking that God belongs to them—will be victimizing themselves. The Bible is the property of everyone. There's to own, for salvation if they read daily; the spirit of the living God will intercede to them rather than inflict severe curses through Westerners' wrong interpretations and attitudes.

Nimrod, who was he? Was he Godly or evil? The word 'before' in Genesis 10:9 should be translated to 'in defiance of.' Even his name—Nimrod—denotes one who rebels or lets rebel. Nimrod was a hunter, a mighty one on the earth, a hero of the people. With his skills of hunting and war, he protected the people against wild animals, thus causing people to turn to him for protection instead of God.

The Jerusalem Targum (a Hebrew translation into Aramaic language which was used in Christ's day) says that he [Nimrod] was powerful in hunting and was wicked before the Lord, for he was a hunter of the sons of men. He said unto them, depart from the judgment of the Lord, and adhere to the judgment of Nimrod! Therefore, it is said: "As Nimrod [is] the strong one, strong in hunting, and wickedness before the Lord." This Aramaic language is closely related to the Amharic language(s) spoken today in Ethiopia and Eritrea. In Acts (26:14, 15), they called it Aramaic, whereas, in NIV, they called it Hebrews. Does Aramaic, which was used during Christ's time, have a connection with Ethiopia's and Eritrea's Amharic? Or was the Hebrews language called Aramaic?

From a Biblical standpoint, no single scripture had described that Cush and his sons had made a single rebellion against the will of God. "Yes, they had been describing sending ambassadors by the Nile in vessels of papyrus on the waters! To a nation tall and smooth, to a people feared near and far, a nation mighty and conquering, whose land the rivers divide. At that time, gifts will be brought to the Lord of hosts from a people tall and smooth, from a people feared near and far, a nation mighty and conquering, whose land the rivers divide, to Mount Zion, the place of the name of the Lord of hosts" (Isaiah 18:2 and 7). If having power makes people rebel against the Almighty God, that's exactly what is happening now in Western societies. Because of the technology they have acquired in the Twenty-First Century, Western Nations have created and operated a corrupt system. Power has allowed western nations to interfere in other countries' affairs because of the maximum power they have, especially on a financial basis. Power has made Western countries legalize killing infants in the name of freedom and not criminally charge the doctors. Power also allowed Western countries to legalize gay marriage, which is contrary to Almighty God's creation. Finally, Nimrod, as a son of Cush, never introduced any of those when he was mighty before the Lord. Some are just trying to defame the image of Cush and his descendants simply because Western arrogance does not want to accept that the origin of mankind was black, and as such, they want to create the wrong thinking to let the followers believe them. The Creator created the anus to eliminate waste products and not for sexual use; it's precisely unacceptable, nor should it be allowed for practices at all levels of human beings. Horatius Bonar D. D 1808-1889 wrote this context. "Some of the old translations render the word giant, identifying Nimrod with the old race of giants of whom we read not infrequently in scripture, and still more often in fable. But mighty as Nimrod was, raised up in his greatness above the mighty of generation, there is mightier than he among the sons of men of whom he is but the type." This might be relevant information certainly because mankind was composed of giants in those days. They have inherited their children into our race; it is scripture facts, not based on opinion. Giants have intermarriage with humanity, and this happened before the flood took place. It states this: "And it came to pass, when men began to multiply on the face of the earth, and daughters were born unto them, that the sons of God saw the daughters of men that they were fair; and they the wives of all which they chose. And the Lord said, my spirit it shall not always strive with man, for that he also is flesh: Yet his days shall be hundred and twenty years. There were giants on the earth in those days and after that when the sons of God came in unto the daughters of men, and they bore children to them, the same became mighty men which were of old, men of renown." I agree with that description; the Angels of the Lord were on earth before the creation of human beings. Therefore, Nimrod's grandfather might be from the race of giants through his mother or father because when they went into Ark, there was no clear explanation about their wives. Either Cush was from the giant's race before Adam (check Genesis 2:11-13). The word 'mighty' began to appear in the Bible after the flood, the son of Cush Nimrod was a mighty hunter before the Lord. Therefore, it is said, Even as Nimrod the mighty hunter before the Lord. Israelites are the chosen people of God who were given the Promised Land, which was inhabited by seven nations. Four Kings attacked Sodom and Gomorrah, destroying the two cities capturing valuable weapons, including Lot, Abram's nephew. When Abram heard the news of Lot's captivity, the word Hebrews appeared in the Bible for the first time. Abram was living by the Oaks of Mamre the Amorite, brother of Eshkol and Aner; these were allies of Abram. Abram mobilized his men and made attacks on the Five Kings, and he managed to recover some goods and his nephew back. After news reached Melchizedek about the defeat made by Abram over their enemies, Abram brought some goods and men.

Melchizedek asked Abram to give him some of the recovered men, but he refused and offered some goods. From there, Melchizedek blessed Abram for his success and said: "Blessed be Abram by God Most High, maker of heaven and earth; and blessed be God Most High, who has delivered your enemies into your hand." And Abram gave him one-tenth of everything" (Genesis 14:19-20). These Seven nations were butchering themselves within these two cities, Sodom, and Gomorrah. Also, Melchizedek was among them, but he hid himself with remnants you could see above. They started wars with Abram before his name changed to Abraham, so the conflict in that area was almost after the flood. These seven nations are detailed like this: Hittites, the Gigacities, the Amorites, the Canaanites, the Perizzites, the Hivites, and Jebusites—seven nations mightier and more numerous than you.

Now let me explain the seven nations, who were grandsons of Ham (go back to Genesis 10:6&15 to see how my claims match the descriptions of the seven nations). These seven nations were sometimes called Anakim, Ammonites, and their description matched with the descriptions of Cush, in Isaiah 18:2&7 on how tall they are (read Deuteronomy 1:28 and Deuteronomy 9:2; also read Joshua 11 and 14). Their descriptions, in my analysis, matched how the pyramids were built. Because their cities were large and fortified up to heaven, we saw there the offspring of the Anakim. Those seven nations were living on the land flowing with milk and honey in the promised Land. Now, God heard the outcry of Israelites and came down to rescue them. Then the Lord said, "I have observed the misery of my people who are in Egypt; I have heard their cry on account of their taskmasters. Indeed, I know their sufferings, and I have come down to deliver them from the Egyptians, and to bring them up out of that to a good and broad land, a land flowing with milk and, to the country of the Canaanites, the Hittites, the Amorites, the Perizzites, the Hivites, and the Jebusites. I declared that I would bring you up out of the misery of Egypt, to the land of Canaanites, the Hittites, the Amorites, the Perizzites, the Hivites, and the Jebusites, a land flowing with milk and honey" (Exodus 3:7, 8, 17). Also, the same description was made in Exodus (13:5). I believe these Mighty people were the first to domesticate cows because their land was the only place described as one flowing with milk and honey in the Bible. After God drove out seven great nations before them and mightier than themselves, to bring you in, giving you their land for a possession, as it is still today, remark on this word from God. When Moses was struggling with the Pharaoh to get the Israelites out, the Pharaoh was refusing because the Israelites were among the workers who were preparing the bricks. I think that was the time of the preparations for building the sophisticated pyramids in Egypt. "You shall no longer give the people straw to make bricks, as before; let them go and gather straw for themselves. But you shall require of them the same quantity; do not diminish it, for they have made previously; do not diminish it, for they are lazy; that is why they cry, let us go and offer sacrifice to our God" (Exodus 5:7-8). These powerful people maximized their time toward work to the degree that they were not praying to God, who could give them maximum power. Of course, they were industrious and self-sufficient because when starvation hit Israel during Jacob's time, the Israelites ran to Egypt for food. I wish they could have inherited such spirit among our African leaders; we would have superior maximum power now. Nimrod was categorized to these people,

54

who have rebelled against God, but the rebellions of Israelites were not considered harmful to God, and I do not know why. Israelites frequently rebel even after God gave them a land flowing with milk and honey, yet they struggled until they became a powerful nation. When God made the restoration and protection promised to the Israelites as described below, Egypt, Ethiopia, and Seba were given in exchange for them. "For I'm the Lord your God, the Holy one of Israel, your savior I give Egypt as your ransom, Ethiopia, and Seba in exchange for you. Because you are precious in my sight, and honored, and I love you, I give people in return for you, nations in exchange for your life" (Isaiah 43:3-4). These Israelites might be in captivity of sins, otherwise there was no point that these two nations were exchanged for them. This God was our Lord before them; as I explained, the Two Rivers started from Egypt through the Land of Cush, watering the Garden of Eden. Adam and Eve lived there, so the ancestors of the Cushite's were His flocks before the Israelites. The values and characteristics of the Cush descendants were closely connected with the logic of the Bible. Although many scholars have defamatory remarks about Africans, let it not discourage us to fall apart. Being White or Black has the same coins as a black cow with white milk. No black cow has black milk, and interestingly Almighty God does not favor any color. The Creator's ways have many principles to follow, and demonstrating energy of faith is the key to pleasing God. The Nilotic people have similarities with Israelites, socially and spiritually. Social similarities, like the duties of the family of a deceased person among the Nilotic of South Sudan and other Africans, are still carried on until today. The rituals are performed for a deceased brother as well as a maternal or paternal uncle. Spiritually, the Israelites have the spear for their spiritual leaders in those days. The Nilotic's of South Sudan still practice like this today. Why they are related to these two issues is not known for sure, but we are at the corner of the Lord ever since; although spoilers tried to lie that race has a connection with God, that's a white lie. If two races were created, He is responsible for how He will treat them according to their behaviors, not by racial segregation. We are not evil as others had believed a black man is evil; we are better off than any other race because our attitudes have no problem with races. I request a voluntary DNA test between Nilotic's and Israelites to verify this because we have many similarities in all aspects of life through the Bible. People of real faith will be able to prove whether my claims might be true or not. Also, it will nullify whether there were two races in creation.

The prominent preachers or Western evangelists traveled across thousands of miles to the Third World to bring people to Jesus, yet they left their houses not yet saved. Suppose they do not preach the disadvantages of gay marriages, abortion, and legalizing whoring as being against the will of God. In that case, they are carrying nothing to the Third World because your houses are in rotten shape in the eyes of the Lord. In superpower countries, individuals do not challenge themselves for bad behavior; they just follow without saying why.

In 2001, one of my co-workers had asked me if I was married and had kids. I said yes, and I asked, "What about you?" She said no. I said, "Why?" She replied that she did not want kids. I asked her, "Do you think that your mom and dad were stupid to have you?" She looked at me! And she went to her work area without answering me. To her, that conversation was fruitful between us that one day she came, and she said, "Lat, if I would have met somebody like you, I would have at least a child, but now it's too late because I'm forty-two years old and can't make one anymore," and then she cried. That's what is meant by rebuking one another; we reshape our behaviors to the right directions toward Jesus..

CHAPTER SIX

Exposing Out Hiding Facts

Haran died before his father Terah in the land of his nativity, in Ur of the Chaldees. Terah and his son Abram moved from Ur Chaldees to the land of Canaan. They settled there peacefully with Canaanites; no Promised Land was mentioned by that time. Ishmael, son of Abram, was born in the Land of Canaan after Abram lived there for ten years. God's power began to possess him through Ishmael when an Angel of Lord rescued them and told Hagar and son Ishmael "He shall be a wild ass of a man with his hand against everyone, and everyone's hand against him; and he shall live at odds with all his kin. As for Ishmael, I have heard you; I will bless him and make him fruitful and exceedingly numerous; he shall be the father of twelve princes, and I will make him a great nation". Now the starting point of differences between women over husbands started with Sara. However, in the beginning, Sara began to show us the concept of multiple wives for one husband because her generosity and love for Abraham's resulted from blessing Abram through Ishmael. Not only that, the three of them were black because a white couple couldn't have accepted a black slave-girl to share her husband.

Israelites originated from Ham, the son of Noah, who was the father of Canaan, and that was the reality of the indigenous exodus who became Jewish and Israelites. Ezekiel Chapter sixteen proves my consciousness of why we were close to Israelites with regards to the Bible. "And say, thus says, the Lord God to Jerusalem: 'Your origin and your birth were in the land of the Canaanites; your father was an Amorite and your mother a Hittite'" (Ezekiel 16:3). Chapter three stated that if my readers are not lazy, they will be on and back from Genesis Chapter ten verifying verses six and fifteen to see my claims. It is well articulated that Israelites are grandsons of Ham according to verification, and therefore Israelites were black if they claimed Jerusalem to be their daughter. "I passed by you again and looked on you; you were at the age of love. I spread the edge of my cloak over you and covered your nakedness: I pledged myself to you and entered into a covenant with you, says the Lord God, and you became mine." (Ezekiel 16:8) This word nakedness has connections with the nakedness of her grandfather in Genesis 9:22 when

Ham saw his father Noah's nakedness and inherited uncertainty to some descendants of Ham because it is shameful to see both parents in their privacy. "You are the daughter of your mother, who loathed her husband and her children, and you are the sister of your sisters, who loathed their husbands and their children. Your mother was Hittite and your father an Amorite" (Ezekiel 16:45). The statement referred to when Jerusalem was born. Her mother left her without being cleansed, nor was her belly button cut, but God cleansed her, clothed her, and gave her sandals of fine leather. (Oholiab) Jerusalem was a beautiful girl and tall; I believe that is why the place was called the Holy place for God before prostituting herself, which made God so angry.

When Joshua crossed to the Promised Land after he defeated six from seven nations, one nation made a peace treaty with Joshua, which were the Hivites. "Here is our bread; it was still warm when we took it from our houses as our food for the journey, on the day we set out to come to you, but now see, it is dry and moldy; these wineskins were new when we filled them, and see, they are burst, and these garments and sandals of ours are worn out from the very long journey" (Joshua 9:12-13). No town made peace with the Israelites, except the Hivites, the inhabitants of Gibeon; all were taken in battle. Suppose you visualize the treaty between Joshua and Hivites people. In that case, it represents the Communion of Jesus Christ's body, which is why they have Christians in other Muslim countries in the Middle East. "Your elder sister is Samaria, who lived with her daughter to the north of you, and your younger sister, who lived to the south, is Sodom with her daughter. You not only followed their ways and acted according to their abominations within a very little time, but you were also more corrupt than they in all your ways." (Ezekiel 16:46 and 47). These famous names Jerusalem, Samaria, and Sodom were sisters in the promised land. We should use their names with the background to understand what it means. As explained earlier, they were the origins of Israelites and Arabs because God made a covenant with them. Oholah was the name of the elder, and Oholiab, the name of her sister. They became mine, and they bore sons and daughters. As for their names, Oholah is Samaria, and Oholiab is Jerusalem (Ezekiel 23:4). To accept it or not to accept those above, read Joshua and Ezekiel to verify my allegations. Why were the Israelites butchering themselves in the

Promised Land? It was because those living in the Promised Land were so wicked that they slaughtered their children to an idol and practicing prostitution within them. They were prostituting themselves with different men while they had their husbands. They paid gifts to all workers for sex activities; however, they did not understand prostitution was a great mistake to their God. These two points show disobedience to their God, and as such, Jehovah called Moses to restore the dignity of the Promised Land. And therefore, Lord removed them from his presence, as He had warned through all His servants the prophets. So, the people of Israel were taken from their homeland into exile in Assyria, and they are still there. However, the tribe of Judah was left in Jerusalem. Those who made a peace treaty with Joshua were the origin of Jerusalem; you could see above how the treated represented Communion of today. Egypt, Cush, Put, and Canaan were brothers; you can imagine how the Egyptians made the tough decision when the Israelites defeated them in the October war of 1973. Both Israelites and Egyptians negotiated peace settlements of withdrawals from Sinai and autonomy for the Arabs of Samaria, Judea, and Gaza. Anwar Sadat, for example, would talk in private about the Arabs as if he were someone who did not feel a total identification, "Those Arabs," he would say. Both he and his countrymen thought of themselves as a little separate, a little distinct. In their own eyes, they were the inheritors of the great ancient pre-Arab world of Kings and pharaohs, Arab, yes, but at the same time something more than Arab (Ariel Sharon, An Autobiography Warrior page 393.) That statement was an indication that Egyptians were by spirit consciousness of not being Arab. If the African leaders evaluated Biblical facts, then the problems of Arabs and Israelites could be resolved within twenty-four hours because we are brothers. Jordanians are descendants of Lot's uncle's son of Abraham because those called Whobites originated from Moabites Ben-Ammi, and that's why Arabs marry within the circle families (read Genesis 19:30-38). The peace they made for themselves lasted forever because that was like the one made by Joshua and his uncles after he defeated them all. The point of my clarification was in Genesis (15:16) and Joshua (24:15). So those who went back with Abraham were fourth generations, which means other Israelites were already in the promised Land. As doubtful or comparison, any remarks I made have concluded that we are brothers, unless those concerned with race may raise their nose and deny. The African countries who forged a relationship with the state of Israel should embrace each other through Biblical Foundation, which may normalize the relation between Arabs and Israelites rather than encouraging strife differences.

The Holy Book is not focusing on the prayers alone to us. It is a source of discovering why we exist on this planet. Using the Bible for prayers alone, the majority will neglect the significant part of their lives. The sick element is trying to push us out of the history of humans, telling us different stories simply because we do not read the Bible for our benefit. Human beings have been concentrating in Sudan, Ethiopia, Egypt, Iraqi, Iran, Damascus, Lebanon, Turkey, part of Southeast Asia where Indians are located, and the contention places between Israelites and the so-called Arabs today for thousands of years. These Kings below and their descendants lived in those areas before million years after the Great Flood or the destruction of mankind for immoralities.

Nimrod was allegedly the first king to wear a crown. "For this reason, people, who knew nothing about it, said that a crown came down to him from heaven." Later, the book described how "Nimrod established fire worship and idolatry, then received instruction in divination for three years from Bouniter, the fourth son of Noah."

Comments: I want to briefly emphasize the crown's point because Nimrod is a son of Cush, and Cush was well-known to be the origin of African nations. Most Africans still have kings (Collo King, Anyak King, and Zande King, who are in the new Republic of South Sudan now) who wore crowns. Are these marks a continuation of that described above? Is there any other way people may dispute the reality regarding the kings and wearing crowns that did not originate from Cush? If that might be true, did the British steal it from us during the colonization period? No other person in the Bible has established a kingdom besides Nimrod, the son of Cush. The so- called traditional beliefs of an ancient Nilotic had become the way of worshipping of today.

When Nimrod commanded people to build the tower of Babylon, they had one Language because Nimrod was the ruling clique, and it means they understood him because of one language. Nimrod communicated with Abraham on how he should accept his instruction to worship fire, wind, and water.

KING NIMROD

Copper Portrait compiled By Dee Finney

In Rabbinical literature: "As he was the first hunter, he was consequently the first who introduced the eating of meat by man. He was also the first to make war on other peoples, and his great success in hunting was due to the fact that he wore the coats of skin which God made for Adam and Eve (Gen. 3: 21); these coats were handed down from father to son, and thus came into the possession of Noah, who took them with him into the Ark, whence they were stolen by Ham. The later gave them to his son Cush, who in turn gave them to Nimrod, and when the animals saw the clad in them, they crouched before him so that he had no difficulty in catching them. People, however, thought that these feasts were due to his extraordinary strength, so they made him their king." Before the Industrial revolution of the Western world, Nilotic knew of some trees to get fire. What I'm driving at is the introduction of eating meat by Nimrod. He might be the one who also introduced how to get fire among the specific trees. If you go to South Sudan now, if there are no matches, they will use their abilities to bring fire as soon as possible from any tree they know.

Is the picture above the continuation of what is found from the Nilotic in South Sudan, or is it different from them? Where did the tattoos originate from, like the one on Nimrod's face and the ones on the Jewish faces from those found in the tombs? Do the Jewish people have blood relationships or common cultures previously with the Nilotic? Is this the notorious guy mentioned above influencing black genetics of today around the globe? "An estimate was compiled by the German ethnologist Richard Andell and published in 1881. Around 402,996 in Africa were Jewish, the descendants of Jewish exiles who married African wives. Because the Jewish profile among the brick makers, whose faces are painted upon the ancient tombs of

Benin-Hassan in Egypt, among them may be mentioned the Jewish Negroes of central Africa, the black Jews of the coast of Malabar, the Afghans, and the Nestorians of Persia" (H.L. Hastings (ed.), The Christian, Boston, Mass.). Are those Flashes part of the Flashes exiles back in 1984, from Eastern Sudan to Israel? Of course, nobody is sure, but there are many Jewish people among Africans because many similarities are found in the Bible.

Since many scholars believe that Cush created civilization, what written language was used? They stated that the Cush established rules of government, a religious way of life, organized how people live in groups, and moral laws. Why do many scholars say we don't have written documented stories when they trace civilized culture through the records of Cush and his descendants? Do they mean the African people of today, or do they tell with 'unrecorded stories'? Is the history of mankind reversed from Adam to be Cush, who was mentioned before Adam?

Why is there no significant story after Adam? he lived for 930 years because no creditable account had been able to explain his lifetime on earth except being a father.

Text of the Midrash Raba Version

The following version of the Abraham vs. Nimrod confrontation appears in the Midrash Raba, a major compilation of Jewish Scriptural exegesis. The part relating to Genesis, in which this appears in Chapter 38, 13, is considered to date from the Sixth Century.

נטלו ומסרו לנמרוד. אמר אלא
אברהם לו אמר "לאש עבוד:
את שמכבים ,למים ואעבוד
למים עבוד:נמרוד לו ?אמר האש
לענן ,אעבוד כך :אם :לו אמר!
עבוד ,לו ?אמר המים את שנושא
לרוח ,אעבוד כך אם :לו אמר !לענן
:לרוח עבוד :לו ?אמר עננים שמפזרת
שסובל ,אדם לבן ונעבוד :לו אמר!
מכביר אתה מילים לו ?אמר הרוחות
,לאור אלא משתחוה איני אני
אלוה ויבא ,בתוכו משליכך אני הרי
הימנו ויצילך לו משתחוה - .אתה שם
נפשך מה :אמר עומד הרן שם היה!
'משל מר או - אברהם ינצח אם,
מר או - נמרוד ינצח ואם',אני אברהם
אברהם שירד כיון.'אני נמרוד משל'
משל :לו אמרו ,וניצול האש לכבשן
אברהם משל :להם אמר ?אתה מי
לאור והשליכוהו נטלוהו.אני
פני על ומת ויצא מעיו בני :ונחמרו,
על הרן וימת נאמר וכך .אביו תרח
רבה בראשית". (אביו תרח פני

(...) He [Abraham] was given over to Nimrod. [Nimrod] told him: Worship the Fire! Abraham said to him: Shall I then worship the water, which puts off the fire! Nimrod told him: Worship the water! [Abraham] said to him: If so, shall I worship the cloud, which carries the water? [Nimrod] told him: Worship the cloud! [Abraham] said to him: If so, shall I worship the wind, which scatters the clouds? [Nimrod] said to him: Worship the wind! [Abraham] said to him: And shall we worship the human, who withstands the wind? Said [Nimrod] to him: You pile words upon words, I bow to none but the fire—in it shall I throw you and let the God to whom you bow come and save you from it!

Haran [Abraham's brother] was standing there. He said [to himself]: what shall I do? If Abraham wins, I shall say: "I am of Abraham's [followers]," if Nimrod wins I shall say "I am of Nimrod's [followers]." When Abraham went into the furnace and survived, Haran was asked: "Whose [follower] are you?" and he answered: "I am Abraham's!" [Then] they took him and threw him into the furnace, and his belly opened and he died and predeceased Terach, his father. [The Bible (Genesis 11:28, mentions Haran predeceasing Terach, but gives no details.]

63

Let me support some of which are related to the Nilotic on the point above. Some tribes believe in fire, water, wind, lions, snakes, and others not pointed out in that content. If correct, then those who respect the three explained might be descendants of Nimrod. But who was the translator between Nimrod and Abraham if that is true information? If that translation from what language to Hebrew, if not, then the main language might be from Cush, the first name mentioned before Adam. There are three things to be explained here: Firstly, many scholars believed that the origin of civilization belongs to Cush, and at the same time, they do not believe the origin of human beings is black. Secondly, as it was mentioned before that Nimrod is the father of Azurad, the wife of Eber, mother of Peleg if that is confirmed to be true; therefore, the origin might be Nilotic, or those who are existing in part of Southern Sudan now and in other parts in Africa.

Thirdly, people are running away from their real origin simply because Westerners do not believe something originated from black skin, which is not true information. But then again, think wisely: why did Cush's name appear first? We are descendants of the first King after the flood that made his Kingdom in Babel, Erech, and Accad; all of them were in the land of Shinar. Tracing genealogy is an attempt to know where human beings have originated. Even still, certain gaps in tracing genealogy cannot account for every ancestor. For example, when I trace my genealogies, I manage to account for up to eleven generations. Still, that was not the beginning of the existence of my ancestors on Earth. As I elaborated in the references to King Nimrod, he established his Kingdom in many places, and after that, he started waging the worst wars with different kings. These famine-related wars eliminated a considerable number of brilliant African groups, and that's where the records of the writings had disappeared in Africa.

Records of my claims are available in the Bible, where the entire confrontation between many kings can be traced back to Nimrod, who made himself the King of the people in Assyria. Those living in Assyria knew how to write before us, and certain generations got wiped off either because of wars among themselves or disobedience to God. I believe those generations had made creditable information discovered now by archeologists in Africa and Asian countries. Many references are in 2 Chronicles (from Chapter one to the last chapter). Our Nilotic ancestors were brilliant human beings, intelligent to the point all archeologists have collected numerous pieces of evidence in Africa. Thousands of generations have paid prices due to the word Mighty from Nimrod, making them inherit something like a curse. But since God remembers us in Isaiah and Zephaniah, we had to fix ourselves to please Him. The only things that put us back are our leaders who have crowned themselves into an authority where they rule their flocks as agents of Western powers. They make themselves so cheap to the point where they spend a lot of time gossiping about one another to their colonizers. Assassinating those brilliants, men of 'nos, and a bunch of 'yes' men remain, so our resources are looted at daylight while they laugh with them.

Today's generation may change direction from being an agent into our common heritage where they focus on our welfare. We are much bigger than that, as Dr. John Garang said: "We have an ankh in the history of human beings in the Bible if we unite today, something bigger will appear because the Land of Cush is the center of Africans' common heritage cultures." It is ridiculous why we went backward while the history documented that our grandfathers discovered the entire visible phenomena. Ethiopia or Cush fought Israelites in the worst war in its history, where Ethiopians mobilized one million men and three hundred chariots. It was a major army in the history of mankind, they were about to destroy Asa King of Judah, but they managed to defeat the Ethiopians because God helped them according to the Bible. The Cushite's were probably defending their Mighty (Read 2nd Chronicles 14:9-15, NIV). Despite all the help from God, Israelites continued to rebel against Him. Each king of the Israelites came and did not obey God, and, as such, they paid a great price in life during the wars' period. In the book of Stuart Stevens narrated by Edward Holland entitled, The Big Enchilada, this information was stated: "Ethiopian history was often interwoven with that of Egypt" (2nd Kings 19:9 and Isaiah 33:9). "Because of their attacks upon the Land of Israel, the destruction of the Ethiopian Kingdom had become a certain (lesson foolishly ignored by Israeli enemies today). Many prophecies dealt with their coming ruin" (e.g., Isaiah 18:1; 20: 3-5; 43:3, and Jeremiah 46:9 and 10). There was an indication that the Ethiopians may have held territory other than in Africa, on the east of the Red Sea in what is today Arabia" (2nd Chronicles 21:16). Ancestors have confronted each other, as well as helped one another in wars with the Israelites. Those kings of Assyria, Pharaohs, and Ethiopians had either fought simultaneously among themselves or fought with the kings of the Israelites. " Different sources suggested that Nimrod was called Amraphel and Hammurabi, who was born 252 years after the Great Flood (of Noah). He was the son of Cush, grandson of Ham, and grandson of Noah. Nimrod was blessed by God and won all the wars he fought. After winning the war between the sons of Ham and sons of Japheth at the age of 40, he was made a king over the people, and built the city of Shinar and ruled from there. This was the same year Abraham was born". Because of that notoriety, our grandfathers had paid great punishment from that time onwards. Even today, many brilliant leaders are subjected to assassinations by so-called brothers in Africa.

CHAPTER SEVEN

Is Polygamy Sinful More than the Same Sex?

While I am still asking God for more wisdom, knowledge, courage, and strength, I will make a conclusion of why same sex marriage is not sin to the Western cultures, whereas polygyny is. Though homosexuality may exist in Middle Eastern countries and in some parts of northern Sudan, according to the reports.

The term polygynous is a Greek word, which means the practice of multiple marriages, and is used in related ways in social anthropology, sociobiology, and sociology. Polygyny can be defined in any form of marriage or having more than one wife. In social anthropology, polygamy is the practice of being married to more than one spouse at the same time. David Friedman and Steve Sailor have argued that polygyny tends to benefit men most and is disadvantageous to most women. Friedman uses this view points to argue in favor of legalizing polygyny, while Sailor uses the above to argue against legalizing it.

The idea is, firstly, that many women will have husbands rather than be prostitutes. Secondly, discouraging polygamy will put several women into the disadvantage of being sellers on the streets. Now because of that comparison, polygamy might be good to reduce prostitution rather than legalizing it. In fact, sex in Western countries is not meant for mating. For them, it is enjoyable until the two parties agree on whether to get pregnant or conceive. Western cultures always attempt to appreciate negative things by making them positive such as the legalization of prostitution, abortion, same-sex marriages, and using condoms to sleep with different men or women. As a result of this, God gave them over to shameful lusts. Even their women exchanged natural relations for unnatural ones. In the same way, the men also abandoned natural relations with women and were inflamed with lusts for one another. As a result, men committed indecent acts with other men and received in themselves the due penalty for their perversion.

They have become filled with every kind of wickedness, evil, greed, and depravity. This is senseless, faithless, heartless, and ruthless. Marriage in Western societies is a social contract between two individuals without involving parents, and no dowry payment made to the parents. Because both parties feel that paying dowry is just like buying and selling, and as such, human beings should not be sold to the loved one. I totally reject this foolish opinion. There is nothing in the Bible that tells us marriage should be free or not pay dowry. Paying the bride wealth connects people of God because marriage has the foundation in the Bible, and we should not adapt immoral attitudes of Western elements. Love is not about kissing one another in public places; love is secret practices between the two partners in their respective places, and the Creator is their witness in what is done in secret.

Below is what the Bible tells us in references to the old marriages up to our present time: "Then Shechem said: 'Dinah's father and brothers, let me find favor in your eyes, and I will give you whatever you ask, make the price for the bride and the gift I'm to bring as great as you like, and I will pay whatever you ask me. Only give me the girl as my wife'" (Genesis 34:11 and 12, NIV and again Genesis 29 :17-22 NLT, 1 Samuel 18:23 NLT). "Dinah was a daughter of Jacob while Shechem is a son of Hamor—both fell in love in order to form a family. The boy was aware that someone's daughter could not be taken without paying whatever her father demanded as dowry. He discussed the issue with his parents, relatives, and friends about contributing to his marriage. The bride's groom was so proud to the point he wanted to pay whatever the girl's father asked for dowry; he and the relatives will be ready to pay". Was that a matter of selling and buying to those proud that God's principle belongs to them and avoided paying dowry to someone's daughter, or was it a principle laid down by God? Would it be better if they just said, "I love you" and kissed, but in less than a week, you see them in on divorce court demanding a divorce because nothing cemented the marriage? Paying dowry among the Nilotic and Africans generally is why our marriages last because dowry is prestigious to both couples. They have to respect each other to the point they cannot depart from each other easily. Valid marriages had also saved Jewish catastrophes in the days of King Ahasuerus, who deposed Queen Vashti and replaced her with Esther.

Esther was adopted by Mordecai when both her father and mother died, and all of them were Jewish. This king was probably from India; he was a ruler there up to Ethiopia. One hundred twenty-seven provinces where under his kingdom. His spies or advisors were running day and night, informing him that there are people disobeying the laws of his kingdom. King Ahasuerus instructed all the governors under the command of Haman to destroy the Jewish elements. Queen Esther as the king's wife, could not permit such destructions to happen to her Jewish fellows while she was the wife of King Ahasuerus. Esther averted the evil design and plot to kill her Jewish people and requested a revoking letter which was written to destroy the Jewish. That's an example of the benefit of official marriage. If she were a girlfriend like what we are practicing now, she wouldn't have rescued her Jewish fellows. It is not our doctrine in Africa. It's God's system to obey. If people doubt the dowry doctrine, they have a right to dispute it Biblically and not based on opinion or intellectual argument. You should not be proud that we are children of Abraham, while his rules are thrown away. Does requiring education mean to change our cultures or to be assimilated into baseless culture? Socially, Westerners have a misfortune of conduct; DNA tests identify one-third of their children due to random sexual behaviors. But in African cultures, underage girls who become pregnant are condemned. Why do they teach sex in schools? What is the usefulness of teaching sex? If they were trying to avoid the early practices of sex, why do they teach it? Do they think their children are dumb to an extent that they do not know sex for themselves? Westerners criticize Africans around marriages, whereas they have their wickedness which needs to be exposed. Why do they use DNA test for identification for the bunch of kids? This means they use sex like animals who entertain themselves without knowing one another, and as a result, they do not know who slept who. They don't have proper motives of engaging besides having material which can push her to sleep with anybody. Maury Show and Jerry Springer are my witnesses of what I stated above; I'm always shocked when I see such a show of identification. It is total bankruptcy of society, both morally, and socially. Ladies cry when they find out that they brought different men to the show. Morally, Westerners are not better than Africans at all.

They see anything with money as the best idea regardless of how harmful the consequences are in God's eyes. If the Western pastors think polygamy is practiced because of the primitiveness, why are they legalizing prostitution, abortion, gay marriages, medical motivation, and condoms? Is it because of the revenues they get from the above categories? Are they good in modern

Christianity? Did God permit those? Western pastors never condemned gay marriages more than they condemned polygamy as a sin. Where in the Bible does God permit gay marriages and legalizing prostitution for revenues? Check the consequences of prostitution in Hosea (9, NIV) or in any translation. Polygamy has been practiced since the creation of man, before Noah and after the Great Flood. The same pastors who condemned polygamy are blessing gay marriages in their churches today in Western countries. Is this what the Bible tells us in (Genesis Ch.2:24), which says for this reason a man will leave his father and mother and be united to his wife, and they will become one flesh? Who will go to hell now? Are they polygamists or gay marriage people? according to the Western pastors? Even though God the Creator did not condemn polygamy, yet those who are wicked morally have condemned polygamy with stranger terms while they are blessing gay marriages in the house of God without shame.

WESTERN STYLE, NOT GOD STYLE: CONSEQUENCES OF THESE PICTURES ABOVE ARE EXPLAINED IN SODOM AND GOMORRAH CITIES IN GENESIS NINETEEN.

Gay marriage, in my view, is the freedom of enjoying whatever you like, whether God allows it or not. In Africa, gayness is a criminal act and immoral. It is Western intellectual choice, not God's choice. Choice and freedom (by definition) is an act of choosing power, right or liberty to choose, option of something best or preferable, an alternative. Freedom is the state of being free, unrestrained liberty of the person from slavery, oppression or in concentration, apolitical independence, and so forth. That's what freedom means, never mentioning freedom of marrying another man or woman with the same sex. If I shot a person by an accident, will the police arrest me even if I did not intend to kill him? But if two couples approach a medical doctor for the intention to make an abortion of six weeks without any reasons, will both be charged of murdering, or will they walk away under the name of freedom? I'm guilty of killing somebody by accident while medical doctors and couples are protected by law because of freedom. You People of goodwill wake up because faith is under the heavy attack of Western technology, and at the same time social welfare where many ladies dislodge their husbands because social welfare may assist them. Social welfare is a tool for dismantling social life in western cultures. I think the way it was designed is no longer there because Westerners are waging a cold war on Africans Americans to dismantle their houses while laughing at them. Marriage is like bee and honey, when a bee stings you, you will come again and take another while in severe pain. It might not be easy to understand the parable.

Already, they have staged a war within the previous African American cold war of deforming marriages, and now it has become a new phenomenon with immigrants. If a boy or girl is insulted for being a bastard, it is a severe insult in our countries. The word itself may cause losing a life among the community because of the hate of being called a child of a prostitute. Now, it has become prestigious among women in Western countries where they are proud of being divorced. Lord saves your kingdom; marriage is under the serious attack of an atomic bomb to be eliminated totally. Marriage is a beautiful thing we should be proud of. However, it's just now like smoking cigarette where two friends share one cigarette, and that's totally immoral to have two husbands simply because welfare may assist you. Africans Americans are not respected because they have been considered children who do not know their fathers or are being raised by single mothers. This has hurt them to the point where they lost confidence of reaching leadership positions. Africans' American ladies do not have the ethics of thinking that having another man who is not the father of these children will hurt their future emotionally. The taste of having sex with different men is the same whatsoever the style may be. Stick with your husband like bee and honey no matter what because this is your prestige to being married rather than depending on social welfare, destroying one's reputation. You guys have tied your pants that also has reduced respect, and that's why many children are imprisoned without no legitimacy cause, because once you are wearing loose pants, you are categorically among the criminals, no question whatsoever. There is no point of showing us your underwear, we did not ask to see it, wait until someone asks you whether you are wearing underwear or not. You girls must dress in an appropriate way to close sweet eyes out of lurking clients. Showing a part of your breast is an indication of being suspected of being a prostitute. This is ultimately why African Americans revisit humiliation by our own accords; there is no reason for wearing loose pants, and, in the end, people blame the system. It may not be possible to accept my appeal to refresh conduct if you want a husband, or a wife involved with your parents. Let them know who he is or who she is. Let us refrain from adapting illicit sex to those who believe in themselves and undefined freedom of same-sex marriages, destroying the social norms of those who respected Christianity. We should not adopt baseless cultures based on lies and misleading, not only that based on a doctored God. Losing our rich cultures means you have no basic foundations in life because you have adopted different attitudes based on ignorance and pretension. Rich cultures in Africa are likely dying out because of emigration. We are losing our languages, losing our norm in marriages, and at the end we will be people without any values. Political differences among our leaders cause all these potential losses. And as a result, emigrants are looking for safe havens in Western countries. However, it turned out to be misunderstood by our children and their mothers. These categories are easy to be manipulated by others culturally because they feel that they were hostages without freedom in their countries. Westerners pass moral values, and because of that passing, people who are still running after values are behind the times, and that's why we are called Third World countries. Getting a cheque and losing moral values are the first priorities in American cultures. How do I prove that? Ladies expose their secrets just to be paid a lump sum amount. She is ready to expel secret information between her and somebody running to be President. The man has no problem provided, that both will divide the cheque equally. No one cares about the shameful aspect because the value of the cheque has erased shame.

CHAPTER EIGHT

Disadvantages of Various Contraception

Minimizing adultery among Dinkas or Nilotic generally has some psychological effect, where both adulteresses are prevented from seeing a sick person and holding newborns. These categories are very sensitives to their views. They believed once unholy, touching them may intensify the sickness. That was a psychological condom protecting personalities and reducing immoral conduct before the physical condom was introduced in recent years. Because of Western influence, Dinka's do not emphasize this practice as much anymore. But to go forward, you must understand that you must have a historical background; otherwise, going forward without fundamental beliefs will end in vain. Are condoms helping prevent endemic diseases? Yes. But does it protect loyalty amongst the couple? No. Because of the influence of technology, people who engage in these behaviors are not prevented from seeing their loved ones who were sick or newborns. Technology is fighting with essential norms and cultures because generations of technology have misused sexual contact. Now, what will happen to condoms and other medicines, were introduced to prevent pregnancies? Loyalty and the dignity of having sex with unknown people have disappeared among our communities in the name of freedom. Previously, in the Dinka life, if you are a divorced woman, you could not have friendships with married ladies, let alone girls, because they were given a certain necklace to wear so that they may be known. That was the way random divorces were minimized within our communities.

Divorces with legitimate reasons are supported. For example, suppose a wife committed adultery. In that case, it is because her husband is very physically abusive or not providing her needs, or if he accuses her of being a prostitute although she is not. All these narrated above, and the rest were legitimate factors of divorce, not just for seeking being recruited by the groups of infidel women. Believe me, a good life between couples is not about the wealth they have, it's about being patient with each other, it's understanding why your partner was so irritated today.

Sex has no power of superiority; it was designed by the Creator to protect the dignity of being a daughter of Mr. and Mrs. It's about not being married again by another without a legitimate cause and it's about 'I cannot leave my child to another lady to bring her/him up in Dinka life.' I beg you to stay with your husband to protect the dignity of your children previously You are free using pills to prevent pregnancy, and therefore, there is no way to catch you at the corner of adultery. I can estimate from 1800 to the early 1970s that active sexual relationships with another's spouse have been very rare in our societies in South Sudan because family planning was well-known to Dinka's before others made it as a subject. When a child is weaned, a couple must spend six months without any sexual relations; this is the family planning of today. Now, other individuals may say that was a primitive way of life because enjoyment is number one topic, they might be right since sex has been motivated by pills, and they could not stay without sex because sex had been influenced by medicine and been legalized in other countries to get revenues. Dinka's were aware of the consequences of having many kids without having proper food security although we were living in small huts. You must make sure that you know how many cows you have for milk. Since the world of materialism has dominated life, human beings are not under the mercy of "De Cik" (Creator) any longer. Abortion is the killing of innocent babies, yet we preach in churches. "Don't hate people, don't kill," but killers are among us in the church. We teach others not to engage in sex before marriage, however, hypocritically, we forgot that those in the choir may be carrying a bunch of condoms in their bags. This is the ridiculousness in modern faith of today where people abandoned prestigious proud just because we want to be like western societies.

I don't understand how the Western pastors of modern Christianity believe in gay marriages because Sodom and Gomorrah were destroyed because they were attempting to have sex with God's Angels. Lot and his wife were preparing the meal for them, baking the bread without yeast, and they ate. Before they had gone to bed, all the men from every part of the city of Sodom, both young and old, surrounded the house called to Lot, "Where are the men who came to you tonight? Bring them out to us so that we can have sex with them" (Genesis19:5, 6, and 7, NIV). Lot went outside to meet them and shut the door behind him and said, "No, my friend.

Don't do this wicked thing. Look, I have given two daughters who have never slept with a man. Let me bring them out to you, and you can do what you like with them. But don't do anything to these men, for they have come under the protection of my roof." Lot gave them his two daughters as an alternative, but they rejected an offer insisting to let them have sex with God's Angels. Consequently, God punished Sodom and Gomorrah because of the wicked morals (Genesis 19:24 and 25, NIV). Verse Twenty-four and Twenty-five, respectively, illustrate the events. Then the Lord rained down burning sulfur on Sodom and Gomorrah—from the Lord out of the heaven. Thus, he overthrew those cities and the entire plain, including all those living in cities—and the vegetation in the land (read Genesis 18 and 19). During the Great Flood, the Almighty God knows the importance of being with one's wife; he told Noah and his three sons with their wives and each living thing male and female to be in the Ark. "De Cik" (God) never left a female out. Why? Because He was aware that male and female had to live together for the purpose of mating. Even though others chose not to have children, it's not God's choice.

Throughout the Bible, all the people of today came from polygamist descendants, yet God blessed them. Some of the examples we use are from polygamist families, who were Abraham, Jacob, Moses, and much more. Polygamists will die out naturally, not by condemning it as a sin because we love money more than having children. When God destroyed those cities mentioned earlier, it was not because he hated freedom. Those gentlemen were crossing His boundaries or going against His principles, in other words, violating the way He created us. There is no logical argument in gay marriages because the second helper to Adam was a woman, which indicates that he was in the right direction. If the second person was another man, I think there would be a genuine argument answerable to gay groups.

There is no doubt in my mind that the sign of destruction is knocking on our doors sooner than later. The deteriorating world economy, Iran, and North Korea testing weapons of mass destruction plus the continuing demonstration demanding the right for abortion and gay marriages are signs of punishment. Nobody knows why God was grieved by that time when He first wiped-out mankind and second time in Sodom and Gomorrah. The Lord grieved that He made man on the earth, and his heart was filled with pain. So, the Lord said, "I will wipe mankind, whom I have created from the face of the earth. Men and animals, and creatures that move along the ground, and birds of the air—for I'm grieved that I have made them" (Genesis 6:6 and 7, NIV). Lot made a counteroffer to the wicked young and old because he knows the consequences of disobedience to the Lord, Lot was also aware sex is between man and woman. I do believe the outcry which reached Him from Sodom and Gomorrah might be the same things of gay marriages and abortion we are proud of today. The wealth and technology we are proud of, as advanced nations, do not belong to us. It's God who gives us wisdom of technology and how to produce wealth. "You may say to yourself, 'My power and the strength of my hands have produced this wealth for me,' but remember the Lord your God for it is He who gives your ability to produce wealth and confirm his covenant, which he swore to your forefathers, as it is today." (Deuteronomy 8:17-18 NIV). Let us minimize our understanding because an ancient Egyptian pyramid has articulated our little knowledge while other scientists attempted to dismiss that there is no Creator. The pyramids themselves are and were challenging Scientists to predict when it was built and how it was designed.

Government recognition of same-sex marriage is presently available in eight countries: The Netherlands, the first country to legalize same-sex marriages in 2001, Belgium, Canada, South Africa, Spain, Norway, the United Kingdom, and the U.S.A.

Now, in developed countries when you discipline your children, they have a choice in freedom to call the police. If you have any disagreement with your spouse; he or she has a choice in freedom to call 9-1-1. However; because of the choice of freedom, he or she has the right to marry the same sex regardless of its consequences. Because of the choice of freedom, various governments have a right to give licenses to girls for prostitution, subjected to taxes. How will having faith in God work in such conditions? My appeal to fellow Africans is that although we are under criticism of being from undeveloped countries, we have not crossed God's boundaries to choose such freedom. Our communities have a right to discipline our children; our marriages are spiritually governed by God, not by choice and freedom of the world. I beg you to boycott such norms, let us not cross God's redline through the Westerner's elements. "Theologians of the African Institute churches, for instance, rejected the historical missionary effort to divorce

78

them from their traditions of honoring their ancestors. This effort tore apart their social structure; they feel, with no scripture justification: As we become more acquainted with the Bible, we began to realize that there was nothing at all in the Bible about the European customs and western traditions that we had been taught. What, then was so Holy and sacred about this culture and this so-called civilization that had been imposed upon us and was now destroying us? Why could we not maintain our African custom and be perfectly good Christians at the same time? We have learned to make a very clear distinction between culture and religion.... (For instance) the natural customs of any nation or race must never be confused with the grace of Jesus our savior, redeemer, and liberator" (Living Religion by Mary Pat Fisher, p.370). This has totally cleared the understanding of the Holy Scriptures; they should not be allowed to damage our rich cultures in the name of wrong translation of the Biblical scriptural way into their ways. Africans must refrain from being blindfolded by money. The ultimate wisdom is a spiritual way rather than an intellectual knowledge of the self. The holy scriptures are regarded as the divinely inspired word of God. The Gospel is not just the Holy Scripture, but also a symbol of Christ Himself. When Jesus said, 'I'm the Way, the Truth, and the Life, he meant the spirit we possessed in the lifetime because when our death comes, our spirit goes back to God regardless of being believers or not, our spirit goes back to the Holy place.

Several churches teach love and compassion towards people, regardless of their sexual practice while there are still teachings against homosexual relationships. My final conclusions are, this generation led by superior technology cannot listen to our previous norms because they believe that what they get from the computer is satisfying their enjoyment, regardless of the consequences. Maintaining your husband to them means you are not beautiful enough to be engaged because there's a story I may not translate very well in English. It says: "Good generation comes and go, reckless generation replace to destroy the perfect norms." Tasting many men or women is just a prestige of many styles in a youth's life, irrespective of how bad it is. It is a generation that is proud of getting divorced. From then on, social security will practically be your husband, in a sense; they will take care of you in the daytime, whereas at night, you might bring some handsome guy to satisfy you properly. But the reality is this, after three months exactly, both husbands (social security and her actual husband) will quit their duties quietly because social welfare is business; other telephones are ringing with new similar cases, too. Therefore, the old ones should stand on their feet with no more assistance.

The prestige of being a husband and a wife elevates personalities between both families; it's precious to your parents, relatives, and friends rather than being a prostitute or unopened clients to anybody who needs sex that night.

CHAPTER NINE

African Leaders Lack Compassion

Everyone must submit himself to the governing authority, for there is no authority except that which God has established. The authority that exist have been established by God consequently, he who rebels against the authority is rebelling against what God has instituted, and those who do so will bring judgment on themselves, for rulers hold no terror for those who do right, but for those who do wrong. Do you want to be free from fear of the one in authority? Then do what is right, and he will commend you" (Romans 13:1-3, NIV). Opposing the elected officials after you fail in an election is not the solution to our crisis in each country in Africa.

Though we know elections are rigged, we should observe the rules of democracy where opposition work together with forged elected officials for sustainable stability of the political atmosphere and economic sustainability. There is a lack of national agenda for elected officials. Instead, governance is based on ethnicity, not on the agenda of national interests. We should give their time and a chance, as the authority has been given to them by God. Although some are not aware that the logic of authority is provided to them to supervise people's lives, we should not be in opposition as an alternative. There must be the point of compromise to move forward, rather than to make a drawback. "If it is encouraging, let him encourage; if it is contributing to the needs of others, let him give generously; if it is leadership, let him govern diligently; if it is showing mercy, let him do it cheerfully" (Romans 12:8, NIV). Do elected officials govern our people diligently? Do they provide for the needs of vulnerable people and lead them into a harmonious life rather than kicking one another because of being bloodshed-thirsty leaders?

Our leaders have chosen the wrong directions since most African countries gained their independence in the early 1940s to about the late 1960s, but they still have the same mentality as before the colonists left them. Submission to God brings desire of a divine mind to us; old desires must be changed to new habits of having compassion towards their fellow countrymen. When human desires conceive us, then the birth will be in, and sin will produce death. Installing inept leaders because of ethnicity has become an advantage to the so-called "advanced nations." Their prosperity is because of us; the slavery of the seventeenth and eighteenth century is still being practiced today towards undeveloped nations. Seventy-five percent of our failures have promoted evil spirits to enslave us in the Twenty-First Century.

All promises given to Abraham belong to everyone, but the problem is how to activate the promises into realities—which is to have faith in God. The same supernatural powers still exist in each nation, but they don't know how to operate them. We are subjected to others who have turned on their engine of life properly. We shouldn't run to Americans or Europeans for solutions; let us run to God.

Why are we still poor, as people say? The problem is simple: we lack spirituality, and our finances and resources have been manipulated by the "Superpowers" of the world. Patience was how Christ set us free from the devil, and that is where we need to take our destination. Our emotions run out quickly; such behavior is a behavior of the enemy. When we accept Satan's suggestions into our minds, our emotions are affected, and bad decisions eventually pop up. We need to stand on our own feet. Hope cannot come without asking the Holy Spirit to manifest within us.

According to our oral history from our Great, Great, Great-Grandfathers, we were told that a particular sea was crossed to the place known as Africa, where we settled. "They were all baptized into Moses in the cloud and the sea. They all ate the same spiritual food and drank the same spiritual drink, for they drank from the spiritual rock, and that rock accompanied them, and that rock was Christ. This is another indication of the existence of Christ as the spirit of God; it was a biblical logic story" (1 Corinthians 10:2, 3 and 4). This oral story confirmed that what was inherited by many Cush descendants was a Biblical fact. If you were a son who chatted with one of the village elders, you would be aware of the story of crossing (Adakdit), which is the Dinka word for the Red Sea.

"There is a time for everything, and a season for every activity under heaven: a time to be born and a time to die, a time to plant and a time to uproot, a time to kill and a time to heal, a time to tear down and a time to build, a there is a time to weep and a time to laugh, a time to mourn and a time to dance, a time to scatter stones and a time to gather them, a time to embrace and a time to refrain, a time to search and a time to give up, a time to keep and a time to throw away, a time to tear and a time to mend, a time to be silent and a time to speak, a time to love and a time to hate, a time for war and a time for peace" (Ecclesiastes 3:1-8). God knows our activities on earth; all the times of the above are His words. My interest was the last verse. Peace is essential to us at all times, and when there is no peace in our continent or any country in Africa, people are at the mercy of aid. Can we not shift our attention to God rather than focus on others? The moment we focus on others, the more we are fueling our conditions. World forces have different interests, and if their interests are not served, they will give guns to other parties to fight severely. But God does not have an interest in the suffering of His people; He likes us to be in peace; see how He narrated the last verse time for peace. No one will fix our house, which is Africa, except us with the help of God. Let us get rid of the crazy idea of pointing our guns towards each other. No one has guns; precisely, we end up destructing ourselves and wasting our resources. However, the Superpowers of the world were laughing at us while accumulating wealth in the name of hungry people and diseases in Africa. In other cases, they will eliminate the acceptable leader as a dictator because there is a slogan that many brilliant leaders were killed under that pretext.

Why do Western countries accept peace calls? Peace is a source of being rich materially and spiritually; war is a source of poverty and slavery. Prosperity cannot prevail unless we have made peace with God. Our spirits are constantly with grief, and spirit belongs to God. "But the fruit of the Spirit is love, joy, peace, patience, kindness, goodness, faithfulness, gentleness, and self-control. Against such things, there is no law. Those who belong to Christ Jesus have crucified sinful nature with its passions and desires. Since we live by the Spirit, let us keep in step with the Spirit. Let us not become conceited, provoking, and envying each other" (Galatians 5:22-26, NIV). The moments we lose one of those above, then we are indefinitely fighting amongst ourselves. It is an obligation to everyone to restore these precious words. Spirit is like fire— it can burn us as well as warm us during the cold. Authority of the world will not change people except the word of wisdom from God, who gives forgiveness and prosperity.

If the so-called Third World maintains peace for six months and creates middle-class jobs, you will see how the main power will restore itself into their respective countries. However, that hope will not come unless pastors and lawmakers develop strong prayers and draft laws. We cannot overcome our difficulties with our own brains without help from the Almighty God.

We cannot overcome our difficulties with our brains without help from the Almighty God. There's no way to disarm western forces if we are not cooperating with the Holy Spirit. Working on our power has reached deadlock. No one had called for justice, none pledges his case with integrity. Instead, they rely on empty arguments and speak Lise. They conceive trouble and give birth to evil. According to Isaiah, this is how we are, no justice, accountability, and integrity. An argument is not to be winner; an argument is to meet a compromise with one another. But if we don't compromise, the other side has steps up, looking down, saying, you cannot touch me.In other words, you are not a man to lead to the promise Land. This arrogance will result in disaster if the leaders refuse among them as equal stakeholders.

CHAPTER TEN

Spiritual Leaders Delimit?

Being a spiritual leader has nothing to do with your tribe; you are beyond the region you came from. Possessing the Holy Ghost had purified the heart so that you act spiritually as far as your decision is from heaven. When the Holy Ghost qualifies you, you are out of the circle of human nature. As a result, you were not selected a leader by human nature. You have been crowned into the Kingdom of the Almighty by the power of the living God. As such, you have no boundary to stay in Uganda, Kenya, Ethiopia, or Congo without mobile preaching. All administrative decisions are influenced by heavenly thinking, where you act with conviction of faith that is controlling you. Keeping silent while the majority are struggling with dictators, the Holy Spirit will walk away, leaving you to implement your policies of injustices. You must motivate spiritual progress by moving around the believers to discipline them. The spirit of the Living God did not call you to preach what pleases the politicians even if his kingdom is in a horrible situation. Tell them the consequences of injustices because you are God's ambassador who is delegated to protect His peoples so that they may live in prosperity, peace, and spiritual progress. If you do not tell them about Biblical facts, they will consider the church a club, not a spiritual place where they are challenged. The spiritual voice may sound louder than an atomic bomb. As far as you have references in the Bible to show, you have been given the mandate by Holy Ghost to air the truths out. Spiritual Leadership is a capacity that will rally men and women to the common purpose, the character that inspires confidence. I am not familiar with the spiritual constitution of Africa as well as South Sudan, which says you had to remain in a particular country to serve. I am, however, familiar with God, who doesn't divide people by His Word because of tribes, language, or colors. I am also familiar with what the Bible says, "Go and make disciples of all nations, baptizing them in the name of the Father, the Son, and of the Holy Spirit." It is clear to make disciples in any village, region, state, and continent in this context.

Why are we accepting assistance from foreign countries while we localized ourselves to the extent that we become a bishop in our villages forever?

Meanwhile, we are internationally begging, and we localized the power of God. Is it because money is important to us, whereas preaching the Gospel to different tribes is unimportant? Are we preaching to our men and women not to accept forgiveness from other tribes because this is what you are teaching in your villages?

Why were we making noise around the globe that we want to be separated while we have even decentralized or limited God's vision? Why were you not rejected in your villages like what happened to Jesus in Capernaum when he told the truths? Maybe you are not telling the truths of God; otherwise, you would have been rejected. We cannot be successful if spiritual leaders cannot accept being ignorant about condemning injustices. We cannot be successful if spiritual leaders cannot condemn injustices of all forms among our communities and the ruling leaders.

Our politicians cannot unite us if the church leaders localize themselves. Politicians have their own agenda of unity, but spiritual leaders do not know who is an intellectual and who is an average person since God does not accept us in those categories.

The Lord is the spirit, and where the spirit of the Lord is, there is freedom. If the spirit told you to ignore people's suffering, you are entertaining the demonic spirit inside you. I believe these corrupt social structures are built while spiritual leaders stand behind them and the Kingdom of God suffers. The growing moral bankruptcy within the civil society system had been sentencing and condemning us to brutal captivity in a tribalistic structure. Church leaders must step up as video surveillance that sees things in the darkness. Being silent in a time of human crisis is equivalent to being a traitor to the cause of people. Dr. Martin Luther King said this during the civil rights movement, "Darkness cannot drive out darkness; only light can do that, hate cannot drive out hate, only love can do that."

Commenting on these issues of darkness and hate, it's true that they cannot bail themselves out from corruption, darkness, and tribalism because they are guilty of past mistakes. They are in a prison of propaganda where corruption becomes an epidemic disease to be eradicated. They are wearing the same shoes as the first thieves who protested in the historical reconciliation meeting in Rumbek. The South Sudanese are very unfortunate. There are nowhere our people can run to for safety. They fed us so much with empty promises of democracy, justice, and equality without anything that has been put into practical action. If you examine their empty speeches, you will realize how they were misleading the Southern Nation.

Seriousness is not a long speech of two hours. It's in the actions of what you say. The Bible says in Ecclesiastes: "Again I look and saw all the oppression that was taking place under the sun: I saw the tears of the oppressed— and they have no comforter; power was on the side of their oppressors—and they have no comforter. And I declared that the dead, who had already died, are happier than the living that is still alive. But better than both is he who has not yet been, who has not seen the evil deed that is done under the sun. When you make a vow to God, do not delay in fulfilling it. He has no pleasure in fools; fulfill your vow. It is better not to vow than to make a vow and not fulfill it. Do not let your mouth lead you into sin. And do not protest to the temple messenger." My vow was a mistake. "Why should God be angry at what you say and destroy the work of your hands? Most dreaming is meaningless. Therefore, stand in awe of God". People of the living ghost are made to be hostages in the prison of hatred, whereas the leaders are enjoying themselves with many prostitutes, and nobody is on their side.

Spiritual leaders must warn politicians that they should not take advantage of widows and orphans. It is dangerous to them; if they cry, God will hear their voices. This is not a joke or opinion; it is practical. Read Exodus below for your guidance: "Do not take advantage of a widow or an orphan. If you do and they cry out to me, I will certainly hear their cry. My anger will be aroused, and I will kill you with the sword; your wives will become widows and your children fatherless" (Exodus 22:22-24 NIV). "The great God, mighty and awesome who is not partial and takes no bribe, who executes justices for the orphans and widows, and who loves strangers providing them food and clothing." I'm not calling God for punishment, but my point is that the moment orphans and widows are in a bad mood or not reaping the fruit of their dads and husbands who passed away, then heaping sins upon sins will occur continuously. As far as the human beings' stomach is the source of happiness and anger, you cannot be happy if you are hungry; subsequent dynamics must be considered. "The rulers of the early farming communities were thought to have been religious leaders, rainmakers, and, in due course, organize in all levels of their societies." If civilization refers to those contents above, we Nilotic or Africans generally were well civilized, economically, culturally, and especially in our marriages of paying dowry.

All relatives, clans, and friends contribute to the marriages of their sons to preserve the relationship between the relatives. The history of man was running around these areas of Ethiopia, Sudan, Eritrea, and Egypt, which they sometimes call the land of Cush. We should not follow the wrong step of the Western world concerning biblical facts. They do accept the Bible partially, and introduce nasty things to use the anus for sexual enjoyment. Does this give good credit to accepting their advice? These people have no foundation in the Bible, which they claim is related to their present life; they want to push us out of history. However, we must defend our history based on biblical facts.

Africans have failed in every situation to be independent or to diagnose the realities, especially God as a creator. I don't understand why Western Church leaders have monitored our spiritual leaders. Does it mean that the God we worship belongs to the Western churches? Does God have regulations with Westerners, whereas others have none? When we accepted God as old and new, this is where we missed the point. God does not have two faces as old and new. Still, because we do not distinguish or critically analyze deeply, we are subjected to slavery ideas from a borrowed faith with no African roots Biblically. Now there are some contradictories that innocent people accept blindly, in other words, those who are dead by heart. What are the things? When you reference some logical ways of life in the Old Testament, they argue that it is the old way of life. Jesus has changed them. In the first place, people did not practice baptism in the Old Testament, but polygamy was being practiced. No one was baptized in the Old Testament. The names of Moses, Abraham, and others had a different meaning altogether. They baptized innocent people in the name of the Old Testament, the names of polygamists, which they have rejected. Again, the reference to the blessings given to Abraham, a polygamist, is the basis of the blessings.

I'm not against baptism, but my point is not to select according to your taste. In Revelations, God said: "I warn everyone who hears the words of the prophecy of this book: If anyone adds anything to them, God will add to him, or her plagues described in this book." And if anyone takes words away from this book of prophecy, God will take away from him his share in the tree of life and the holy city, which are described in this book." So, exalting yourself to the extent that you legalized killing babies in the name of freedom will not justify you being believers. Is that the meaning of being better believers? These are hypocritical attitudes. God did not give us the freedom to kill a fetus; he gave us the freedom to be out from sin, not repeating the same sins Jesus died for. So how do you accuse others of not being believers while killing fetuses? Are you a believer because of organizing crimes in the name of freedom? And you are calling yourself a believer of blessing gay marriage, intensifying sex behaviors through using condoms to womanize? And you think you are safe more than womanizing people?

Yet, they reject polygamy and accept homosexual marriages as a choice of freedom, whether their God likes it or not. This is what I call we are living on slave ideas from others. When they say we are poor, they do not mean by materials, but they mean poor ideas. People are in a weak position on everything. When you have isolated ideas from Western ideas, they will not allow you to accomplish the mission. But I appeal to those who have African ideas not to be influenced by tribal agendas to conceive you. Biblically, possessing an evil spirit is when you apply wrong thinking into action; the results will be evil. I think the serpent in Hebrew or Greek is a spirit because when you examine it thoroughly, you will believe that what spoke to the woman was her spirit. When God said, because you have listened to the voice of your wife, He meant the spirit of his wife Eve, which directed her to eat the fruit of the Tree of Knowledge and Wisdom.

Temptation is both spiritual and physical. When one of the two things accepts the choice, then we are in one of the two. Either you made an excellent choice answering the spirit opposing murdering, adultery, and corruptions of all forms, or you chose to accept the worldly choice. Then you are opposite to the above, and the answer is the so-called evil spirit. Who was tempted in Deuteronomy (8:3)? It was Moses' spirit; look at the statement he said, it's the same when Jesus Christ was tempted by his spirit in Matthew (4:1-10). In the Bible, there is not a single chapter in Genesis which indicates what date Satan was created. I do not believe the allegation of Satan existing in a particular place rather than living within us daily. Was Satan created in the New Testament or the Old Testament, and in which book? To give you my opinion with regards to Satan, these are the examples: gay marriages, homosexuality, tribalism where innocent lives perished without any legitimate reason, pride (where others think that they are much better than others), unjust governances where certain tribes are milking the resources of the country by themselves leaving others in poverty, and much more. Whatever does not please God is the work of the evil spirit. If you say the above are choice or freedom, as many of us say, then we allow evil into our communities, which is how we entertain evil. That is where they come in and assassinate our leaders in the name of being dictators. An anointed leader cannot localize his ideas to tribes or clans. You must get Africans out of poverty in views and spirits. Each nation has a language, and they know God from in their languages. Read Genesis (10), the Table of Nations. The so-called local languages are political words and should not be accepted in modern times. God did not create superior languages or superior cultures to others. However, financial power and military power could eliminate other civilized ways. The name of God has become popular because of civilizations, but that does not mean it was the beginning of knowing the Creator in Africa and other parts of the world. The reality is defamatory images of the black communities worldwide; we have never associated with demons since God created human beings in Africa.

After Babylonia was left in disarray, the Creator gave each nation the way they could know the existence of God. The Creator cannot be given regulations in western countries. The Creator gives rules to be followed by each nation if you read from Genesis to the end. You will ultimately understand the structure of today was structured out from the Hebrew Bible. African churches cannot manage their faith in a way they should judge themselves what it means to be a son and daughter of God. During the dialogue between SPLM/, and NCP on power-sharing and wealth, both had spent a lot of time discussing the fate of our currency. SPLM rejected Dinar because it is an Arab currency, which was not true Biblically. Denarius was mentioned in Matthew (18:28, NIV). But because we follow what Westerners say, we believe that is the right to think. From a Biblical standpoint, Denarius is a Christian currency; there is no logic that the Denarius currencies belong to the Arabs. Ask them where they had because Quran came after Bible unless they have borrowed it from us. If both spiritual and political leaders were not following the footprints of the colonization, they would not have changed the Denarius.

The pound may not be superior by itself. It's how much you produce and export out of your country. Political stability makes your currency strong, not American Dollars.

Spiritual leaders do not have sustainable evidence or have established reasonable ground that the faith we believe does not exist in the Western world alone. We must change the mindset in that way. Deliberately, we are inflicting the curse into our hearts. The moment we go to the Western world attending conferences, God will attend the mission together with us. After the conferences, we come back, and his principles are not implemented; accordingly, God's power will go back.

Why?

This is what we believe, as far as our flesh and interests lead us, despite having the same eyes, ears, hearts, and how to analyze what God needs from us. Yet, we are still depending on other people to support our spiritual leaders. Nothing will come out of those conferences if we do not establish our relationship with God in African identity. How many times have we attended spiritual conferences in the West? It's almost been three hundred years. Why do we not ask the Ugandans? They refused to be slaves spiritually.

Do we think God has abandoned them? A spiritual relationship based on materialism is dangerous. They believe in their hearts that Africans do not have God because the way of our lives has been controlled by borrowing faith. It will not be easy to let us stand on our own feet. To reach a goal, an individual must have a strong motivating force and an intending desire and belief that it can be done by the Nhialic (creator). Every inside situation reflected the external conditions. Let us change on the inside because a changed person can become a new man or woman, and that change comes through words by our relationship with Him.

CHAPTER ELEVEN

Ridiculous, No Justification of White Race

The English naturalist Charles Darwin first proposed his theory of evolution in 1859 (The Origin of Species). When he applied his theory to the origin of human beings (Descent of Man, 1871), he suggested that the birthplace of humankind was probably Africa. Many Europeans found it hard to accept that their ancient ancestors had originally come from Africa. Since the 1950s, however, scientific research in the dry savannah grasslands and woodlands of Southern, Eastern, and Northern Africa have provided sufficient evidence to confirm the truth of Darwin's proposition: Africa is the only continent in which evidence has been found for man's early evolution. The material evidence for human evolution depends largely on recovering and examining ancient bones, fossils, stone tools, and other artifacts. Since the earliest Homo sapiens came from tropical Africa, they were probably brown-skinned and similar in appearance to one or more of the many variations of African peoples of today. As they spread throughout Africa, they had colonized the other continents of the world and adapted to variations in climate and environment. Those in the heart of tropical Africa had developed the darkest skin to protect them from harmful rays of the direct tropical sun. Those moving to cooler climates developed paler skins in rays to absorb more sunlight. The so-called racial differences between the various people of the world are thus literally only skin-deep, which are local adoptions to climate and environment. All humans belong to the same species, and the origins of that are found in Africa (Shillington, Kevin, History of Africa, Rev. Ed., p.1). "The method used is interdisciplinary and is based on multi-faceted approach and a wide variety of sources. The first among these is archaeology which holds many of the keys to the history of African civilizations. Thanks to archaeologists, it is now acknowledged that Africa was very probably the cradle of mankind and the scene in the Neolithic period of one of the first technological revolutions in history.

Archaeology has also shown that Egypt was the setting for one of the most brilliant ancient civilizations of the world." (UNESCO Report, Vol. 1-11, 1880-1935.) These indigenous Africans were so brilliant even the famous

Moses of Israelites was instructed in the wisdom of Egyptians at those days (check Acts 7:22). This explanation has confirmed the origin of mankind was not in the West because most evidence of mankind has been found in Africa. All the evidence of old human information is discovered in Africa, where many Black races live. The other fact is that in today's Middle East, Southern part of Asia, Europe, South America, and even Australia, you find Black Aboriginals. "The Name Egypt occurred later on, and it was originally called simply the two lands upper and lower kingdoms or the Black land in contrast to the red desert surrounding it. How pyramids were built is not known up to now for sure. During the last centuries of the late period, Egypt was invaded by the Nubians of the Upper Nile or black people whom the Egyptians called Cush. They overran Egypt in 750 BC. And lower Egypt around 720 BC., the role played by these black people in the formation of Western cultural tradition particularly their influence on Greeks has recently become the focus of discussion among scholars" (Shillington, History of Africa). Those blacks living in that area called Sudan today have an ankh in the history of mankind; we are not living in this place called the land of Cush by accident without concrete information in the Bible. "Dark am I, yet lovely, O daughters of Jerusalem, dark like the tents of Kadar like the tent curtains of Solomon. Do not stare at me because I am dark, because I am darkened by the sun. My mother's sons were angry with me and made me take care of the vineyards; my own vineyard I have neglected" (Song of Songs 1:5 and 6). Solomon is a son of David, describing himself to his loved one how he is dark. He did not describe how white he is or how he changed from white to dark. In Genesis Chapter 2:7, this is what God had said: "The Lord God formed the man from the dust of the ground and breathed into his nostrils the breath of life, and the man became a living being." Now I did not understand the claim of westerners. It's clear that the man was formed from dust. Are they claiming that dust is white? Or are they claiming themselves the Holy Spirit might be white? How do they prove it to others such claims? In other words, that dust was not even from America or Europe. Again, the Lord God had planted a garden in the east, in Eden; and there he put the man he had formed. Where is the Garden of Eden in the first place? The Garden is in the Middle East of today, not only that, the two rivers running from an ancient passing through Sudan watering the Garden of Eden where Adam

94

and Eve had once lived. But for Adam, no suitable helper was found. So, the Lord God caused him to fall into a deep sleep; and while he was sleeping, he took one of the man's ribs and closed the place with flesh. Then the Lord God made a woman from the rib he had taken out of the man, and he brought her to the man. The man said, this is now bone of my bones and flesh of my flesh; she shall be called Woman, for she was taken out of man. This formation of Woman also has dismissed lies claiming that the mother of Jesus is white according to the pictures of Mary around the globe. Being nice or mean is not determined by skin; it is our acts and judgment since human blood is the same as Dr. Charles R. Drew had confirmed. He was protesting the practice of racial segregation in the donation of blood from donors of different races since it lacked scientific proof that blood from a white man cannot merge with a black man's blood. Some facts are to be given to our white brothers because Black communities around the world missed the right way of behaviors, such as sagging, being homeless, tribalism in Africa, which has cost many innocent people their lives in their origin place; these are terrible examples to us. It's now time for Black communities to change from sagging and being homeless, having random sexual or immoral attitudes, and having unnecessary divorces. Strong leadership comes from a strong family; the so-called freedom has misled you. Yes, freedom is there in politics, but not freedom of divorce and sagging. When we are addicted to bad habits, that's slavery; we believe in something that is destroying our reputation. Now, if we think back according to biblical genealogy, some great grandson's father might not be white because, logically, Solomon cannot be dark while others' grandfathers might be white. I do not doubt the possibility that human beings were created black. The white color came because of leprosy. "Naaman healed of leprosy was commander of the army the king of Aram. He was a great man in the sight of his master and highly regarded because through him, the Lord had given victory to Aram. He was a valiant soldier, but he had leprosy; Naaman's leprosy will cling to you and descendants and forever."

"Then Gehazi went from Elisha's presence, and he was leprous, as white as snow" (Read 2 Kings 5: 1, 2, and 27 for the complete story). "When the cloud lifted from above the tent, there stood Miriam—leprous, like snow. Aaron turned toward her and saw that she had leprosy" (Numbers 12:10).

These two verses also have the same explanation for the white color. It stated white color came as sickness of Leprous, which changed Naaman and Miriam, Moses' sister. This was an indication of the origin of black. When Moses married a Cushitic girl, he wouldn't marry the black girl if Moses were white. When his sister turned leprous—white like snow—was an indication she was not white. I need help from those who know exactly how the leprous changed skin, which will lead to the discovery of leprosy from somebody. I remember this is how we diagnose leprosy, as even our dark skin will change to having light skin in Southern Sudan, and as such, you are categorized among the leprous people. Have a clear understanding of the word to your descendants forever and white as snow!! Do the white people assume that these two words mean it increased being white more than what they already had?

Forever it means started from Naaman, and they will be white indefinitely since of healing Naaman from leprosy. Another color that has been mentioned in the Bible is the color red. In those races, no one has the right to present pictures of the Son of God and his mother Mary as something related to their picture. This is arrogant behavior. You cannot imagine the God Almighty as white according to your picture. If that might be true, where is the Black God or Red? Believing in that way than we are proud of ourselves, God does not love his people or reject them according to their images. "Then Peter began to speak: 'I now realize how true it is that God does not show favoritism but accept men from every nation who fear him and do what is right.'" He loves us when we obey his rules regardless of our colors. Sometimes we think about our skin very much to please God. Black ladies in South Sudan think that being white or orange may make them attractive. In other words, Almighty God made us ugly because of my skin.

Being attractive to your man or Lord Jesus has nothing to do with your color; it's the attitudes of our hearts toward both. Those who are trying to adjust their skin need to remember that you are not ugly in the eyes of the Creator. God doesn't love his people because of their skin; we are all his citizens regardless of our skin color. "But our citizenship is in heaven, and it is from there that we are expecting a savior, the Lord Jesus Christ. He will transform the body of our humiliation that it may be conformed to the body of his glory, by the power that also enables him to make things subject to himself" (Philippians 3:21, NIV). Suppose you succeed in making a cosmetic change to your skin! What do you think about genetics? As well as your man to be attracted, too, plus children you have already? "Isaac prayed to the Lord on behalf of his wife, because she was barren. The Lord answered his prayer, and his wife Rebecca became pregnant. The babies jostled each other within her, and she said, 'Why is this happening to me?' So, she went to inquire to the Lord. The Lord said to her, 'Two nations are in your womb, and two peoples from within you will be separated; one people will be stronger than the other, and the older will serve the younger.' When the time came for her to give birth, there were twin boys in her womb. The first to come out was red, and his whole body was like a hairy garment; so, they named him Esau. After this, his brother came out, with his hand grasping Esau's heel; so, he was named Jacob. Isaac was sixty years old when Rebecca gave birth to them" (Genesis 25:24-26 NIV). This is where the red color was mentioned in the Bible; it was when Rebecca delivered twins, presumably where the two nations were mentioned. Having faith in God is an abstract thing you cannot touch or see, but you must believe that He is a Creator. On the other hand, faith is what we hope for and is uncertain of what we do not see. By faith, we understand that the universe was formed at God's command so that what is seen was not commanded out of what was visible. Faith is the hope of what we do about our future; we must proclaim with high hope that God will help us to achieve our dream. Affirming those in many chapters before I read Dr. Nana Darkwah's book was a fact revelation. Still, the question is: how we verify your predictions while the Bible was silent because of the assumption that it a reference of everything's.

CHAPTER TWELVE

Crossing the Red Sea

I had stated precisely virtual factors disqualifying where the Bible originated and whether readers should follow the story closely. Whatever stories were done by each famous Name like Moses, Abraham, Jacob, Jesus, Isaac, and the rest of other names were written differently in both Old testaments and New testaments. They were not Jewish based on intensive research by Jewish scholars and Europeans to prove whether they wrote the Bible as Jewish or copied information from an ancient Egyptian African. Their outcome and the findings of Dr. Nana Banchie Darkwah, who knows how they were called based on his linguistic skills, prove that they were not Jewish.

Even though scholars knew they were hiding Africans being writers of the Bible. All stories in the Bible were written by Africans, and those who defined themselves as Jewish copied from previous documents. All different religions of the world branch out from the ideas of African religions, for example, Buddhism and Islamic religion. Crossing the Red Sea was the tremendous turning point for Moses to trust God's instructions according to how he was educated by Egyptians wisdom (see Acts 7:22). This verse remarks that the wisdom of the Egyptians instructed Moses, and Africa Christians couldn't figure out to question that above due to the fear. Why did Moses' parents allow their child to be educated according to the wisdom of black Egyptians? Acknowledgment of the origins of Jewish existence before the Bible was written was entirely acknowledging Africans who wrote the Bible otherwise; debating who wrote psalms, proverbs, song of song, and other books was nonessential. The focal point should be where Jewish originated. If they are unfounded, they were Africans because they lacked their original identity before their leaders spoke with God "Nhialic" as they claimed to generate a sufficient part of ancient Egyptian Africans. Moses never hesitated to believe that God's power could deliver the Israelites from pharaoh if the Egyptian army pursued them. "Then Moses stretched out his hand over the sea, and all that night, the Lord drove the sea back with a strong east wind and turned it into dry land. The water divided and the Israelites went through the sea on the dry ground will a wall of water on their right and left" (Exodus

14:21). Moses believed in the instructions from God because the God of the People of Israel chose their father. He made the people prosper during their stay in Egypt; he led them out of that country with mighty power. He endured their conduct for about forty years in the desert. He overthrew seven nations in Canaan and gave them their inheritance. This took about 450 years to fulfill the promise to the Israelites. When Jesus was doing miracles, it was not because He was a white Son of God, but he possessed the power of the Almighty God, which has nothing to do with colors.

When we give our selfish motives to the word of God, rather than looking through proper details of spirit and word by itself, for example, we ask who the Creator of the Universe is. How do we sleep and wake up in the middle of the night or get up in the morning? Why do we eat good food, and it turns out after twenty-four hours, like something you would not like? Why do we die? All those things are God's work. Although other scientists have their own opinions on the above, God moved you to the level of being a scientist. You were not born as a scientist; you learned to be a scientist after God took care of you.

In other words, God was the first person to perform the very first surgery on Adam to make the first lady, Eve. Do we believe this is what had happened to Adam and Eve? Jesus and his Father were neither white nor black nor whatever color, as people think that the Son of God was white. I call this a ridiculous assumption; God is the Creator, period. The more we believe the good news in that corner of the Whites, then we have pride and arrogance in ourselves.

Consequently, we get much resistance around the globe. People looked at God as a God of white people. "The Lord appeared to him at night and said, 'I have heard your prayer and have chosen this place for myself as a temple for sacrifices if my people, who are called by my Name, will humble themselves and pray and seek my face and turn from their wicked ways, then will I hear from heaven and will forgive their sin and will heal their land. Now my eyes will be open, and my ears attentive to the prayers offered in this place. I have chosen and consecrated this temple so that my Name may be there forever. My eyes and my heart will always be there.'" (2 Chronicles 7:12-16, NIV). In these four verses, God did not elaborate on a particular nation; He addresses the whole universe that He created, not the white people who believed that God is white.

Why do Westerners break the rules of God now if they were sure He is like them? Because they have disrespected the norm of the Creator, paying close attention to revenues more than their God as they alleged. Jesus does not show up in a human body until the New Testament. Isaiah's prophesied about the Messiah: he predicted the Messiah would come from David's birth line. He will be the cornerstone, a strong foundation for those who believe. Throughout the Bible, all people worship one God in the Old Testament. The word Christianity was not mentioned at the time of Adam and the time of Noah and his descendants. Before people were wiped out by the flood, Noah and his children were chosen because of their righteousness to God. The word "Christian" was first mentioned in the Acts of the Apostles. "Then Barnabas went to Tarsus to look for Saul, and when he found him, he brought him to Antioch. So, for a whole year Barnabas and Saul met with the church and taught great numbers of people. The disciples were called Christians first in Antioch" (Acts 11:25 and 26). Paul wrote to the Roman people saying that no human being is righteous; Jesus Christ is perfectly righteous. If we have faith in Jesus, we are freed from the power of sin, given a new life, and returned to a right relationship; we should live Christian lives that are holy and pleasing to God. Whenever you disagree with your spirit, you are conducting a different business. God is the spirit you breathe today, and we call it Christ; whether you like it or not, what you're living is the Holy Spirit that conceived Mary, the mother of Jesus.

God had to be glorified just as a Creator because all these denominations have corrupted His Name. He will not judge us according to denominations. Our goal is to worship Him as a God, not a denomination. Denominations are selfish praises or selfish beliefs; He has nothing to do with rubbish which has taken much criticism for nothing. God is God, He has never changed since He created us, but our selfishness has brought many names under His Kingdom. Faith is the product of the spirit; when faith in God declines, the spirit also declines. The faith in being alive is a reputation of human beings. In the Old Testament, Jesus was a spirit because His Name never appeared in the Old Testament, but the power of God was their thousands of years ago.

You become vulnerable to others when you have lost your faith, but what faith do you have to let others believe in you? Get rid of being inferior; follow God to your purpose.

Let us check the balance sheet of our capacity, thinking if there are some errors, we had to readjust the balance sheet of having God who created you, not evangelism. Our attitude needs to be checked so that the people of God can live in peace rather than in destruction to one another. Unless we submit ourselves to the Creator, we will not be set free because of being Christians, baptized, or born again. The center of submission is our heart to accept all the above. If our heart does not agree with us, there is nothing in you and me. Before Adam was given the fruit of knowledge in the Garden, he was blind spiritually, not physically; he couldn't recognize the difference between good and evil.

But as soon as the first fruit was given to him by Eve, they began to realize that they were naked. In the Gospel of John (chapter 8). Jesus was having a conversation with the Jews. At this the Jew exclaimed, 'Now we know that you are demon-possessed! Abraham died and so did the prophets, yet you say that if anyone keeps your word, he will never touch death. Are you greater than our father Abraham? He died, and so did the prophets. Who do you think you are?' Jesus replied, 'If I glorify myself, my glory means nothing. My father, whom you claim as your God, is the one who glorifies me. Though you do not know him, I know him. If I said I did not, I would be a liar like you, but I do know him and keep his word. Your father Abraham rejoiced at the thought of seeing my day; he saw it and was glad.' 'You are not fifty years old,' the Jew said to him, 'and has seen Abraham!' 'I tell you the truth,' Jesus answered, 'before Abraham was born, I am!'" (John 8:52-58 NIV). Understanding the meaning of that statement will give you an idea that Jesus did not exist physically, but he was there as a spirit. Nevertheless, Abraham was breathing by the spirit of God. Furthermore, reading the First Gospel of John and Genesis Chapter One may give you more ideas. Here is how it is written: "In the beginning was the Word, and the Word was with God. He was with God in the beginning." When interpreting the Bible, you must connect the Old Testament with the New Testament. It is not even easy for a pastor to explain clearly how they are related to one another.

CHAPTER THIRTEEN
Working Hard and Dedication

Now, this is what the Lord Almighty says: "Give careful thought to your ways. You have planted much but have harvested little. You eat, but never have enough. You drink, but never have your fill. You put on clothes but are not warm. You earn wages, only to put them in a purse with holes in it. "This is what the Lord Almighty says: "Give careful thought to your ways. Go up into the mountains and bring down timber and build the house, so that I may take pleasure in it and be honored," says the Lord. "You expected much, but see it turned out to be little. What you brought home; I blew away. Why?" declares the Lord Almighty. "Because of my house, which remains a ruin, while each of you is busy with his owned house? Therefore, because of you, the heavens have withheld their dew and the earth its crops. I called for a drought on the fields and the mountains, on the grain, the new wine, the oil and whatever the ground produces, on men and cattle, and on the labor of your hands" (Haggai 1:5-11). This was the message to those who refused to build the house of the Lord at that time, saying that the time had not yet come to take care of the house. It was also telling the believers not to beg to build His house. He tells those believers to let them build His house with their own resources. When we fail to comply with His instructions, He will not open the windows of the heavens to give us abundant rains for our fields. The land will remain dry, and whatever we get from others will not satisfy us, as declared from His Word. It might be the beginning where God knows Ancient Egyptians declining from us or wishes of Jewish translators! Remember what the Gospel of Matthew says in 19:30 &20:16: the first will be last and the last will be first. Did we note the logic now? In Jieng Agar, we have these parable which say: the first wife's kids serve the second wife's kids and vise visa.

How often have we called a spiritual leader to pray for us because we have been promoted to the high ranks official? When did we give God praise when our daughters were married off by one hundred cows? What portion did you give to God because you believed it was God who gave you all of those, and as such, you had to give Him a portion? Do not look up and say you know God while you pay nothing during the time of offerings. Who is taking care of you if you lose your job? Who is taking care of you day and night? Have westerners built a bridge between God and us? The answer to that above is simple; they are making their wealth on us because God has rewarded them. My friends, if we do not pay close attention to the house of the Lord and pay us tithes and offerings regularly, it will not be easy to become a millionaire as we wished. Paying tithes and offerings is the secret. Evangelists did not teach us this. They trained the early pastors to believe that they worked voluntarily without pay. On the contrary, they come back building churches without telling us who gave them the money to fund the projects. The secret behind it is that teaching us to those standards will make us independent spiritually, politically, economically, and financially. Now they injected being poor into our thinking to the degree we cannot bail ourselves out of the bondage of poverty because spiritual leaders failed to dispute the allegations of being poor. People did not take the word of God seriously because missionaries didn't have suitable methods of presenting the message correctly, and African people have become poor spiritually, not materially. Preaching the word of God as the savior without explaining in detail where people can prosper through working hard was not being taught in Africa now. Now it is high time to understand the gospel in detail of prosperity. There is an open door to allow God to crush bad attitudes in our communities (example: word of life can overcome tribalism, corruption, and nepotism because He is a loving father who does not divide his people based on race or ethnicities).

These are the most common diseases that plague Africans, particularly Sudanese. A new approach will break all the cycles above if equipped people present it. We have tried many things hoping that it will bring change, such as tribalism (to kill each other in the hopes of becoming the most superior tribe), corruption (to make those of your clans rich quickly), and nepotism (to employ your immediate relatives). All these have brought many disasters in Africa.

We are not yet independent spiritually because most churches were built by a friend's assistants or funded by European countries or the Americans. This contributes to the negative side of being believers, we cannot be believers, and our spiritual houses are built by others. We cannot be believers while British churches are paying our pastors. For Asians to come to the level they are at now, they isolated themselves in their own countries to think hard of overcoming the challenges. They made critical thinking of faith prosperity, critical forgiveness, and critical repentance. Critical emigration back to our respective countries will signal our father (who is Madhol). Our failure begins as a thought when we criticize our countries; we agree with Madhol to destroy us more because we have no clear direction for him. In the fight with the Babylonians: they will be filled with dead bodies of the men; I will say in my anger and wrath. I will hide my face from this city because of its wickedness. "Nevertheless, I will bring health and healing to it;

I will heal my people and will let them enjoy abundant peace and security. I bring Judah and Israel back from captivity and will rebuild them as they were before. Then this city will bring me renowned, joy, praise, and honor before the nations on Earth that hear of all the good things I do for it, and they will be in awe and tremble at the abundant prosperity and peace I provide for it." "The sound of joy and gladness, the voices of bride and bridegroom, and the voice of those who bring thanks and offerings to the House of the Lord, saying, 'give thanks to the Lord Almighty, for the Lord is good; his love endures forever. For I will restore the fortune of the land as they were before,' says the Lord." Restoring healthy, healing, abundant prosperity, and peace cannot knock on our doors if we are unwilling to throw back the old ways of life. Westerners are like us; they have nothing other than love for themselves. They put their nation first before tribes; God did not give these names of tribes or different languages of ruining us rather than having the joy of peace and prosperity. Let us change the culture of fighting into a culture of peace. Let us change the culture of hatred into the culture of love. Let us change a culture of distrust and suspiciousness into a culture of confidence in one another because teamwork brings progress. "For God did not give us a spirit of timidity, but a spirit of power, of love and self-discipline" (2 Timothy 1:7). Let us change the culture of corrupting into having compassion and concern for the national interest of justice and equality. National interest cannot be narrowed down to selfish individualism. National interest is the pride of generations to come; its footprint is where others will follow. We should thank God who gave us the beautiful land called Sudan with many resources, for example, cows, honey, plentiful oil, and the Nile River. All those need better distribution among them without any fear for themselves. Loving ourselves can attract different nationalities around the world to invest in growing a strong economy. The whole world has changed from running counterclockwise toward the right direction of justice for all. It's high time for us to run toward the freedom of justice; otherwise, Almighty God will deprive us of freedom and prosperity. Do not open the door where people feel they are coming out from minority clique into another "Dinkanization". That is a bad image that has harmed us for so long, and it might put the New Republic of South Sudan into pieces. Do not agitate to become a minor leader; you will remain a minority leader. Cross that corner to the national issues, you can be a minority, but your ideas are not insignificant. You may be the majority leader; however, if you have ideas of building up tribal leaders, you may become a minor thinker. This is the actual reality facing each country in Africa, and that's a flawed imagination. There is nothing called majority and minority in the eyes of the Almighty God. Saying it will qualify you and encourage you to think like a minority. Change is taking place in each corner. Barrack Obama, the son of a black Kenyan father and a white American mother, has fulfilled Dr. Martin Luther King's dreams. Now that he has been sworn into office, one can truly see the possibility of anything, no matter the demographic that you may face. Using negative advertising backfires on candidates. I do not know about you, but I feel sick and tired of the politicians' negative political promises.

Producing and airing harmful ambition will not convince people. Being a politician, have some faith in the public. Do not tell us why your opponent should not be elected. Tell us what you think about the issues on the table, why we should support you, and why you should be entrusted to represent the people. Being a leader shouldn't be a matter of where you come from, but more so what you have prepared to give. Distrustful leadership can engulf you into clan tribes and will not qualify leadership to the national center. Advisors will direct vision locally, but opening the room to many influential wills strengthens leadership to cross the local ideas. A leader's motto should be high to the nation's survival, not only tribes.

A nation should always be above tribes; tribes cannot exist with the nation's interest on the sideline. When throwing a stone at someone's camp, always be ready to receive the consequences of reply. For example, the SPLM secretary-general said, "The government he was in as minister of cabinet Affairs was corrupt and a failed institution." I think his statement might be true because Arthur Akuen Chol was fired three years from then because of sixty million dollars. The investigating committee was set up for fact-finding, but there was nothing that has been shown to southerners to justify or dispute it. This is a sign of a failed institution because southerners remain in limbo while nothing has been brought forward to nullify it.

Let us conceive a positive spirit of joy, a spirit against nepotism, a spirit against tribalism, a spirit against spiritual poverty, and have a spirit of prosperity, "In Madhol' Name, Amen."

The Bible says in Jeremiah this is what the Lord says: "Cursed is the one who trusts in man, who depends on flesh, or strength and whose heart turns away from the Lord. He will be like a bush in the wasteland; he will not see prosperity when it comes. He dwells in the parched places of the desert, in a salt land where no one lives." "But blessed is the man who trusts in the Lord, whose confidence is in him. He will be like a tree planted by the water that sends out its roots by the streams. Its leaves are always green. It has no worries in a year of drought and never fails to bear fruits." "The heart is deceitful above all things and beyond cure. Who can understand it?" "The Lord searches the heart and examines the mind, towards a man according to his conduct, according to what his deeds deserve" (Jeremiah 17:5-10).

Our choices if we continue to follow our fellowmen from where we belong not to trust God, then we are reaping Verses five and six; and if we turn and entrust all our success into his supreme authority; then we will reap peace, love, justice, and prosperity. How many lives have been lost after the accord was signed on January 9, 2005? All these losses are activities of the flesh, pride, and exalting ourselves to one another instead of his Name as the Creator. We exalt him by the flesh, not by spirit. Let us humble ourselves and have a new spirit and a new beginning to go forward. "From beyond the rivers of Cush, my worshipers, my scattered people will bring me offerings" (Zephaniah 3:10). This statement has disputed the so-called Cush descendants were not believers some time back. Zephaniah did not say that we were worshipping witchcraft or magic, but we were worshipping God, and that's why we paid offerings into the house of the Lord. The Westerners evangelize in a way that does not credit our relationship to Almighty, how we were related to God. Our pastors have contributed negatively to their alleged lies that we did not know God before they came despite Isaiah mentioning Almighty God would reclaim us. How will God reclaim the people who practice witchcraft if he does not know that we worship Him before them? Bible addressed the past, present, and future.

Cush and Canaan were mentioned in the Bible before the Table of Nations; Cush was mentioned earlier in Genesis (2:13), and Canaan was in Genesis (9:18). Noah, a man of the soil, proceeded to plant a vineyard. When he drank some of its wine, he became drunk and lay uncovered inside his tent. And Ham, the father of Canaan, saw his father's nakedness and told his two brothers outside. But Shem and Japheth took a garment and laid it across their shoulders; then, they walked in backward and covered their father's nakedness. Their faces were turned the other way so that they would not see their father's nakedness" (Genesis 9:20-27).

There is an important illustration I want to remark here because there is a point of missed information from many scholars. They misinterpreted that people became black because of the curse from Noah to one of his children, who is called Ham. Biblically, this is not accurate information because Noah was not a prophet to curse. In other words, the word curse has not been mentioned to the black race in the Bible. Some scholars say Israelites have originated as a subculture of Canaanites. That is accurate information; see the Table of Nations to verify. Some have confirmed that Cush was a large part of the land that included Northern Ethiopia, Eritrea of today, and most of present-day Sudan. The capital cities of Biblical Cush were in Northern Sudan. The rulers of Ancient Egypt were known as pharaohs. They claimed to be the earthly incarnation of their gods. The idea of where divine kinship originated is unknown, but it seems to have come from inner Africa to the North. The rulers of the early farming communities are thought to have been religious leaders, rainmakers, and, in that course, controllers of the flood.

They studied the sun, the moon, and the stars to understand the seasons and calculate the time of the flood. They developed the world's first annual twelve-month calendar of 365 days in doing so. Comments: This calendar type was related to our yearly sacrifices according to the year's season. Even today, Dinka's have four seasons in their languages. I'm not claiming they might be Dinka's, but there are similarities in explanations. It was believed that the origins of all the ancient world's earliest farming communities were to be traced back to Mesopotamia for a long time. Christianity came into Africa supplementary to a spiritual way of life that had already existed. Today's Royal Kingdom's family originated from Cush's descendants because he established the Kingdom in Babylon. I believe that the word "kingdom" was stolen from those of the Cush by the British. As most scholars confirmed, Canaan came from Ham's descendants, including Cush, who fled to Africa. As you can see in Zephaniah before, Cush played a significant role in worshipping. Cush descendants were worshipping the living God paying their offerings and tithes, yet our brothers in the western world were not convinced. Now, what is the first fruit? The first fruit is offerings to honor God so that He may give you power and anointing to get wealth according to the word of God. God's grace is filled with many benefits activated through precious faith or trust around giving rather than receiving from others. He wants us to enjoy our life and spread His Word out to those who have not yet heard of His son Jesus Christ. When we do not tithe our first fruits, we open ourselves to a dangerous life. The first fruits are the most significant investment to the Kingdom of God. Our God can pay dividends beyond our imagination success. He will give us the power to be prosperous and enjoy the fruits of our sweat simultaneously, requiring us to give Him a portion to establish His Kingdom and continue His work in the Kingdom. Even Solomon, the richest man of his time, knew the importance of honoring God with his substance and the first fruits of his increase. Our first fruits contribute to many things: First and least, it supports spreading of the Gospel, feeding of God's people, saving of souls, healing of sicknesses and other diseases, and development of future ministries

PART TWO

Current Leaders Never Learn Positives and Negatives from Previous Presidents

Part two will be dealing with a diagnosed sickness called tribalism, nepotism, failure to manage diversity, and corruption in Africa! Why is it challenging to cure or eradicate comprehensively? What are the factors diagnosed or reasons for Africans preventing their progress? The absence of an efficient and professional civil service and competent civil servants has been cited as an essential contributor to corruption, tribalism, and nepotism in the continent. Each country needs a competent, efficient, and professional civil service as a necessary condition for sustainable economic growth and development.

Furthermore, chronic poverty and inequality in income distribution have caused conflicts over resources. This poverty is because by the emergence of military power after the civil war, an important impact in resources allocation has had a significant negative impact on income and resources distribution in each country. However, what the dictators loot during the civil war causes collateral damage to the economy due to chronic poverty, not lack of resources. Another factor is how African culture contributes to corruption in the continent. We condone unlawful injustices in all forms and harbor corrupters within ethnicities because of no accountability and transparency.

A budget to the Ministry of Defense is just buying weapons for killing opponents or ethnic groups because of existing injustices. However, African countries have never fought each other besides supplying weapons to the opponents of the other countries. Three quarters of national resources of each country in Africa are put in the ministry of defense instead of High Education for research so that when epidemic disease surface, we shouldn't warry where to get a vaccine. According to some scholars, corruption arises from the clashes between traditional African cultural values and norms and other values and norms brought from abroad with political, industrial, and economic development. On the other hand, tribalism was a major problem. It

111

was necessary to have a political system that could bring together competitive ethnic groups to provide the appropriate environment for peaceful coexistence and sustainable development. Instead of engaging the people in a national debate on state construction, the so-called big ethnic groups undertook opportunistic forms that enhanced their ability to monopolize power and allocation of resources for their benefit.

A one-party system and interference of the tribal armies have created an unstable political atmosphere in Africa. But the ruling clique in each country in Africa has the same mentality, which does not allow such professionals because they might not support the Junta agenda. Many African are well qualified at this moment. But the professionals were not allowed to apply what they acquired in different fields. Also, another major problem is the proliferation of political strife and genocide. These problems are often engendered by greed, ethnic animosities interest groups who desire vengeance, and the highest illiteracy rates where their generals influence them to join the tribal army to defend them. The intervention of military dictatorship and rebel governments that control the countries in the political strife show no loyalty to the people they claim to serve. The bulk of the people suffers while the gun-wielding few benefits. These are the most formidable problems because of our economic underpinnings. Several past leaders, present, and future could not get rid of these diseases mentioned by many researchers abroad and African themselves as one tearing Africans apart. The difficult diseases our leaders didn't cure were how many times previous leaders enjoyed power and ended up in miserable conditions. For example, Muammar Qaddafi of Libya, Mobbutu Sek Seko of Congo, Zine El Abidine Ben Ali of Tunisia, Muhammad Honi Mubarak of Egypt, and finally Omer Hassan Ahmed Al Bashir in Sudan. All those leaders ignored and disrespected the supreme constitution of each country and the time allotted, yet the will of people compelled them to run away or die in action. On the positive side, few countries have term limits for their leaders, such as Tanzania, Zambia, Nigeria, Gahanna, Senegal, and South Africa. These countries where leadership changed hands progressed because of competition with multiple visions and economic and delivery agendas. The rest of the leaders asked them why did they leave offices? The answer will be simple: many of the leaders who refused to learn from past experiences are spiritually blind, and as such, they could not see the consequences of the above leaders. Isaiah 56:10 and Matthew 15:14 are references to those in falsity and ignorant of the truths; therefore, both are called spiritual blindness. Spiritual blindness is more dangerous than physical blindness because even dogs are trained to show the proper pass way to blind people. Spiritual blindness is tearing the continent of civilization into nothing because its prosperity should be based on spiritual thinking. Disillusion with trusting tribal supporters has never yielded the fruits of prosperity in decades in each country in Africa. Therefore, a viable solution is to leave the office.

If your term is over so that others will invest in new ideas rather than repeating rotten ideas repeatedly. After ten years of American independence, Lawmakers sat and discussed how America should look like in centuries to come. The critical question at the constitutional convention in 1787 was not "who should be president? Who should lead us? Who is the wisest among us? Who should be the best King?" No, the country's founders concentrated on "what processes can we create that will give us good presidents long after we are dead and gone? What type of enduring country do we want to build? On what principles? How should it operate? What guidelines and mechanisms should we construct, that will give us the kind of country we envisioned?" They created a constitution to which they and all future leaders would be subservient. This constitution convention was after ten years exactly. Numerous African leaders failed to develop such a conscious vision to save thousands of generations in each country. The lack of these conscience thoughts was the central failure of several Africa leaders because they did not have a moral obligation. Their interests and conscientiousness are influenced by their ethnicity rather than rebuking them to save the lives of innocent people. The vision of our leaders is to create tribal egotist superiority where others are prepared to be the best fighters, in other words, those who liberate the country, while it was done collectively. Reckless leadership is destructive; specifically, exalting and praising certain ethnic groups destroys African people.

After looting our resources, they create unnecessary civil war to prevent people from asking for essential promises they made during liberation. They became robbers, sex offenders, and killers of their own citizens. Precisely, 98% is usually the winning percentage of each presidential election in African countries composed of all ethnicities. Was that competitive competition really between the winner and loser? Did they have the same opportunity, likes debating programs of each on National Television of the country? Do leaders debate within their party so that the party nominates one according to their program of economy, international politics, social-economic policies, Health Care Issues, improvements of equality education, and road infrastructure?

Furthermore, a payback of 98% goes back to some individual families of the elected president, not to citizens who elected him to the office! Is it not pathetic and sad? Another ridiculous thing is when the president is supported by Diasporas, who know competitive elections. Are we not so ashamed to ask this logical question why the elected president won by such a percent and paid back selectively? Staying in office more than the allotted constitution period is a problem in Africa. A Leader's positive thinking has a limited timetable, and that's why there should be a two-term limit. Being a referenced president is better than being forced to leave by mass demonstrations, coup d'état, or exile. Constant amendments of the constitution are disastrous to progressive thinking if the elected president fails in two terms. For example, he would not think positively apart from being coined up. An attempted coup resulted in ethnic cleansing genocide of ethnic groups for an unjustified coup. Nevertheless, less developed countries' leaders quickly mow down thousands of innocent lives. They are quick to blame regional leaders and superpowers for sowing their own seeds like the Republic of South Sudan. Ignorant attitudes of our leaders are subject to distinguish between them and us because slaughtering your citizens and blaming others while it was your own belief to kill them are unacceptable. Let us be realistic to address our failures logically rather than blaming others. Furthermore, their interference was based on weak leadership exploited by superpowers. For instance, stealing billions of dollars and depositing them in European countries and American banks was a sign of exposing our ignorance to them. Such an attitude and behavior show that we deny our citizens better services. Howewer, what we manufactured for ourselves is more than their interference because making ourselves, as tribal leaders, and clans, is deplorable, unspeakable, and excusable from African leaders. We should know our wounds before they tell us to cure cancers of being tribal leaders and corrupters. Denying ethnic cleansing on December 15, 2013, in Juba anyhow was an obvious phenomenon among the southerners. On March 28, 1987, the Aldazine massacres happened.

Southerners denied that there were no massacres, even though two professors at Khartoum university documented it. Suppose Uganda, Angola, Cameroon, Chad, Eritrea's president, and many others failed to render tangible services apart from Killing innocent civilians. What will make Kiirdit an exception not to be on the same page with them? In conclusion, competition and limited terms should be the best way and reduce the number of political parties, debating within the parties, and equivalent opportunities during the campaigning elections. Otherwise, 98% and payback zero percent and blind support will continue to be the order of undeveloped countries. The time African leaders learn to value their diversity as a strength, their prosperity and African unity would surface immediately because they have not recognized the strength of diversity in each country. Utilizing diversity properly promoted Western countries economically and socially to make them powerful. Though discrimination still lingers here and there, they understood the strength of diversity and leveraged the manpower of the economy, specifically in American society.

Failure to manage diversity was the cause of failing to pay debts of promises to the citizens during Liberation in Eritrea, Zimbabwe, South Sudan, and other countries.

CHAPTER FOURTEEN

Third World Countries

Mindset after colonization had many various forms in humanity's survival. Suppose elements of individuals of yesterday are campaigning in our names for our sufferings caused by our leaders. In that case, we become liabilities under the same mercy of who is campaigning for us, and a stolen God will bless their hands and ideas to prosper. Raising our flags in our own countries, the United Nations, African Unions, or other organizations while the masters still control us economically. The flags are just political ways of deceiving our opinions. If we are independent, why are our leaders stealing and running away with huge amounts of money and depositing them in foreign countries? Why are they suspicious after securing political independence to the extent that they loot their resources while ruling the country? Why shouldn't they use the huge resources they pillaged inside their countries for better investments for the welfare of their fellow countrymen? Are they not yet independent in our resources? Such leaders lack confidence in themselves, for there's no point in robbing ourselves, leaving the rest into the mercy of somebody we waged war against yesterday to help. At the same time, we enjoy ourselves with international clients. Now colonialism is still in the minds and hearts of our leaders, and that's why they don't invest the money in their own countries. If Africans cannot help themselves in times of their crises, then what independence do they always speak about? We are still being divided by suspicions and ruled as if we are not independent politically. Even those in Western countries couldn't compromise with their brothers at their original homes in their respective countries. As a result, black people have genetic problems of not valuing the lives of their own brothers and sisters. Israel is surviving because of their brothers and sisters living in advanced countries. Still, black communities were given false pictures about Africa not helping their own brothers.

The African Union is ineffective where our leaders raise their voices to whatever may concern them because of the financial crisis attached to European Funds, United Nations funds, and problems of ideologies between English speakers, French speakers, and Arabic speakers. They are being monitored by their colonialists so that they may not make meaningful unity among themselves. Should the 'masters' fear if we realize the benefits of unity, it will amount to fear among them. Of course, Africans are brilliant. If we come together, it will send fear signals to the Westerners. It is already well known that we are capable and intelligent, which was obvious.

It is mentioned in the Bible even though other individuals tried to push us out based on their ignorant facts of the Bible. Even Moses, famous of the Israelites, was instructed in all the wisdom of the Ancient Egyptians and was powerful in his words and deeds according to how we are intelligent check (Acts 7:22).

Did God give us the title above? No, God didn't create us with classes, but we accepted the title to be ours from generation to generation because of our ignorance. When God created us, He didn't create us as Africans, North and South Americans, Europeans, Asians, and Australians. He created us according to His image, all of us. Who were among the first, or second, and third? The answer is simply misleading us into the false misinterpretation of many verses and taking the wisdom of our Lord that had qualified them to the title we believe today. "The fear of the Lord is the beginning of knowledge: but fools despise wisdom and instruction" (Proverbs 1:7, KJV). We misunderstood the rules and regulations of the imaginative God our Ancient Egyptians created and gave a mindset of praying for five hours, working 24/7 while others work less than eight hours, hoping long prayers may seal the gap. They misinterpreted other verses like the one below, which has affected us spiritually and emotionally. We felt like captives or people have who done wrong to God. It was a lying interpretation. We were not ransomed for the sake of Jewish; it was their wishes after stealing our God Tor (Torah in Jewish) and owned to be their God. Jewish and Europeans knew secretly through their scholars that Africans wrote Bible, but they were ashamed to confess until African sons dug thoroughly and surprised them.

Jewish and Europeans had assassinated us spiritually and emotionally. As stated below, God made Egypt, Ethiopia, and Seba be the ransom for the sake of the Israelites. That was the beginning of evil wishes to us. Being brilliant during those days hurt us because His word says those who were first will be last, and those who are last will be first. This is precisely what happened to us in Africa. With that, the indigenous took tribalism of killing each other, thoughts of nepotism of employing naïve groups, and corruption of all forms. These were deadlocks to prosperity, not only that they are against the will of the Almighty God. Let us come back to seek the Kingdom of God; the rest will be given to us. "But seek first his kingdom and his righteousness, and all these things will be given to you as well" (Matthew 6:33, KJV). This verse above also has been misinterpreted by European evangelists, and we didn't analyze the proper details. In their interpretation of us, you are praying in the order you receive, which is precisely what we are doing. In other words, they injected that to those who assumed to preach to us about being poor.

"Therefore, if anyone is in Christ, he is a new creation; the old has gone, the new has come" (2 Corinthians 5:17)! Where are we now in Africa? Are we still of the old creation or new? I think we are still old because during the Rwandan genocide, and a similar one of South Sudan, people were killed in the house of the Lord—this is an indication that we are operating the word of life by the flesh, not by the spirit of God. The word of the Lord will not make sense in our life unless we structure ourselves, in other words, to be renewed in spirit. "You were taught, with regard to your former way of life to put off your old self, which is being corrupted by deceitful desires; to be made new in the attitude of your minds." (Ephesians 4:22-23, KJV); Cultivating all these things, then we will be functioning by the wisdom of God, not by intellectual or tribal basis behaviors.

According to how we have been running it for so long, African prosperity will never prevail. Unless we come to know the truths of the Bible, we will be subjected to poverty forever. I believe we have received the wrong message; however, it is never too late for us to come back to God, not God of Europeans thinking! Our own God if we are willing to do so. The windows of opportunity are open for us to return to "Nhialic Wende Madhol" because Europeans and the Americans turned our poverty into their blessings. "But love your enemies, do well to them, and lend to them without expecting to get anything back. Then your reward will be great, and you will be sons of the Highest, because he is kind to the ungrateful and wicked. Be merciful, just as your father is merciful. Give, and it will be given to you. A good measure, pressed down, shaken together, and running over, will be poured into your lap. For with the measure you use, it will be measured to you" (Luke 6:34, 35, 36, and 38). "Although we are not their enemies, they lend us many things without expecting a payment in returns for the borrower is a slave to the lenders always" (Proverbs 22:7). Their money is a weapon against us or any Third World country; however, our debts are a huge weakness to dictate our prosperity. We cannot prosper because so many debts tie us up. If God knows that debts make you slaves to the master of wealth, then the Third World countries had to accept Biblical principles. Faith and politics are surviving side by side should faith support political prosperity, and politics support faith as the foundation of man's existence. Misunderstanding the relationship between faith and politics had denigrated prosperity in the Third World countries badly. There can be no prosperity if we do not abide by faith that respects human beings regardless of where they come from. How do you comprehend the Bible? In Biblical ways, it means those who understand the Word of Life would be continue helping us without expecting payment. Still, Nhialic Madhol's father will continue to give knowledge to their leaders to move forward, so their wealth will increase. This is a powerful statement consulting your pastor. Are we ready to be Lenders in Africa? Yes! Let us bow our heads down to repent. Let us not be stubborn to the Lord. "But because of your stubborn and unrepentant heart, you are reserving wrath for yourself on the day of wrath, when God's righteous judgment will be revealed" (Romans 2:5). African leaders must set perfect non- discriminative laws and transparency and accountability to engulf more investors and the labor force. This is how the so-called super nations came about; the dream laws, as many of us say America is a dream country. Even though discrimination is in a different uniform, it is not easy to be on the surface. Blessings can be bought or stolen from you. Study Genesis (27) the case between Jacob and his brother Esau: Our blessings were either sold because of our ignorance or stolen from us through the popular sovereignty- good laws which attracted everyone to advance nations.

Setting good laws needs strong faith and prayers from lawmakers. Suppose you study the case of refugees and other political issues of giving asylums. In that case, you may think it is positive for humanitarian bases, but the reality is an economic purpose and blessings to them. Why? Because we failed to treat ourselves humanely and transparently, they exploited the opportunities of human rights bases to engulf many individuals. If we set accountability rules in our respective countries, you will see how immigrants will return to their countries and contribute effectively to the nation's buildings. Let us stop fighting each other and ask God for forgiveness to achieve our dreams. Otherwise, all the Third World countries will be empty in the next hundred years because of immigrants going to super nation countries, and that's what they are dreaming and praying for. They expect the world to be less than one nation; that's a big dream, and they may achieve it through our weak spirit.

In Hosea, the Bible says: "My people are destroyed for lack of knowledge; because you have rejected knowledge, I reject you from being a priest to me. And since you have forgotten the law of your God, I also will forget your children. They shall eat but not be satisfied; they shall play the prostitutes', but not multiply; because they have forsaken the Lord to devote themselves to whoredom. the idolatry of Israel wine and new wine takes away the understanding" (Hosea 4: 6, 10, and 11). There is no difference between the statement above and our cohesion in the Third World today. For instance, investigate the problems of HIV/AIDS and other common diseases in Africa. All of those were a result of the lack of knowledge from God. Though other diseases are manufactured to be tested on us, we were not prepared to protect our well-being, and therefore, many different aspects have combined our failures. Our politicians cannot bring change. Change comes by hearing the word of God and putting it into life; change of having compassion, change of having concern for our people, change of having peace rather than shooting at our people throughout all the time as answering grievances.

How many agreements have we signed between ourselves in Africa, and they failed? Do we know why? This is because those who signed such agreements were led by political motivation, not spirit. Let me give you some agreements signed by those who were anointed. First, the American civil war and slavery during Abraham Lincoln's time, the Civil Rights Movement led by Dr. Martin Luther King, and finally end of Apartheid in South Africa. Although Mandela was a politician, he was supported by a man of God, Rev. Desmond Tutu. All these agreements have lasted peacefully because spiritual leaders led these noble causes. Spiritual leaders can set Africans free if they are anointed because God's word cannot fail if fixed accordingly.

Our failure started in the churches should we not believe in what we worship. Is it the pastors or God? People must be encouraged to pray in their houses. Thanking God cannot be practiced only on Sundays. Everyone has an obligation to pray at whatever time is acceptable to them.

Pastors must fix three prayers a year with leaders, for the Bible says, "The weapons we fight with are not the weapons of the world. On the contrary, they have divine power to demolish strongholds. We demolish arguments and every pretension that sets itself up against the knowledge of God, and we take captive every thought to make it obedient to Christ" (2 Corinthians 10:4 and 5). If we set our prayers as I emphasized above, the weapons of the living spirit will intercede in us in our difficulties. Previously, before the emergence of Christianity, our spiritual leaders made sacrifices at the beginning of the rain season and when we reap our crops as thanks to God for a successful harvest.

Our negative side has become positive to helpers, and God looks to the positive side to the lenders or helpers. All African people are everywhere looking for a better life in advanced countries, promoting their economy with cheap labor. Being stubborn has opened the door for evil to capture our thoughts and spirit to the point we cannot repent. God does not like being prideful; he works with humble people; not arrogant people like us. We must accept His call as He said in Second Chronicles: "If my people, who are called by my name, will humble themselves.

And pray and seek my face and turn from there wicked ways, then I will hear from heaven and will forgive their sins and will heal their lands. Now my eyes will be open, and my ears attentive to the prayers offered in this place. I will have chosen and consecrated this temple so that my name may be there forever. My eyes and my heart will always be there" (2 Chronicles 7:14-16, NIV).

Now God is calling us back into His Kingdom; our ways have led us to an end. Nothing fruitful has come from our tribalism, regionalism, and fighting. Therefore, let us denounce arrogance, pride, corruption, nepotism, tribalism, and much more so that God will heal Africa as a whole. In particular, the people of New Sudan need to adopt the principle of the word of life.

Regardless of race, continents, and languages, we are all his citizens. He is the Father of all. God does not love people of specific colors or matters. He loves those who obey his commandments. Have faith in God, his power, and that power will transform us to higher thinking of love, peace, grace, and precious life we have missed for so long. He will give us confidence in ourselves and the ability to produce our wealth. "He gave you manna to eat in the desert, something your fathers had never known, to humble and to test you so that in the end, it might go well with you. You may say to yourself, 'my power and the strength of my hand have produced this wealth for me.' But remember the Lord your God, for it is he who gave you the ability to produce wealth, so confirm his covenant, which he swore to forefathers as it is today" (Deuteronomy 8:16-18). God is giving more abilities to our lenders or helpers to let them produce much wealth so that we will receive from them constantly. Remember my quotation in Luke 6:35, 36, and 3): God rewards them because they operate on his line.

"Anyone who listens to the word but does not do what says is like a man who looks at his face in a mirror and, after looking at himself, goes away and immediately forgets what he looks like. But the man who looks intently into the perfect law that gives freedom, and continues to do this, not forgetting what he has heard, but doing it- he will be blessed in what he does" (James 1:23-25; 3:5-6, 9). In the same way, the tongue is a small member and yet has great pretensions. Consider how small a fire can set a huge forest ablaze.

The tongue is also fire. It exists among our members as a world of malice, defiling the whole body and setting the entire course of our lives on fire, itself set on fire by Gahanna. With it, we bless the Lord and Father, and with it, we curse human beings who are made in the likeness of God. African churches preach something different, which does not change people. Pastors believe that Africa is a poor continent, and they do not know what they say impacts human life. Those who believe that we are poor are the real killers of African spirit and prosperity; you cannot look down on yourself and think assistance will make a difference.

Tongues have the power of blessing and cursing. Whatever you claim you will reap because it is what you wish to have by preaching the content of the poor, then you agree with God. "Truly I tell you, whatever you bind on earth will be bound in heaven, and whatever you loose on earth will be lost in heaven. Again, truly I tell you that if two of you on earth agree about anything you ask for, it will be done for you by my Father in heaven. Again,

I tell you that if two of you on earth greed about anything you ask for, it will be done for you by my father in heaven for where two or three come together in my name, there am I with them" (Matthew 18:18-20).

The gracious God is telling us whatever we believe in our hearts, as a fact. You will receive it if you ask for the blessing, and you believe it will be granted to you. Therefore, we are part of why things go wrong sometimes rather than encouraging ourselves in God. The Bible says in John: "Then you will know the truth, and the truth will set you free" (John 8:32). When we know the truths, faith comes, and you have confidence in divine power, you're operating in Him because God has never changed his power ever since. The power he gave to Moses, Joshua, and the power which raised Christ is still in us.

But the problem is how to press it or turn it on. The nature of power is to communicate with God in prayers, not prayers for five hours; seasonal prayers, as I indicated before. He never changes that power. In Hebrew (13:8), "Jesus Christ is the same yesterday and today and forever." So, if you turn to Hebrew (13:8) with confidence, you can change the circumstances around you, as well as in the whole country. But turn on the wrong interpretation power to lead you.

Catastrophes such as the Rwanda massacre, Nairobi disaster, and Sudan genocide will result from your actions.

CHAPTER FIFTEEN

Quick Riches, Quick Bankruptcy

"Dishonest money dwindles away, but he who gathers money little by littlest, it grows. A good man leaves an inheritance to his children's children, and the wealth of the sinner is stored up for the righteous" (Proverbs 13:11 and 22). When we try to get riches quickly, we will not inherit anything. Nobody is against being rich. Even the Creator wants his people to be rich, for He Himself said the house of laziness would fall apart. "Now I commit you to God and to the word of his grace, which can build you up and give you an inheritance among all those who are sanctified. You yourselves know that these hands of mine have supplied my own needs and the needs of my companions. In everything I did, I showed you that by this kind of hard work we must help the weak, remembering the words the Lord Jesus himself said: It is more blessed to give than to receive" (Acts 20:32, 34 and 35). Precisely, that's what we should do. Be hardworking to be independent economically rather than inherit millions in debts. In the Less Developed Countries, the wealthiest clique doesn't donate to the churches, for they know where their wealth comes from, and as such, they do not have relationships with church leaders. God is not against being wealthy, but the sign is, where do we get wealth? Stealing public resources will not be inherited by your grandchildren. Think about those who robbed public resources before in South Sudan previously. As soon as they go back (death), resources disappear with them; that means they are not coming out from their hard work, and therefore kids waste them immediately after their parents.

You cannot master two things at a time, corruption, and justice; you just have to choose one. We have passed the period of deceiving public opinion because citizens living under colonization have been wiser than dictators for many years. At the beginning of 2005 in South Sudan, most government officials were relocated with their families in neighboring countries, deserting the country they were fighting for decades for the farmers supporting the struggle. However, even Almighty God was behind the cause because the legitimate war was supported. However, richness has turned into sorrow.

With very few exceptions, our rulers are utterly corrupted and self-serving. Not surprisingly, they are surrounded by equally corrupt supporters who have been put into positions of authority to increase the amount of suffering or the size or decoration of the entourage. The brightest minds are naturally drained away to the Western countries. They can practice their talents in different fields, not because the continent is poor, but because the rulers have judged the situation before listening to the argument. "Therefore, in the present case, I advise you: Leave these men alone! Let them go! For if their purpose or activity is of human origin, it will fail. But if it is from God, you will not be able to stop these men; you will only find yourselves fighting against God" (Acts 5:38 and 39). The Book of Acts was filled with the Holy Ghost, and many disciples got baptized. It was also a book of miracles to the apostles because many were filled with the Holy Spirit, and they spoke many tongues. If the spirit of the Holy Ghost inspires us, we will provide better services to our communities and our countries. If we are motivated by the world to become a leader and fail to exert much to render the needed services, we will either exile ourselves where we end up in exile or be gunned down by crazy elements thirsty to take over.

We must use God's criteria of humility and listening attentively so that we may overcome evil from our clans, tribes, or region. If we apply the worldly criterion definitely; we will fall into the hands of evil advisors because they are directing us according to their interests. Be inspired by the Holy Ghost so that people will fight the win while Almighty God leads you to the Promised Land. "After the death of Moses, the servant of the Lord, the Lord said to Joshua, son of Nun, Moses' aide: 'Moses my servant is dead. Now then, you and all these people, get ready to cross the Jordan River into the land I am about to give to them—to the Israelites. No one will be able to stand up against you all the days of your life. As I was with Moses, so I will be with you; I will never leave you nor forsake you. Moses interpreted the will of God for them. Truly many elders served under him, but there was not another Moses. Precisely to the sense of crisis was the timing of his death. The people could hardly believe that God had a new leader in reserve. But Joshua was in preparation, and the crisis brought him forward'" (Joshua 1:1, 2 and 5). The death of a leader is the ultimate test to inferior leaders like those who submit their resignation during the toughest time test to their lead-

126

ership. They walked away thinking that Garang was the one who was defending the marginalized cause. They were an infantile leadership built up with inferiority, but I may not blame them very much because they were not told death could not be calculated, it can come anytime to take a leader, and as such, the cause cannot die with him.

Leadership inspired by God, and built on spiritual principles, will survive like president Kiir when he was out of the "Gogrialism" kitchen. The shock of leadership change may even prosper as a result; we all have witnessed this during the last eight years. Though some challenges still existed, there were signs of unity. An organized body is like a pregnant lady, leaders must be cautious in handling it. It might set out an abortion of unity or unhealthy pre-term baby. This is the same thing with a leadership founder. If leadership foundation is based on tribalism, then killing innocent civilians will become its future because each replacing leader will put their foot in the same shoes. That's why Africa is not united as a whole and in its respective countries.

Great moments are often thrown into crisis at the death of a founder. During the last decades, our case was not known as the case of certain regions or tribes. Our struggle was supported overwhelmingly by peace lovers as fundamental rights to the people of South Sudan. Why are we trying to throw away legitimate rights for personal gain? SPLM/SPLA are paying themselves selectively and forgot the real revolutionaries—the farmers—those who supported the movement for twenty-one years by their cows, goats, sheep, and whatever they could produce.

SPLM/SPLA does not have sympathy with such commanders, as they call themselves. You couldn't be a commander if you were not fed well by those farmers. You have forgotten them and failed to provide services and peace within states. SPLM/SPLA has forgotten to pay regular salaries even to their own soldiers, those who have been constantly on the frontlines, those who were guarantors of the CPA. It's horrific, blind heart leadership. Nelson Mandela spent twenty- seven years in prison. After he came out, he became a hero, the first African President of South Africa. He never took revenge against white people who ruled them for almost 300 years. He never took revenge against the Zulus collaborators, and he never compensated his party leadership ANC financially like SPLM Leaders. He did not treat other South Africans people as traitors like our case in South Sudan. But what about the farmers where they were also traitors? Why are their children not in better schools like the time of Addis Ababa when students enjoyed three meals from Elementary to university, and Sudan did not have plenty of resources like today? How have you rewarded the farmers? It is just a flag, national anthem, and valueless currency whose ministers and generals don't even use as much as American dollars. Why are you treating your families abroad while others are left without medicine, like the Addis Ababa Accord of 1972? "What does God expect from the person who holds the most powerful office in the world to do? It is to provide life necessities to them because you are a servant or overseer. In one of the chapters, I explained swearing-in is a commitment to citizens. If you think you are deceiving us, no, you are deceiving Almighty God, for that book does not belong to the pastors. Less Developed Countries accumulated unimaginable debts when they inflicted heavy casualties with unnecessary civil war, which have nothing to do with citizens as they claim. The wicked borrow and do not pay back, but the righteous are generous and keep giving, and what made us wicked are debts and is a fundamental issue in Africa. Remember what God says in Deuteronomy chapter eight verses 17&18 always was and is the principle of being wealthy.

Swallowing somebody's earnings or a country's resources, then you are undermining God's instructions, and you will reach the dead-end when reshuffling takes place anytime. While in Debt, leaders live in fear because lenders are always directing what to do and not to do. Our local currency could not compete with foreign currency because of the many debts accumulated during the civil wars within the government itself. Before the meaningless war erupted in South Sudan, the local currency was competitive in the region compared to the time of the war. Just being a debtor was ashamed and disgusted to pass near the native of our court in those days. If the creditor saw you, he or she might demand his due. So, those known to accumulate people's properties were avoided for marriage, and that's how our ethics were. Today being corrupt is prestigious and honest; not only that, doing a huge reception by sectionalist appointees was a signal of corruption because the appointed person was not appointed by constitutional sectionalism to serve them. We should all learn this lesson: "Debt is not good. Debt as a way of life will lead to a multitude of problems and spiritual ills that will ultimately bring any nation to its knees. America has been swallowed in Debt to a nearly unbearable point to finance homes, goods, and lifestyle. The American people could not afford the required dependence on nations like China and Saudi Arabia to buy and hold bonds, treasury notes, and dollars. They financed an unparalleled orgy of spending that has resulted in trillions of dollars of Debt, mortgaging future generations. Written in the instruction God gave to ancient Israel is a financial principle for the ages" (The Good News, January / February 2009). "The borrower is the servant to the lender" (Proverbs 22:7). Borrowing money and ideas might be good if you utilize both properly. But suppose we have no time to study the meaning of having a mortgage. In that case, it means a temporary and conditional pledge of property to a creditor as security for performing an obligation or repaying of Debt. Nevertheless, if we fail to meet the timeframe for payment, we are subjected to pay the so-called late fee. In advanced countries, they hate to be a slave of borrowing. If they borrow money, they must utilize it properly to avoid borrowing next time to be their own boss. By borrowing money and ideas, we do not have time to study them for our welfare generation. Instead of inherited Debt, we need to study some terms before we take action: it's dangerous if we fail to fulfill the deal. "Therefore, the kingdom of heaven is like a king who wanted to settle accounts with his servants. As he began the settlement, a man who owed him ten thousand talents was brought to him. Since he was not able to pay, the master ordered that he and his wife and his children and all that he had be sold to repay the Debt. The servant fell on his knees before him. Be patient with me; begged, and I will pay back everything. The servant's master took pity on him, canceled the Debt, and let him go. But when that servant went out, he found one of his fellow servants who owed him hundreds denarius. He grabbed him and began to choke him. Payback what you owe me! He demanded. His fellow fell to his knees and begged him. Be patient with me, and I will pay you back. But he refused. Instead, he went off and had the man thrown into prison until he could pay the Debt. When the other servants saw distressed and went and told their master everything that had happened" Matthew 18:23-31).

That's the situation debtors were facing in Biblical times, and that's precisely how we are with our lenders. They choke us not to move through anywhere because we owe them so much.

Borrowing money and ideas financially, socially, and politically are coups to the Less Developing Nations; see the quotation above from the Bible. God knows how money has been essential to our lives ever since. Let me illustrate how the Superpowers' treat the leaders of the Third World under the umbrella of so-called democracy, and these are their own words. Much of the funds go into private pockets rather than for development. Economic dependency: "This is why most oil-rich countries are poor, corrupt, and undemocratic. The big, bad United States keeps Latin America poor. The United States controls economies of weaker countries through local middlemen who do the bidding of the U.S. Corporations argues dependency theorists. The poor country must sell its agricultural and mineral products cheap and buy high-priced U.S.- made goods. This conically siphons off the wealth of the country and keeps it poor. When the United States doesn't get its way, it uses dirty means, such as encouraging rigged elections and military coups. On the other hand, intervention is usually a lot cheaper and subtler than war. It can include bribes to government officials, foreign aid, secret subsidies to political parties, destabilization campaigns, encouragements coup palters, arms shipments, proxy armies, and if nothing else works, invasions will be the last alternatives" (Roskin/Berry, International relation, page 150). This is the game the super nations play when we see them broadcasting development or help; they mean recruiting alternative leaders if their honeymoon is almost over with the present gang or junta. The democracy they activate is for their benefit first before we use it properly in our country. Let us think seriously of how to be wealthy men and women differently, not by robbing through American lobbyists so that we will be able to inherit our blessing. A sphere of influence is a tool where a major power molds the policies of other states while directly controlling its government. "Threat bribes keep local rulers to be submissive to powerful States. Major powers create and maintain spheres of influence for their security, economic well-being, and save for prestige." Is Jehovah-Jeer against such practices? Yes. "He says do not pervert justice or show partiality. Do not accept a bribe for a bribe blinds the eyes of the wise and twists the words of righteous; Justice, and only justice, you shall pursue, so that you may live and occupy the land that the LORD your God is giving you Deuteronomy" (16:19&20 NIV see in many translations). I categorically explained how we were running with the bone of being Christians while we didn't precisely have the correct way of connecting people with God.

Europeans' leaders have practiced these two verses above and the rest. They told us to let us baptize you and be good at accepting bribes and practicing injustices. Our own native chiefs' administrators were far better than independent of SPLM Oyee! Citizens are dying in hundreds across the liberated country. Yet, leaders are busy dividing the resources in bribes. Money will not go back with us, whether by robbing or hard work. But we want to inherit faith to our children so that they may live in peace in the next generations.

In other words, educate them to be honest, trust God, be confident in themselves, be peace lovers, and forgive people. We want to inherit the justices from the Kingdom of God, and the Holy Father will provide the rest. He wants us to be the wealthiest; that is his desire. He doesn't want us to be hungry or have diseases. We are part of the temple of His house. By acquiring wealth incorrectly, we will hate one another and be arrogant and haughty. Therefore, a nation falls into crisis because of no wisdom.

CHAPTER SIXTEEN

Lack of spiritual Maturity

"If you become willing and obey me, you will eat good crops from the land. But if you refuse to obey and if you turn against me, you will be destroyed by your enemies' sword,' the Lord himself said these things" (Isaiah 1:19 and 20). Having spiritual maturity is not for those who are pastoring to us. It is an obligation to whoever should have compassion and concern for the life of others.

When we are growing in spirit, how will we spread the word? Through services and loving each other unconditionally. For example, church infrastructures within the community, school infrastructures, medical infrastructures, pay the bills of widows and orphans, and any other member within the congregation who may be entitled to help. This is how churches are blessed and aimed for the Gospel. While Preaching the Bible without services means nothing to the people of the Gospel because feeding the mind and the stomach must be intertwined. By doing this, people who pay their tithes and offerings are blessed, and the entire country is blessed too. Transparency must be solid in tithes and offerings to avoid the embezzlement of tithes and offerings. Solid eradication in church funds must be a goal to win the lost soul completely.

Otherwise, our Gospel would be a dead case, as we witnessed in previous centuries. When there is no accountability in tithes and offerings, then there will be no accountability at all levels of the government because injustice had already captured the house of the Almighty God. As such, it will not be easy to preach justice. Church resources shouldn't be used by the pastors as their private entities, like an ATM personal card, which we use any time for withdrawal. The Catholic Church had a vision of rendering services to their members, but Episcopalian churches, especially in the New Republic of South Sudan, are badly organized and do not work to give services to their members. Instead of embracing each other, they have jealousy among themselves. They are just showing their collars running from country to country, looking for assistance while pocketing tithes and offerings with their wives, who are their financial managers. Church or faith survival should not be based on assistance while the congregation contributes its tithes and offerings; meanwhile, they do not know where their money is going.

These tithes and offerings services should be rendered when any congregation member is sick, or something difficult happens; church leaders must assist them. The believers must correctly address church funds' mishandling in Episcopal churches because money is not meant for pastors. Money should be used to build the Kingdom of God and to provide assistance for those who may be in a vulnerable situation. Preaching for more than thirty years oppresses others. You are not the only man called by God. Thousands in line have the same calling; there must be a limited constitution of guidelines for being a pastor. Preaching for forty years doesn't mean that your calling is the only one acceptable to God; you should show how the authority can be rotated among the believers. This is how our leaders will learn to give up the authority to others, but maintaining your position and attempting to rebuke government officials as spiritual leaders will not convince them to step down because you have not shown them the ways of justice. Most pastors preach and do not ask to govern the Kingdom of God as Solomon did.

Solomon showed his love for the Lord by walking according to the statutes of his father David, except that he offered sacrifices and burned incense in high places. "Now, O Lord my God, you have made your servant king in place of my father, David. But I'm only a little child and do not know to carry out my duties. Your servant is here among the people you have chosen, a great people, too numerous to count or number. So, give your servant a discerning heart to govern your people and to distinguish between right and wrong, for who can govern these great people of yours?" The Lord was pleased that Solomon had asked for this. So, God said to him, "Since you have asked for this and not for long life or wealth for yourself, nor have you asked for the death of your enemies but for discernment in administering justice, I will do what you have asked. I will give you a wise and discerning heart so that there will never have been anyone like you, nor will there ever be. Moreover, I will give you what you have not asked for—both riches and honor—so that in your lifetime, you will have no equal among kings. And if you walk in my ways and obey my statutes and commands as David your father did, I will give you a long life." The first ruling Solomon made after he asked the wisdom from God was the case of two prostitutes (Read 1 Kings 3, NIV). Do we know why people pay their tithes? It is to help build up the Kingdom of God. Tithes are also the main source of funds for building the kingdom of God and helping needy people in all forms. Pastors need to provide physical needs to the believers before they pretend to provide spiritual healing. How will God trust you to such levels of healing while you provide nothing to his people from tithes and offerings? Turning tithes and offerings into our personal benefit has consequences and abuse the power of healing and obedience. Tithes and offerings should be checked because we have failed to define what tithes mean.

When we give tithes and offerings, we trust God and obey his spiritual law of demand and supply to the givers. It is not because we have so much wealth, but in the Commandments, we should pay tithes so that he will send us rain in its season, and the ground will yield its crops, and the trees of the field will be fruitful.

"Will a man rob God? Yet, you rob me." "But you ask, 'How do we rob you?'"

"In tithes and offerings; you are under a curse—the whole nation of yours—because you are robbing me. Bring the whole tithe into the storehouse, that there may be food in my house. Test me in this," says the Lord Almighty, "and see if I will not throw open the floodgates of heaven and pour out so many blessings that you will not have room enough for it" (Malachi 3:8-10, and Proverbs 3, respectively). "Honor the Lord with your wealth, with the first fruits of all your crops; then your barns will be filled to overflowing, and your vats will brim over with new wine. First fruits are a form of tithing—a way to honor God simply because of who He is" (Proverbs 3:9-10). When we offer our first fruits to God, we express our faith and appreciation for what He has given to us. Giving him first fruits is making an investment into the Kingdom of God that produces future dividends that God guarantees. The Bible says that the first fruits of our increase are what God desires from us (Proverbs 3:9). God has trusted us to give back to Him as an expression of faith, honor, and appreciation for all He does for us. The first 10% is God, and He allows us to have stewardship over the remaining balance of 90%. Remember, this tithe is a way to thank God for the many blessings He provides for you. Tithes are for our benefit and the benefit of others, not God. God doesn't need our money, but He has established a system whereby He could open the windows of heaven and pour out a blessing in our life (Malachi 3:10).

Tithes are a spiritual law in the Old Testament and the New Testament. It is a blessing to God, not a Bishop, as in our case in Africa. Tithes are also a spiritual law established before the Law of Moses in the Old Testament by indigenous Africans. Tithing was practiced by Cain and Abel, which was 430 years before the law was given and was later made as a part of Moses' law. This was also practiced by the churches in the New Testament in 1 Corinthians. "On the first day of every week, each one of you should set aside a sum of money in keeping with his income, saving it up, so that when I come, no collection will have to be made" (1 Corinthians 16:2). It is clear now, everyone should put tithes and offerings aside before every Sunday so that when an offerings basket passes through, you shouldn't hesitate to give them up.

Let me give you some verses in both the Old and New Testaments. "Which is says blessings and obedience? The Lord will grant you abundant prosperity in the fruit of your womb, the young of your livestock, and crops of your ground in the land he swore to your forefathers to give you. He, the Lord, will open the heavens, the storehouse of His bounty, to send rain on your land in season and bless all the work of your hands. You will lend to many nations but will borrow from none. The Lord will make you the head, not the tail. If you pay attention to the commands of the Lord your God that I give you this day and carefully follow them, you will always be at the top, never at the bottom" (Deuteronomy 28:11-13).

Now take a deep breath, think very carefully of those lenders—the Americans and Europeans. The tithes they got from their people, they gave it to us, note how they were blessed, that is because churches were transparent of tithes and offerings, and they apply a spiritual law called "give and you will receive abundant blessings." Receiving tithes and offerings is not the responsibility of the bishop and his wife; it's the responsibility of the board of directors. The committee is the people who set up the senior pastor's salary and the other church employees. Our churches do not have employees; the pastor and his wife control everything. Church finances are unknown to junior pastors; the pastor has made the kingdom his private sector, collecting internal tithes and offerings and external donations. The church accounts must be audited by the end of the year because the money belongs to the public, and they should know where their blessings go. Applying these Western rules, as people may say, will open the

windows from heaven for much rain into our lands, and prosperity will come. Stop running to the super countries and turn to God, for He is the God of all nations. There are better things leaders could borrow from Western churches if we think it will benefit us, like auditing the church accounts. In the New Testament (Luke 6:34-36 and 38), it was said: "And if you lend to those from whom you expect repayment, what credit is that to you? Even sinners lend to sinners, expecting to be repaid in full. But love your enemies, do well to them, and lend to them without expecting to get anything back. Then your reward will be great, and you will be sons of the Highest because he is kind to the ungrateful and wicked. Be merciful, just as your father is merciful. Give, and it will be given to you. A good measure, pressed down, shaken together, and running over, will be poured into your lap. For with the measure you use, it will be measured to you." Though we are not their enemies, they are the head, and they borrowed nothing from us. As you can read from Deuteronomy, we have become a tail to them. As I stated early, aid and gift are not free; they have a right to dictate the church leaders into their beliefs and even accept the rules of abortion and rules of gay marriages in our societies because of their aid. It may not be visible in our time, but eventually, we will witness before us sooner than later because those living closely with their parents are Africans. It must be dismantled by aid to live according to them. This day I call heaven and earth as witnesses against you that I have set before your life and death, blessings, and curses. Now choose life so that you and your children may live.

Because of this spiritual law, God has given us a choice to have life or death, blessing or cursing. He even provides us with the answer to choose life, but still, it is our choice, not God's; and since God cannot take back His word, he honors the choices we make. Since the first fruits belong to God and are holy, everyone who honors God by bringing their tithes to him shall reap the benefits of His blessings—bringing the first fruits honors a God who can supply all your needs according to his riches in glory by Christ Jesus. "And my God meet all your needs according to his glorious riches in Christ Jesus" (Philippians 4:19). God is able; to provide his unlimited power from heaven upon you. God possesses unimaginable resources that are not dependent on the world economy or bound by famine or drought. "Don't be deceived, my dear brothers. Every good and perfect gift is from above, coming down from the father of the heavenly lights, who does not change like shifting shadows. He chose to give us birth through the word of truth that we might be a kind of first fruits of all he created" (James 1:16 and 18). When we agree with the truth that everything we own or accomplish is by God's grace, mercy, and blessing, we can then find it easy to honor Him with the first portion of our increase which is the first fruits. It is clear from His words that trusting in Him releases His blessings in your life. He gave human beings the authority of all living things to be responsible for them. Any thinking lined up with the grace of God will yield the fruit of prosperity. When we bring the first fruits to God, we acknowledge that God is Jehovah-Jireh, the Lord who provides.

"He redeemed us so that the blessing given to Abraham might come to the Gentiles through Christ Jesus so that by faith we might receive the promise of the spirit" (Galatians 3:14). Christ is a symbol of pride to us, a symbol of prosperity, a symbol of liberty. Being a Christian means a lot—peace, love, forgiveness, repentance, and a healthier community—because there is no other God who raised the dead, opened the eyes of the blind, and opened the ears of the deaf. This is evidence of the superior God that we have. In conclusion, what I quoted in many chapters in the Bible and what our ancestors performed regarding worshiping and tithing to spiritual leaders or Rainmakers are the same- nothing less and more except prayers after every six days, which is Sunday.

CHAPTER SEVENTEEN

Combine wisdom and knowledge!

"Trust in the Lord with all your heart and lean not on your own understanding; in all your ways acknowledge him, and he will make your paths straight. Do not be wise in your own eyes; fear the Lord and shun evil. This will bring health to your body and nourishment to your bones" (Proverbs 3:5, 6, 7, and 8). There is a difference between having knowledge and having wisdom. Wisdom understands the spirit of the living God to the good judgment and the ability to make wise decisions. Knowledge is material gained through learning and experience over a long period. Because of this, different definitions of our disunity have been put to maximum by doctorate holders. Those who believe in the knowledge they have acquired in a particular field, undermining our father Madhol (who is God), cannot bring better healing into a land by acquiring knowledge without humbling themselves to allow God to direct them. In underdeveloped countries, having a doctorate is a big problem for those who do not have it.

Where as doctorate holders like Hennery Kissinger who made significant changes to American policies, are not so proud of what they acquired, he is resourceful of healthy policies in advanced nations. I am not against having a doctorate, but do not use it for your selfish end disaster, which is not equivalent to your dissertation. Selfishness is spiritually cancerous to the believers; self- importance to the extent that you cannot listen to others; use it as a light to get into the darkness of hearts. To prove my argument on doctorate holders, check the debate of unity or separation peacefully between northerners and southerners at the Sudan tribute website. The doctorate holder defended unity based on his theories and personal problems with some personalities in the SPLM or Dinkas. He was trying to make Southerners' hostages of his thesis' advantage. But, of course, many of us favored unity based on respecting each other, not unity of looking down on ourselves, so the guy was arguing through his papers not concerned by people's sufferings.

Ignoring the wisdom of the Holy Ghost has consequences, and this is what we are reaping in the so-called Third World countries. The Bible says,

"Live in harmony with one another. Do not be proud but be willing to associate with people of low position. Do not be conceited" (Roman 12:16). Accepting each other is a weapon of success; wasting valuable time distinguishing ourselves is a tool of failure. Equal justice is always forward to God's will and prosperity. We were talking about something we were not handling. If the SPLM leaders cannot pay their employees regularly, we are not independent; otherwise, salaries and wages should be without any doubt. Suppose you say people were not receiving their salaries and wages during wartime, which most leaders say. In that case, that's another indication those who claim something for themselves are not for the welfare of others. Telling the truth without reservation is a leadership style centered on success. If the leaders of any party do not have a central structure or vision to challenge their opponents, then the future is in limbo because the truth always hurts your opponent. Don't campaign the truth and not implement what the means. If truth becomes propaganda, you lose public opinion immediately. Our President may lose public support because his speeches are smooth but without follow-up. This may reflect many things—either he is fooling himself or cheating public opinion—which will be negative to his political career or records. Think about what statements mean to the public; they hope for what leadership says might rescue their condition in all aspects of life. for example, leaders touch basic needs, adequate national security, relationships between countries, education system, health services, public transportation, and food security. If you made five speeches regarding that above and without positive results, something must be checked. The Bible says in Psalm 58: "Do you rulers indeed speak justly? And you judge uprightly among men? No, in your heart, you devise injustices, and your hands meet out violence on the earth. His speech is smooth as butter, yet war is in his heart; his words are more soothing than oil, yet they were drawn swords. Cast your care on the Lord, and he will sustain you; he never let the righteous fall. But your o God will bring down the wicked into the pit of corruption; bloodthirsty and deceitful men will not live out half their days. But as for, me I trust you." Smooth speeches of leaders are impossible, some time to preserve lasting peace in any country unless spiritual leaders used Joshua diplomacy to unite marginalized areas. Let us forget about distrusting ourselves, forget the former things, and do not dwell on the past. The past will hold us back from a bright future living as South Sudanese.

Experience is wisdom, not qualification. Anyone with a good heart can deliver the best Governances which are a public desire. Leadership is not about you, but it prepares a foundation for the next generation. Forgiveness is not a signal of giving in the cause; it is compassion and concern. Senator John McCain had to say this during the Republican convention quote: "No success without a good fight to the cause of welfare, we are all American than any other, whoever is going to be President, we will shake our hands for prosperity and peace of our country. Do not work for the party; do not work for special interest. Work for people, and that's the kind of leadership you want. I better lose the election rather than lose the war; we lost the trust given to us by Americans because of corruption among our fellow Republicans." I hope SPLM representatives have learned something about how leadership addresses the issues concerning their people when they are invited. Education is a civil right in the Twenty-First Century. Let us share ideas so that we change all strategies. It's good to be a hero but serve others to prove a hero. True leaders are concerned primarily with the welfare of others, not with their comfort or prestige. They must show sympathy for the problems of others but fortify and stimulate and don't make weak. Southerners are living in a cage of fear! Why should we develop a positive attitude and impose a certain discipline on ourselves? Because we are suffering under aimlessness and senses of defeat, especially from the negativity of tribalism and regionalism. Let us have an attitude of 'good in, garbage out'—this means substituting positive things into our minds and hearts. We shouldn't overload our minds with negative ideas about others; we should not have the heart to control government machinery. Sharing good and bad together is the basis of justice. Why are El Bashir and his teams restless now because of the ICC? The government was controlled by one tribe or group of criminals enjoying its resources so much. It would be good if all of them were given a mandate by the people. The prices of the government-controlled by ethnicity are too high to be paid by innocent people when things turn the opposite direction.

Let God overhaul our minds thoroughly to repair a new spirit, catch up with, and overtake all the unity processes among our people. Otherwise, our future will be uncertain. Let us think big to overcome hard times ahead of us; we remain with three and a half years to transitional period to make critical decisions for our future generation. God can change a thief into an honest man/woman or a drunk into a sober person. God can change mixed-up defeated guys like us into a normal society; we need Him to refresh us, God only can wipe out our tears. "Repent, then, turn to God, so that your sins may be wiped out, that time of refreshing may come from the Lord" (Acts 3:19). Again, let us understand this imaginative faith on our terms, not the borrowing principles that made us a liability of western societies. We shouldn't be worried about how hells looked like and paradise. Those are the primary concerns of African Christianity, not social justice, and prosperity. We knew (Kajoungtheeth) meant hell before Christianity emerged and twisted it to paradise.

CHAPTER EIGHTEEN

Sermon Biblical Truths

Tests are meant to let us succeed, not to fail you. Tests display progress and understanding of the task ahead to be accomplished. Most leaders pass difficulties through their relationship with their father. True leaders step forward to face circumstances and complex problems. If leaders are to survive, they must view the difficulties as commonplace, the complex as normal. "Moses faced an impossible situation when Israelites reached the Red Sea. Moses, a great man of faith, stayed himself on God. "The bracing lesson is that God delights to lead people and then in response to their trust, to show the power that matches every impossible situation. "Therefore, I urge you, brothers, in view of God's mercy, to offer your bodies as living sacrifices, holy and pleasing to God—this is your spiritual act of worship. Do not conform any longer to the pattern of this world but be transformed by the renewing of your mind. Then you will be able to test and approve what God's will is—his good, pleasing, and perfect will" (Romans 12:1 and 2, NIV). In this context, leadership must make transformations and harmony among his flock; he makes impossible things happen with the help of the Mighty. Leadership must believe that change is possible to happen among the defeated people. When we criticize the plan before action, we are already in agreement with fear. Therefore, negative signs have conceived the spirit, mind, and eventually, the result will be sour. Tongue, spirit, mind, and hearing are lined up with the power of success and failures; however, we say the true picture of our thoughts. "Repent, then, and turn to God, so that your sins may be wiped out, that times of refreshing may come from the Lord" (Acts 3:19, NIV). How a leader handles failures or simple feelings of failures will set most of the agenda for the future. Repentance and love can reopen the door of opportunity. Most Bible characters had encountered failures and survived. Successful leaders have learned that no failure is final, whether their own failure or someone else's. Failure and humility serve to remind a leader who is really in charge. Perfect leaders at all-time times face the problem of jealous rivals.

Moses had encountered that test. Jealously is a common weapon of the devil's spirit. Miriam and Aaron began to talk against Moses because of his Cushitic wife, for he had married a Cushitic (Numbers 12:3, 12). "Now,

Moses was a very humble man, humbler than anyone else on the face of the earth. The anger of the Lord burned against them, and he left them. When the cloud lifted from above the Tent, there stood Miriam, leprous like snow. Aaron turned toward her and saw she had leprosy." Yet, Moses maintained a dignified silence; God would not allow such a challenge to the authority of his servant to go without a positive response. Such a drastic punishment points to the gravity of sin, and once again, with Moses, greatness shines. His only response was to pray for his sister, and God graciously responded in mercy, and God healed his sister after having leprosy, which would change her to what skin? To white like snow. This indicates that if Moses was white, he couldn't marry a Cushitic girl, and therefore he was black if Jewish scholars defined Cush as black. Being a leader is about accepting responsibility, being decisive, serving others, and projecting confidence. Leaders are not born but made with character and abilities, not job titles. The way to change people's attitudes is to turn them to faith. Faith in what? In God, in the Holy Ghost, and let them indicate themselves. When an individual develops strong faith, and when in doubt, attitudes of inadequacy are minimized or even eliminated, that group automatically changes from bad to a Good Society. After the indigenous Africans exited from Ancient Egypt heading to Europe, they took God with confidence they knew about the imaginative faith of their ancestor attitudes before they became Jewish. That's why I uttered in the introduction and chapter three that African ancestors were so intelligent to deceive the whole world that they spoke with God. When faith declines, doubt takes over and can ultimately poison any personality. We need to lubricate our minds with hope, and it will operate with power because, with hope, the power of God will change people. When you say we are poor, we are in effect declaring poverty; our word is an expression of our mental image. It's vital when things are not going well. "Submission to God is the way forward to prosperity." Submit to God and be at peace with him; in this way, prosperity will come to you. Accept instruction from his mouth and lay up his words in your heart. If you return to the Almighty, you will be restored: If you remove wickedness far from your tent" (Job 22:21, 22 and 23 NIV, Devotional Bible). Jehovah-Shalom did not create us to be under the mercy of others, rather than to be capable in our own way. He needs us to submit our ideas to him and not be manipulated by others. If we permit ourselves to nurture critical thoughts, hateful thoughts, and mental attitudes than those of goodwill and generosity of spirit, we develop into unhappy people. Church leaders need to eradicate the spirit of poverty from the people. This belief of poverty is killing unity among us; people always believe in that point. Declaring to the people that the house of Almighty God is in poverty, you then block the power of God because of ignorance, fear, anxiety, negative thoughts, and selfish actions that are spiritually cancerous to us. Submission and listening to the spirit of the living God will answer the desire of his people, rather than waging unnecessary war among us. When I say submission and listening, I don't mean tired our hands, not working hard to elevate poverty, and waiting for God to rain down our needs. Previously, the foundation of the wealthiest countries was constructed in God's principles before the revolution of migration from rural areas into the big towns, which spoiled the social life today where many youths' revolts against the laws of Almighty God in the 1960s.

Church leaders must have a big dream to cultivate a new spirit during a difficult situation because most of us have a bad feeling about the past, but thinking about it consistently will keep us hostages of the past. Eventually, we will lose a dream of having the so-called New Sudan.

God has given us the power to get wealth, and this power was given to us freely, by His grace, so that His covenant may be established on the earth. Most of those resulted from a misunderstanding of what wealth means and why God wants us to be wealthy. The purpose of becoming wealthy is to establish God's covenant, to be a witness in the land on behalf of Jesus Christ, to spread the gospel in more ways than one. "You may say to yourself, 'my power and the strength of my hands have produced this wealth for me.' But remember the Lord your God, for it is he who gives you the ability to produce wealth, and so confirms his covenant, which he swore to your forefathers, as it today" (Deuteronomy 8:17).

Pastors must change the attitudes of always begging; this has become an established deposition of mindset or character. It has become an addicted mindset, constitution, or bad habit, inherited from generation to generation, showing that Sudanese churches have nothing. Faith in God will give us the ability to produce potential wealth. That wealth will turn into a more substantial unity among us. The reality is that we did not dig the roots of faith of God toward Him so that God will peep into us. Our minds have been captured by evil thoughts of tribes, regionalism, thoughts of hatred, and we did not allow God's wisdom to lead us, leaving the hole to evil to control us in all processes of our lives. Let us get rid of being helped because aid has many conditions for government officials, and Church leaders must fulfill to aid us. Otherwise, aid is not a free gift; it has some attachments with the obligation to fulfill. Do not be ignorant about biblical principles, and do not let somebody push you away to the degree where other Christians think they are better than us regarding the Holy Book. Accepting Christianity with the mindset of being new things in our life before them and telling us our ancestors did not know the living God was ridiculous. If you follow my introduction and frequent previous questions about how we were overlooking specific facts, African Christians never asked themselves, and evangelists preaching the doctrine were unaware of where it originated. Nhialic's principles were with our Ancestors before those who called themselves Jewish; you could have encountered many analyses I had questions or chapters with verses.

CHAPTER NINETEEN

Complaints and Reconciliation in November 2004

Rumbek's reconciliation meetings between late Dr. John Garang and the current President were an empty scapegoat of a hidden agenda between the two camps because each tried to defend their leader's camp, as you may figure out in the meetings' minutes. The lean majority was supportive of Kiir on mismanagement of the movement resources and administrative issues, whereas some die-hard to Dr. Garang aired their reservations and attacks. Furthermore, some other figures who were there previously are not there now because they respected the President. But there was nowhere to breathe; they might not get support against the President. Fragmentation was still going on, and that's why the President was unable to execute his complaints in the Rumbek meetings. He made the first cabinet according to his camp. Still, others almost exploded an atomic bomb among the innocent people, so Kiir reversed the direction to save the cause as a military man. When President made drastic changes after independence, cabinets where some individual lost their favorite ministries began to wage war in a mosquito net. They opened the mosquito net so that the mosquitoes of insecurity would destabilize the President. The New State corruption and nepotism were complicated to the degree it would not be possible to bombard it. As a result, families of the clique authorities are/were involved in corruption and nepotism employment. Suppose the President stages of reimbursing money from men and women who have squeezed themselves among the cliques, and their immediate families are not questioned. In that case, that will be acts of ignorance unless the President wants to preserve his promise to forget about friends and families who are in circles of corruption. Otherwise, Mr. President is barking while knowing why his directives are not being implemented. You will not hit the real enemies by shooting the bullet outside the enemy unless you shoot from within. The PLO's Yasser Arafat was misleading Palestine and the whole world to become rich in the name of the Palestinians for decades. When he died in 2005, he was discovered to be among the top richest men in the world, and that is exactly what the gangs around the President are practicing. These crocodiles' tears and lips service policies have spoiled the Dinka's image while the majority are suffering. The Dinka name has lost its value because of some individuals benefiting from the names of the Dinka's, and in the facts, we are not people known to like food rather than confront the enemy. When rebellions started on May 16, 1983, under Commander Kerubino Kuanyin Bol, a certain group denied themselves, and the term the rebellion to be Dinka's movement or Nuers emerged. Patriotic elements from Eastern Equatoria under commander Galore Modi and Joseph Oduho joined the struggle early in 1983, followed by Samuel Abu John in Western Equatoria.

Even though other individuals had denied the reality of the struggle, if Kerubino Kuanyin Bol didn't make the explosive fire in Bor, I believe nobody was willing to start the rebellion. Dr. Garang, the founder of his comprehensive global approach to New Sudan, influenced Yousif Kuwa Mekki in Nuba Mountain and Malik Agar in the Blue Nile. Those were the out-of-the-box policies of focusing on the Southern Sudan problem; he addressed the problem holistically to attract intellectual minds across Sudan. I disagree with elements who say Dr. Garang told William Nyuon Benny and Kerubino Kuanyin Bol to start the rebellion; that's a foolish idea from the exploiters who do not know the war's outcome. Akuot Atem de Mayen, Samuel Gai Tut, and William Abdalla Chuol were around with many soldiers between his mouth and nose for ten years. He never joined them and the rest who are milking resources and nonsenses now that the revolution started in Bor. Started in Bor by who? Diarrhea of the mouth and misleading statements are more dangerous than natural phenomenon diarrhea, and that's what I will be emphasizing here according to the article written entitled, "Who is this Aldo Ajou Deng Akuey," by Job Kiir Garang (Kiir Agou), (Edmonton, Canada December 1, 2016, PaanLuel We Media.) "The names of Akuot Atem de Mayen, Garang de Mabior, and Majak de Agot are sacred to be in the mouth of filthy pig like you who never did anything for the country. The Dinka Jonglei deserved respect for liberating the country with their golden brain and manpower; it was not an accident that the SPLM/A founders like Akuot, Garang, Arok, and Chagai Atem came from the same Twic Dinka." I will be responding to two words, specifically brain and manpower. Where were those brains and manpower in the bush before Kerubino Kuanyin Bol and William Nyuon Benny? Why didn't those brains and manpower liberate Jonglei state, let alone the whole country, until 2005 when the enemy was in their state? Does the Author know George Athor Deng, the man who defended the "Panaruo territory" not overrun by "Manguok Nantoc" since 1991? Also, why are Jonglei people everywhere in South Sudan if they were warriors? Should "Manguok Nantoc" or Murle sneeze or blow their noses, people run away immediately into "Mingkaman" in Eastern Lakes State and "Kakuma" in Nairobi. In other words, blaming the government for not being protected while they are the same citizens. Such comments are baseless, and Aldo Ajou may be responsible for answering other allegations. However, Rumbek was liberated by sons and their daughters of Rumbek alone. Not by the brain of Jonglei and Manpower under operation Commander Daniel Deng Monydit. Their martyrs from Agar were Marial Annie Chaman, Marial Majok Ruai, and Buong Malou Rumdhel, to mention a few.

Nevertheless, Jonglei manpower was not there, and I don't know why? Furthermore, another mad dog pooped during their shameless failures and apologized to Omar El Bashier's teams when they visited Khartoum looking for training and weapons. "General Taban Deng Gai apologized for the support he rendered to Darfurian movements and the role he played in the "Hajilij" battle. That Dinka used them in those battles to spoils their relations with the North. But they discovered the mistake of late. Now they are fighting to achieve a federal system or self-rule for each region. I think any self-rule for the greater Upper Nile is good for us regarding borders, oil resources, and trade. In southern Sudan, shameless personalities like the two above and Tut Kew Gatluak are the President listens to because they speak nonsense without reservation. (English Translation of 31, August 2014 High-level meeting, military meetings; Complete text, posted 29, September 2014). Not only that, spoiling the unity of the country and its people. However, those who say the realities are the first enemies to be targeted and marginalized. The two words "self- rule" may spoil the relationship between Upper Nile and the North because these people may one day want to split into their entity. That's an absurdity, even in a small village where ten people may confront each other with sticks; the clan leader could not give an "okay" while he is not there. If you think that opinion was the right idea, then it is precisely the idea of cowardly groups who exploit the energy of others while they do nothing. Of course, there were some rumors that I'm not sure whether there was evidence before the rebellions that he was selected to be the leader. Credit goes to Kerubino Kuanyin Bol and William Nyuon Benny must remain in the history of our struggle as individuals who influenced Dr. John Garang. In contrast, Garang de Mabior remained in the record of world leaders who see things globally. He will remain an exceptional guerilla leader in Africa because when world leaders heard about his death, the United Nations Security Council made extraordinary meetings to discuss how the CPA would survive without him. That was a remark to an exceptional leader to the world peace lovers, and therefore his legacy was beyond South Sudan. Those looting South Sudan's resources were not even on the front line; otherwise, they shouldn't forget their comrade's hero's martyrs, orphans, and widows. In other words, the wounded heroes shouldn't be struggling to get meals of the day, let alone dead ones. They will be ignominious any time because the world now is living under video surveillance where things are exposed within a minute. As the Bible clearly states in Daniel, let them know that our days are numbered under one sun. "This is the inscription that was written: Mene, Mene, Tekel, Parsin. These words mean: Mene—God has numbered the days of your reign and brought it to an end. Tekel—you have been weighed on the scales and found wanting. Peres—your kingdom is divided and given to the Medes and Persia" (Daniel 5:25-28). In other words, whether we are rich or poor, when our days come, we will leave a bunch of wrong wealth we accumulated. In addition, all our funerals or casket will smell rotten regardless of being rich or poor. Let me highlight how these scientists have made critical research efforts on how things work on this earth. They have discovered many things; however, they failed to predict how many years, days, and minutes a person may spend in this world. They tried their best to find out when the Egyptian Pyramids were built and the method of engraving. These Egyptian pyramids were built by those described as TALLEST and DARKEST, and they were influenced by the power of "Madhol" (God). Yet, they failed to know these two in question, and therefore, "Fear of the Lord is the beginning of wisdom where you need to refrain from oppressing His People not to enjoy peace and harmony among themselves. Be aware also, we came into this world naked, and we will leave it in nakedness as we came from the wombs of our mothers," like what Job said. Again, remark on this also. Have you seen our money from the banks, our cars in the parking lot, and cows from cattle camp come one time to see us in the hospitals if the rich guys are sick to say, "how you are today?" What do the leaders enjoy when human beings are suffering?

In 2007, I made a trip to Washington, DC. Before I reached there, I received a call from our boys who were living in Richmond, Virginia. They told me I should pass through their church in Virginia, so I stopped there, and lunch was already prepared for us. After we ate, their friend who visited Rumbek and other places began to explain his trip to us and how suffering was devastating people. He told us that something that touched his spirit was the behavior of one pastor. He stated that during their discussions of the church affairs, that pastor with a big stomach changed his clothes three times in less than four hours. So, he asked, "Did the pastor intend to show us how many clothes he has while some people were naked and starving? How are people who were not Southern Sudanese supposed to help with such behavior? To him, it was irresponsible behavior and, at the same time, bankruptcy—morally and spiritually. This is how foreign visitors label all our ministers. Nobody can smoke them out because their relatives harbor them, and all but a few are Dinka's. It cannot be hidden. As shown in previous sufferings, we are not the majority to misrule like now; they might be good at fighting, but not to rule with nepotism and corruption. We need to adjust our image in misrule. Otherwise, the so- called South Independence will cost many innocent lives in the future. Giving employment based on clans must be changed to achieve the broad aspirations for the absent generation.

Leaders should be able to project into the life, heart, and mind of others, then setting aside personal preferences, deal with the others in a fashion that fits the others best. This skill can be learned and developed through "Wende Madhol," the Creator God, not our knowledge. Leaders need the ability to negotiate differences in a way that appreciates mutual rights and interests and yet leads to a harmonious solution. Fundamental to this skill is understanding how people feel and how people react to what you get from Jehovah Nissi. For example, after the untimely death of Dr. John Garang, people picked you up as Joshua after Moses. Commenting on this, Joshua used wonderful tack when they divided the Promised Land among the tribes of Israel, which was a critical position to deter itself.

"A wrong move would splint an already wobbly nation, but Joshua, to be fair, his tactical beamed brightly again. When the tribes of Ruben and Gad built their own altar, they nearly created the civil war. However, Joshua had wisdom learned in the school of God. His close walk with God gave him the diplomacy to steer a course away from needless bloodshed and toward national healing." Consequently, we need the wisdom to regard ourselves, not with a tribal agenda that may open many previous wounds. "Disappointment with SPLM/GOSS. During the war, we were all united to fight the Arabs," said Yabu, thirty-three, a mother of six in Juba. "But as soon as the peace was signed, people started dividing. Now the ruling clans get the entire job, and we get nothing." It was a very painful remark to hear that, do not get me wrong, even other Dinka's are suffering like you. "Is this where the money is going through, we were supposed to be equal…and the government was going to end the suffering," said Joseph, in Juba, as GOSS $3 billion revenues from oil revenues in the last two years was spent renovating some ministries with marble floor and cherry stained wood paneling" (LA Times, 2007). They were making themselves rich, not knowing that the CPA was in a coma of tribalism because they mismanaged resources. The Bible says: "He who oppresses the poor to increase his wealth, and he who gives gifts to the rich-both come to poverty. Humility and the fear of the Lord bring wealth, honor, and life."

Knowledge is pride that we learn; meanwhile, wisdom is humble, that he knows no more, but God is my helper. Leaders with knowledge pursue the goal; they never look back or calculate escape strategies if plans turn sour. During the tough time, be aware of the magnitude of the tasks ahead to be accomplished. Tribalism and corruption are not easy to eradicate; we have cultivated the spirit of lies before fact prevails into realities, and that's dangerous. Fighting tribalism and corruption, you must have confidence in the assembly members to back you up in a fight. But making political rallies in each state while you have no base to the hand-picked members will endanger your political career. I think what the Southerners or Sudanese people want more than anything is just common sense and smart government. They do not want ideology, they do not want bickering, and they do not want sniping. They want action and they want effectiveness government. In an interview with the BBC, V. P. Dr. Riek Machar Tenny denied allegations in the

152

press that he was corrupt, saying he led a hand-to-mouth existence: "Since I have come back from the bush, I have not opened an account." He said, "My salary is not that big. I have no luxury or enjoyment. Since the agreement was signed, I have not traveled abroad. I'm inside the country I'm more, or less like a sitting duck" (Jan. 2007). Dr. Riek, time will tell the people of South Sudan your claims whether you are clean or not because when the list of corrupters came out from TheSentry.Org, your name appeared in that list with hundreds of millions, and therefore what you were telling BCC was white lies. You are among the politicians, and that was why those of Ezekiel Loul Gathuoth and general Taban Deng Gai spearheaded rebellions. On that list, Taban Deng Gai had three hundred million dollars.

CHAPTER TWENTY

War of Corruption

Actions speak louder than eloquent words in politics without a tangible action; you have underrated the fight against corruption. The Rumbek meetings have explained the bankruptcy of the leadership morally and thoroughly mobilized the people and told them the truths because fighting corruption is not short-term to be pinned down easily. It might be advisable for your information. Do we believe what we previously said and act against it, or do we hate bad practices when we are not responsible? Because looking into the minutes of the historic meetings in Rumbek in November 2004 between His Excellency Salva Kiir Mayardit, the late Dr. John Garang de Mabior, and the entire leadership, you will not believe why the leaders have repeated the same mistakes, including the current president. Some logical points were raised in those meetings, for example, kitchen cabinet, nepotism, and corruption and disinformation against others. The entire leadership might be hypocrites, or they were misleading the public opinions.

For instance, "corruption is zero tolerance" has become a slogan protecting criminals or political propaganda. Prominent leaders who are well-known corrupters have not yet been brought to justice. Southerners are very smart to the extent that when they write and address the suffering of their people, you will believe that if the writers or speakers get responsibility, they will rebuke the situation accordingly, like what they have said before. Unfortunately, it's zero to reflect the reality of the condition they were complaining bitterly about it. This method is ignorant, hypocritical, and deceiving public opinions in general.

Before I further emphasize how the $60 million came into the attention of the southerners was the beginning of lousy leadership. If E.H. Omar el Basher did not air it out, how would the southerners have known it? Mr. President, you have achieved some crucial issues, including absorbing other arms groups into SPLA. Mr. President had to learn from past mistakes. You and your present leadership need to repent because you opposed corruption and kitchen cabinets in the Rumbek meetings. Yet, these two have been intensified more than ever before under your responsibility. You promoted nepotism poorly in the palace and ministry of foreign affairs just from Awan and Kuac.

Mr. President, you must stand on the principles of your protest, combat corruption, and move your party to the national center or level. Compromising or appeasing other leaders will result to defeat in the coming years; you must show your actual colors because you protested in 2004 for the above. Show your patriotism to the South Sudanese rather than be blackmailed by tribal agenda. Politics of accommodation and appeasement is suicide or political self-destruction. You must have the courage to do what you know is morally right. You must present fundamental beliefs that must not be compromised to politically expedient, unifying marginalized forces and moving to Khartoum. Doing so will send a clear signal to the NIF or NCP by then should be a number one fundamental. Suffering twenty years, we have experienced the same brutal suffering our brothers in Western Sudan have tasted now, so do not think back on their participation with the INF; this is how human beings behave if they are still alive when Sudan was one country.

Distance yourself from tribalism; do not base much hope for self-determination because if you do not show patriotic leadership, our dreams will not go through. "Think big, act with conviction, trust God on your action rather than trusting flesh" (Jeremiah 17:5-10). Failure to endorse or instruct the Southern Assembly to table anticorruption laws, then you have distanced yourself from the bulk of national public opinions.

Now, it would be bad enough if you failed to redeem your promise to reduce corruption. The goal should be unifying the country to renew the spirit of marginalized people like a sense of purpose; capturing the public opinions must be a goal of your survival, not nepotism. Instead, you sell yourself to the public; you are just like a commodity to the Sudanese people; others may buy you according to their needs, and some may reject you.

When are we going to learn about being national figures? Our governments are always set up in nepotism, a narrow gate to a big dream of having statehood. What is written in CPA will not qualify us unless you eradicate tribalism, nepotism, and corruption; people may ask why this call was not brought early during the struggle! The answer is simple. You have shown somehow being a patriotic soldier; for the first time in our struggle, you were the first southerner to be given leadership without competition. Those who gave that trust were not from your area alone—it was a collective belief.

Look back to the dark days of division in 1991: "Abraham Lincoln has to say this during slavery in 1860 in America, he declared that a house divided against itself cannot stand." Again, he said, "A husband and wife may be divorced and go out of the presence and beyond the reach of each, but the different parts of our country cannot do this." This statement is essential because you cannot give most of the positions to one tribe by then. CPA was in horrible shape regarding its implementation among the southerners because of imbalance. The beginning of the first cabinets from 2005-2011 was an alarm ringing to southerners because government machinery was controlled by one ethnic group. Leadership loses sight by neglecting their principles in the heat of the political campaign.

To stand on principles, you must run on principles; this much more is a fundamental case to be made that Kiir may fail to become a President at a critical moment. "You walked away in a defending a cause; I think that Mr. President has realized that he was sitting on a hot stove.

However, sitting on a cold stove will not be possible because abandoning the principles will be a severe defeat in your political life," Dick Morris said (in his book, The Power Plays). A party that could not unite itself was not possible to unite the people of New Sudan. Mr. President, check your balance sheet so that you can find the errors; otherwise, things will be out of your control. Historical reconciliation meetings in Rumbek between Dr. John's group and the current president were motivated by tribalism and emotional anger without any legitimacy proud to follow if one of them got an opportunity to lead just like now, as the case at present, under Kiir. The president documents himself with many promises. For example, recently in Addis Ababa: "Given the legacy on our struggle for freedom, democracy, justices, equality, and human dignity, South Sudan will not just be the world's newest state, but its newest democracy" (President Salva Kiir Mayardit, January 31,2011 Addis Ababa, Ethiopia). When one needs drastic change or radical hopes and less appeal to national purpose and consistency of patriotism, the result may be disastrous to the hope you want to accomplish because high motivation collided with self- interests, and that's the real enemy to African leaders. What Kiir promised above was merely empty promising. In other words, illusion attitudes for nothing.

I will end here by giving the meaning of oaths in the Bible. Why do government officials take oaths? Oaths mean formal declarations or promises, often calling on God as a witness. It officially declares them to be overseers to the people of God, to be providers, to commit them to serve diligently. Do our rulers have attentive care that the Holy Book told them to do? How do you provide nothing to those you took an oath for? You are inflicting a serious curse against yourself of nobody to blame. I suggest that government officials should be given the formal meaning of an oath before they take it; to be sure why they are taking it. It is not for fun or showing yourself that you are taking an oath on the camera. The pastors should not be kept in limbo to not rebuke them about their corruption in all forms. "Again, you have heard that it was said to those of ancient times, you shall not swear falsely but carry out the vows you have made to the Madhol. But I say to you, do not swear at all, either by heaven, for it is the throne of God. Let your Yes be Yes or No, no; anything more than this comes from the evil one" (Matthew 5:33, 34 and 37).

CHAPTER TWENTY-ONE

New Nation in Fragments

Fragmentation means the act or process of breaking into fragments, in other words, scattering of the fragments of exploding bombs or other projectiles. This fragmentation of southerners started in earlier days of struggle in 1983 when the rebellion began in Bor under the commander Kerbino Kuanyin Bol and William Nyon Benny in Ayod, respectively. Enemies termed the struggle as Dinka's or Nuer's mutiny. The first Battalions of James, Tiger, Tomas, 104, and 105 were composed of Nuers and Dinka's alike. Koroma division and Mormor, mostly majority were Dinkas and Nuers from 1983 to the earliest of 1987. Although these two divisions were led mostly by Dinkas and Nuers commanders, this outrageous hatred was not on the surface at that time. The outrageous spite started during the split where Nasir faction murdered their officers and men. At the same time, Torit made similar acts slaughtering soldiers and officers in different places, although it was not practiced in Torit. The two tribes collided with one another badly by Dr. Lam Akol Ajawin because he spearheaded the coup destruction. Before they achieved the propaganda campaign of democracy and human rights among themselves, another split emerged within those who made historical setbacks of the struggle. Loyalists among Chollo and Nuers remained in the movement until the Comprehensive Peace Agreement was written. Many doctorates are insulting and complaining that the government had been Dinkaocrated. However, during the hottest time when the Torit faction was in the last corner of Nimule, they never raised their nose that the war was Dinkanized. Instead, they were busy with the enemy in General Headquarters in Khartoum designing how the SPLA should be buried completely, and video clips of Tut Kew are living testimony. Today, the food is cold where everybody becomes a shareholder. Of course, nobody denies that fact because it had been provided by the constitution of the new Republic of South Sudan. But that right should not be claimed with evil rhetoric words where innocents were subjected to brutality catastrophe. After Kerubino Kuanyin Bol discovered (INF) National Islamic Front deceived him of the so-called Khartoum Peace Accord in1997, he made intensive contact with Bahr El Gahazalians to capture him Wau. That move was welcomed by the fueling fighters of Bahr El Ghazal because they were already not happy with how their best commander was humiliated. On January 28, 1998, Wau was captured around Wau's outskirts, and his forces dislodged. Unfortunately, the reinforcements of weapons were prevented for two reasons: First, if the fueling forces captured their town, they would defend the last soldier. However, there would be no formidable forces to fight on other fronts. Secondly, Salva Kiir Mayardit, as Deputy to Dr. John Garang, was nervous because of his ineffective Deputy Commander in Chief. If Kerubino came back, he would assume his place, therefore; Kiir sympathized with Dr. John to hold back reinforcements, not to rescue Kerubino and his forces. All these censorious were also applied to betray William Nyon Beny when he decided to come back in 1993 until he got killed by the unknown. The war of survival or war of Attrition was painful even among the Dinkans where others say, "why should I fight war bravely like Bahr El Ghazalians fighters?". These are hots points; some sections must have zipped their mouths because of how you become conservatives, while other soldiers were sent for studies on expenses of others while others confronted the enemy bravely. The collision of two leaders in November 2004 was almost extremely disastrous if it was not handled with the wisdom of Bahr el Ghazalians people and specifically Agar Community, who see things beyond the narrowed gate of sectional pride. Mrs. Monica Ayen Maguat and David Nok Marial Bout led a delegation to convince Salva in Yei to let the leaders have a dialogue to resolve the issues of lynching. All sectional organizing proved fruitless to the national issues that I and other Bahr el Ghazalians are proud of. The total change of the High Executive council in 1978 in Juba was possible because Bahr el Ghazalians forced Abel Alier groups out in Democratic elections. When painful mutiny happened in Bor on May 16, 1983, it was Kerbino Kuanyin Bol who made it to be possible.

When the disaster of November 2004 was cold down between late Dr. John Garang and the president Salva Kiir Mayardit, Bahr el Ghazalians themselves acted swiftly to bring two leaders on the table of reconciliations for the sake of peace among the southerners. When Rumbek was captured in 1986 by the SPLA forces, overwhelmingly supporting the fifth column from within made it possible. Rumbek was the first Province to be overrun by gallant forces of struggle because Rumbek people from Yriol all away to Tonjdit were the foundation of confrontation to the enemy by that time and beyond till SPLA was born. In 1994, late Samuel Aru Bol and others attempted reconciling approach between Dr. Riek Machar and Dr. John Garang, which couldn't go through because of bad tension from the Torit faction. His constituency voters in Rumbek undermined his initiatives as if he was campaigning for war, not reconciliation processes. Dr.

John was aware power struggles may emerge at any time of peace between Bahr El Ghazal and the Upper Nile. Therefore, he could not allow reconciliation to be done by someone else besides him because it would leverage Samuel Aru Bol and the people of Bahr El Gazal. Dr. John knows his leadership might face challenges if he still has grievances with Nuers, and he had to reconcile with them on his terms, not Samuel Aru Bol. I'm spelling out all those points because certain groups think that we are dummies to the point. We couldn't organize ourselves, but we knew the consequences of the division of regionalism and sectionalism, so we overlooked such sectionalist organizing. To be fair enough, the point I could not trust or praise within Bahr el Ghzalians is financial irregularities in their hands. They have a bad temperament regarding finances; it is in the records. Late Dr. Lawrence Wol Wol had been fired twice in 1978 and 1982 in regional government respectively because of corruptions, and finally Arthur Akuen Chol and Kuol Athian Mawien. These are facts which individuals of us are not proud of handling, but in terms of war, you slow your tail down or unity among the southerners. How many Bahr el Ghazalians were taken from fields and sent for studies like others who went for studies? The innocent majority paid the ultimate price on both sides without anything to reap during the peace agreements. Most of the Southerners loved each other before the political-ideological division that made their arguments ideology on a tribal basis, and that was the recipe of ignorant. On the other hand, those with bad tension with Dinka's had narrowed vision of engulfing the other Dinka's into boats. Instead of addressing the failures as individual groups, they generalized the whole Dinka's. Other nationalists are pushed back to join the clique because of bad tension. The report released by the US Bureau of Democracy, Human Rights, and Labor from January to December 2011 had categories a series of killing, torturing, raping both women and girls, and other inhumane committed atrocities against civilians have remarked the nervousness of the regime to think twice. Either they change their behaviors, or else; they will be placed on the watch list of abusive countries of Human Rights. It is unbelievable if such reports are not ironing out with facts of setting up a committee to investigate the allegation thoroughly should the regime has ignited many problems. The government restricted freedoms of speech, assembly, and association. However, violence and harassing journalists was the order of the day; detaining, intimidating, and harassing for criticizing security forces or government officials are met with arresting and torturing. There are some questions to the Dinka leaders controlling much of the government machinery; why did our reputation lose critical value among the ethnic group in the new republic? How are we comfortable with such criticism regarding misrules and corruption? Since you have many receipts, do you feel that you don't care about losing respect? Are you also in the position you are not respecting human being life? Do you think you are operating in a different world where your mistakes are not known to the world we are in? The Dinka character within southerners has become less than toilet paper value because all ethnic groups in all corners around the new Republic of South Sudan are insulting Dinka's because they have spoiled their respects. What does criticism mean; is to analyze, classify, interpret, or evaluate literary the right way the government should govern its people. If the government doesn't want to be criticized, it should do the right things to avoid being criticized; otherwise, the public will criticize you. How would you avoid criticism while rampage killings were carried out in Yambio, where three senior police officers were killed in 2006. In 2010, Chief Jock Dau Kacuol Dau in Cueibiet county was killed. In 2009, another random shooting took place in Akot, Lake's state, where many civilians lost their lives and properties. Engineer Lewis lost his life because of a plot where general Marial Nuor Jock was a suspect. Finally, Isaiah Abraham was gunned down on December 5, 2012, in Juba. That entire horrific death president issued several degrees for investigation, yet the public was still in limbo to know the outcome and leave the corruption investigation alone. What I want to justify here to Brother Elhag Paul in his response to Ateny! Wek Ateny on South Sudan Nation dated on May 24, 2012, which stated like this: Dinkaoracy is defined as "a system of rule that can be found in South Sudan based on tribalism whereby parliament is either wholly or partially filled by appointment of corrupt members. Institutions and structures that are presently in place are just for face-saving purposes. In this system, consultation and citizens' rights are not respected. The views and opinions of citizens also do not mean anything". In my opinion, Paul and the original author stated the living realities in our Dinkaocrats behaviors, as he defined in his dictionary. However, linguistic or philosopher failed to define how the groups of Dinkaocrats suffered in the hands of both enemies in earlier 1991, down to 2002. However, how did the linguistics get his or her definition in this time anyway should be laughing point to Elhag Paul and the author; unless they have no consciousness of ultimate prices Dinkaocrats paid? I wished if such definitions or complaints were raised during the liberation movement would have made sense. The Dinkaocrats were waging many wars in decades against the Radical fundamentalist's government in Sudan until the country split; it was because of some facts mentioned by definer and Elhag Paul that we were denied not to run some ministries: Interior, Defense, Foreign Affairs, Chief Justices, and much more. If the systems are being Dinkanized like they are now, then our heroes died in vain because other injustices have been applied against other ethnic groups by Dinkaocrats. When slogans with no favorable tangible beliefs run governments, then consequences of social injustices and unfair social-economic will be jeopardizing that system to nail it down soon. The regime should acknowledge the principles of our struggle before the Mohammed Ahamed Mahadi Revolution against colonization all away to the SPLM/SPLA. Southerners (CUSH PEOPLE OR KINGDOM) have been opposing humiliation since the beginning of mankind in the area we are in today. If you visualize the group living around Omdurman Media Broadcasting, you will figure out those are not Arabs by origins.

They are descendants of the soldiers who joined the Mahdi Revolution centuries ago. Some are Nubians, Zandes, Chollos, Nuers, and Dinka's. Therefore, our struggle did not start with liberators of the days, which is SPLA. Our grandfathers have a history of fighting for justice.

These monolithic system attitudes will disintegrate the southerner's base on tribal lines because the president himself sanctified it by appointing his own cousins several times into top government positions without considering what is facing the Old Sudan now on such appointments. It's unfortunate; both countries chose destructive separations because southerners did not enjoy the fruits of their aspiration separation, and northerners never got satisfied with Islamic Sharia either. Clique individuals in both South and North reaped the benefits of destructive disunity. Meanwhile, the majority are confronting each other in both countries.

CHAPTER TWENTY-TWO

Who is sowing the Seeds of Hatred?

"Bear with one another and, if anyone has a complaint against another, forgive each other; just as the Lord has forgiven you, so you also must forgive, and above all, clothe ourselves with love, which binds everything together in perfect harmony (Colossians 3: 13)". Whenever an authority makes a distinction to his clan or ethnicity and undermines the values of others, he is dependently prepared to oppress others, and that is what we are condoning in South Sudan.

Sowing the seeds of hatred! You will reap its consequences whether Dinka's or non- Dinka's because there were no special schools where Dinka's were better qualified than other non-Dinka's in Sudan or abroad. Repeating what martyrs fought to eliminate it is a betrayal and must be fought in the strongest possible way across South Sudan. The only viable approach is to embrace each other to share little or big things equally. The so-called liberators have spoiled Dinka's characters because their arrogant attitudes toward non-Dinka's are catastrophic. The exclusive monopoly controlling government under the blind assumptions by Dinkaocrats must be addressed inclusively by Dinka intellectual elites. Otherwise, the survival of South Sudan as one nation will be at risk. The lynching policies must be dealt with unanimously by all peace lovers across South Sudan; we must value our citizens' liberty, happiness, and dignity based on justice and equality for all. These elites' monopolized systems, excluding others' opinions, will allow yesterday's enemy to laugh at us, where there will be no proper answer to defend ourselves. "Looting and corruption are accepted as a method of wealth gathering with the façade that the government is working to address it. "The police force is predominantly illiterate and come from the ruling tribe. Their job is to administer brute injustice. Violence is routinely exercised freely by members of the ruling tribe (in organized forces) with impunity. Government officials are guarded and protected by their kith and kin as opposed to agents of the sates". This is what the term means, and this definition can be found in www.allafrica.com under the title "Lies and illusion of South

Sudan's president Kiir" published on 26th September 2011." The definition sounds correct to all elites in Africa, not the republic of South Sudan alone. It was copied from other countries in Africa, and the author must be aware of it. I'm not defending the system, but the author should involve other Dinka's rather than delimiting war for themselves.

After I comment on the statement, let's quote the Bible since our daily lives were basic with Biblical facts." Then you will know the truth, and the truth will set you free."(John 8:32). The author had exposed the alarming points that Sudan disintegrated before us because what is being entertained now in ten states was the similar point of splitting the old Sudan into two. The Bible is an important source to be respected on any occasion. Furthermore, if our leaders go to church every Sunday without knowing these quotations, they're attending prayers based on illusions or pretensions of going to prayers. Again, another quotation is written this way "whoever says, and loves his brother or sister lives in the light, and there is no cause for stumbling in such a person. But whoever hates another believer is in darkness, walks in darkness, and does not know the way to go because the darkness has brought on blindness". (1 John 2:9- 11). Corrupting the system socially and financially will result in lynching our citizens when we fought for their liberty and persuaded happiness, for which martyrs paid the price. Why? For that reason, those who got killed around the Republic of South Sudan after the peace conclusion were protesting the system that marginalizes others on a tribal basis. Accordingly, such rulers are in darkness even though they pray five times like Muslims because killing innocent people proves beyond doubt that leaders were blinded by the assumption of going to church while failing to address inequality. The Dinkaocrat leaders live in the blindness of hating their citizens; they were waging the worst suffering in the twenty-first century to free them from Muslims. The southerners voted overwhelmingly for their independence to enjoy the freedom of sharing their own government equally regardless of being a non-Dinkaocrat. The southerners were not voting for the welfare of the Dinka majority to rule them. No, their choice was to share the resources, as their right defined by the Republic of South Sudan constitution. that was the purpose of independence, not to frustrate them where others are losing hope of prosperity. Applying injustices in any form has no color. It is a system of rules, whether, by westerners, radical Muslims against non-Muslims or Dinka's against the non-Dinka's, it will be called an inequality. This cancer must be equally condemned in the strongest terms by Dinka intellectuals and religious leaders to not spread like wildfire among the southerners in the early stages. Otherwise, it will endure our aspirations or our dreams. If you know Tsunami is coming, one will make strategic planning, like evacuating people to prevent unnecessary loss of life. We should be prepared to avoid the eventuality of 1983 divisions again. We tasted the bitterness of tribalism before where each region went and faced the same challenges of marginalization by certain groups. For example, Equatoria Region was dominated by Bari sidelining non-Bari, while Nuers dominated the upper Nile, whereas non-Nuers were never seated in Governorship. Nevertheless, Bahr El Ghazal experienced similar among Dinka's themselves, so the game is well known to us. Even in the ten states, many citizens are complaining of not being represented at the state level. We should acknowledge that it is not possible to represent each tribe in government institutions whatsoever the broad base government. Also, another reality we should bear in mind is being the competitive person to hold any post not based on tribes. Still, their competitiveness should be participation criteria, not of being Dinkaocrat groups. The so-called federalism will not even solve power-sharing problems because, in the federal system, the federal government owns all naturals resources. The drama of federalism will not work if the multi-party system is not involved properly, so that check and balance will take its cause. But suppose the South Sudan liberation movement is still an adamant party in South Sudan. The federal song will not satisfy the demanders because the one-party system may not make checks and balances to their government. Unless South Sudanese federal demands are different from the western system of federalism because those who are enjoining the so-called land belong to the community will not be happy again under the federal system. Land and any other natural resources will automatically fall under the jurisdiction of the federal constitution. Our solution should be how to respect the supreme law of the country and the moral obligation of being savant to serve others rather than our tribal men and women. Those who are sowing the seeds of minority may not rule over the majority will reap that fruit to the point they will not forget it. However, the only umbrella which could accommodate us is being southern Sudanese regardless of being majority or minority because the spirit of that minority cannot rule over are not all Dinka's but certain groups who failed to acknowledge what togetherness means. Governments are not changed regionally or tribally rather than collectively; individual mistakes should not be generalized for the whole Dinka's. Understanding each other is the key to our survival as a nation. But if some elements misunderstood it to be a call of a coward like an apology of Dr. Riek Machar, then you missed the point. Those who pay the higher price are innocent people who have nothing to do with the government. Calling for peace or making an apology is not assigned to being cowardly; however, it is assigned to forgiving each other. The whole world viewed us as anti-tolerance to others.

However, that is not all of us who behave in that manner. We must pull the wheels back together for love, tolerance, and embracement to one another. Otherwise, in my view, the Torit faction leaders must make a similar apology to Nuers and the rest for comprehensive reconciliation.

Those who survive in Torit either have personal friends with leaders or in-laws to some commanders, and therefore equal life was lost in Torit, Bor, and in Rumbek, all away from other parts of the region in Bahr El Ghazal.

CHAPTER TWENTY-THREE

Collision of National Interests and Tribalism

The brave Third World leaders got assassinated because their different opinions collided between them, and the greediness of western leaders will not go without asking "Garang Abuk," God of all, to question why they were killed. They shed their blood when they said, "why do we not deserve to have our resources without your interference?" The network of assassinating Third World Leaders goes with no question from spiritual leaders in the West and Third World Spiritual Leaders. Why have resources subjected their leaders to death? "And the Lord said, "What have you done? Listen, your brother's blood is crying out to me from the ground! And now you are cursed from the ground, which has opened its mouth to receive your brother's blood from hand" (Genesis 4:10 and 11). God is the blood of Dr. Jonas Samvibi, Dr. John Garang de Mabior, Patrice Lumumba, and the rest I may not name all are not crying to you to question those who shed their blood? Are they just dead because Western groups who assassinated Black leaders see that they are nothing to God? If these groups are loyalists to God's spirit, should they assume that Almighty God belongs to them while others are evil? Do they resemble you, God?

Why are they so evil to the point of organizing criminal ways for lynching African leaders, and you do not tell them such behavior is unacceptable to me. Dr. Jonas Malherio Samvibi of Angola founded UNITA Movement, the first guerrilla war against Portuguese colonial rule from 1966- 1974, then confronted the rival MPLA during the colonization conflict 1974/75 and after independence in 1975. He continued to fight the ruling MPLA in Angola Civil War until he died in clashes with Angola government troops in February 2002. How many powerful guerrillas died in 2002 was a great shock to those who knew his abilities in guerilla warfare. These courageous African leaders resulted in negative pride where Jonas Samvibi and George Athor Deng were erased out of history of liberating their people from colonization. Hence, those who did nothing remained to be champions of liberation. Spiritual leaders must address the courage combined with pride because God stands with facts, not self-ambition. When those guerillas were fighting for the liberation of their people, the wisdom of the living God protected them because they were fighting for a genuine cause. But after the genuine cause was obtained, they insisted on their interests. Therefore, God could not stand behind selfish motives. The wisdom of avoiding being assassinated by regional interests must be learned from the Nelson Mandela school because how he compromised with the Apartheid regime was unbelievable to those who do not want Africa to forge ahead. Dr. John Garang and Dr. Khalil Ibrahim Mohammed both got their fate. As a result, they were obstacles to the big brothers' interests. The ideology of New Sudan was a disturbing point as far as oil and manpower in Sudan will make her a legitimate threat to regional powers both economically and in military capacity in the future under his leadership. Dr. John Garang was a compatible element to the point he brought two camps into his boat of support. It was a complicated equation to achieve. The late Dr. Khalil was obstinate in his radical Islamic ideology, where many Darfurians would have an uncertain future in Sudan. Either the regime in Khartoum changes their ideology after Dr. Khalil's death, or they will be subjected to make necessary multi-cultural, multi-diversity of coexistences between ethnic groups in Sudan.

Otherwise, the hunting down of the elements who stood in front of the right of the marginalized will not end. When Daud Yahiya Bolad woke up and joined Sudan's People Liberation Movement while those of late Dr. Khalil was still entertaining their masters, that was an opportunity for the marginalized to inflict heavy loss to the Khartoum regime. But those of the JEM missed the golden time of struggling together with their brothers as oppressive forces.

Maybe the death of Dr. Khalil Ibrahim may make the situation upside down because if the junta celebrates and does not change their ideology, it may result in separation. Since Africa became an alternative to Western interests after their honeymoon with Arabs countries had run out. They had to ensure that they must eliminate any obstacle guerrilla leaders to loot our resources. The elimination of George Athor was good news to the peace lovers. However, it was one eye tears to the corrupters groups because if he had resisted, many looters, like the case of Jonas Samvibi, would have to join the unnecessary guerrilla fight as safe Heaven for them. If the guerillas' failed to share the cake of struggle equally, they dragged the people back to war. Any guerilla in the Third World, who overstepped his mandate of struggle, or tried to be out of the box policies, will pay the ultimate price like Dr. John Garang in Southern Sudan 2005 and Jonas Savimbi in Angola 2002. Whatever confusion in the ten states among the citizens, its root cause came from Juba. Even if the government deployed so many soldiers while the President did not question the confectioners in Juba to the point some lost their positions, peace might not prevail. It is a game of divide and rule because if there is peace among the citizens, they will realize that they are being cheated in terms of no services. To let them be in such confusion, politicians in each state have more opportunity to hold their position, as long as no one realizes their weakness. When these two above collide together, the results are a national disaster perhaps; both national interests and tribalism were enemies of each other. Opposing the government, in my opinion, should be based on how you address the national issues rather than staging change based on tribes and regions. Let us learn some lessons about what price the cliques and their families have paid recently was not isolated to any of the Third World countries. Stepping up to address the national issues will provide an opportunity where other nationalists will support you but narrowing the issues into opposing the government, just being led by Dinka's will cost much bloodshed. You have denied other Dinka alliances. As the regime will mobilize such an innocent majority to defend the name, not the government, in other words, to defend their identity should they feel their being is under attack. One of the opposition leaders said that the Dinka kingdom would collapse very soon, which was completely ignorant because such comments are derogatory to most followers. They will fight to the last man. As a result, they are not defending Kiir per se, but they will defend their abused name, and it will be a recipe for disaster. Even if you succeed, I believe you will use the same mistake Dinka's applied during their time. Then again, certain groups will prepare for the worst change. Therefore, the change will be from tribes to tribes should national suffering have been discarded to the tribe's interests, and such behavior will never move Africans anywhere. If you cannot convince a nationalist to support you, please do not mobilize your tribe into disaster. The ability to address central issues should be a goal of changing the agenda. You may or may not believe what I'm saying. Kiir pretended in

171

the Rumbek meetings in 2004 to address the national issues, but it turned out to be surrounding himself with groups eager to accumulate much wealth. Being a patriotic person, you will not be imposed by your tribe; it should be a collective concern. Otherwise, each attempt will end disastrously. There is another criterion the political leaders need to define to go forward. When you form a party, you need to participate in the government; you should not leave the party as an orphan who has nobody to nourish it. Why don't you stay with the rest and let others participate so that you can correct them when they report the progress or difficulties facing them? If you are there, do you report to your subordinate, or does your subordinate report to the superior? We were joking at home. I have been here in America and observed that the one who contested to be President is not a party leader; somebody addresses the nation's concerns; concerns within the party competition are contested with other party opponents. If this criterion is different from what we are doing in the Third World, then we are still behind in singing the democracy we talk about. I suggest to those who are not convinced that Sudan's people's liberation movement agenda should form a big party across South Sudan. These massive artillery ideas will root them out easily in each corner of South Sudan rather than opposing them as tribes. But addressing their failure as Dinka's will consolidate their being in authority longer and the suffering of our people. Whereas other Dinka's are in the same coin of suffering. We shouldn't allow them to be chauvinistic of liberation, whereas others did not fight the war; they had already failed to be chauvinistic of liberation otherwise of their massive corruptions. "They promise them freedom, but they themselves are slaves of corruption, for people are slaves to whatever masters them" (2 Peter 2, 19). Let's focus on genuine change based on nonviolence because chances of nonviolence are more than advocating our molecules to one another. These leaders have failed to be Joshua; they did not mediate the fact of liberating us. Let us move to the center of healing together encourage our collective ideas in a concerted manner. When Joshua took over, this is what God told him to do: "This book of the law shall not depart out of your mouth; you shall meditate on it day and night, so that you may be careful to act in accordance with all that is written in it. For then, you shall be successful. I hereby command you; be strong and courageous; do not be frightened or dismayed, for the Lord, your God is with you wherever you go" (Joshua 1:8-9). As I mentioned somewhere, promoting you to be a leader of the majority tribe does not advocate national issues. We must meditate and encourage ourselves to be national leaders, also meditate and encourage one another to listen to God. Let the spirit of the living God teach you and me how to respect the human being. Let us submit our ideas of change to God and resist the temptation of the evil spirit to flee from us. Let us draw near to God, and he will draw near to us to defeat evil leaders who do not care about the suffering of their people. This emotional ambition change is dangerous to innocent life, without any objectives to lose your life for it.

Being in Rumbek, Aweil, Bentiu, Akobo, Juba, or Bor is not a qualification of being a nationalist to address national issues. There must be some fundamental objectives to mobilize the southerners to support you rather than mobilizing simply saying that I'm a Dinka and, as such, stand behind me just like that. Those forming many families/parties in the under developing countries for the long-suffering of our people because their programs are just empty to convince the large majority for the change in our countries. Also, their ideas are motivated by hatred agendas, whereas what they say behind closed doors are revenge ideas. Foolish leaders could use wrong artilleries to make mass destructions if he is not monitored properly. However, the chances of arm struggles are not wide to achieve them, especially when they are not well informed on how guerrilla warfare functions. Leading guerrilla warfare is like a drunkard who just passed out propaganda lies, and when ammunition runs out, they will have nothing to say.

Collaborating with the Sudanese junta to overthrow the government in the New Republic of South Sudan is like putting salt into an injury. All regions are standing together with any government in Juba for their interests are so high with them. Investments amongst the superpowers: America and China are a great factor to support who will control South Sudan economically and will be the leading figure for other decades in world power. Therefore, interests in oil and other resources will not allow any guerilla to emerge because of that competition among Chinese and American companies. So far, mobilizing supporters with nonviolence may motivate other nationalists to support you, and this is the best recommendation to those interested in making drastic changes. Making coups is also a useless alternative, as far we are already under the coup of aid and International Monetary Fund coups. The only viable alternative is to have patience with one another. These two organizations have choked us to the point we have kneeled economically as other Third World nations. Relying very much on Almighty God to return us back to the Nineteen Fifties is another viable way so that farmers can cultivate to support for themselves. The easiest things are complaints when we are looking for a change. However, if you get what you were complaining about, leaders will begin to change strategies or principles. For example, in 1978, a group staged a serious campaign against Abel Alier groups for a change in South Sudan. After God allowed them to change the High Executive Council and set up their government, rumors began to leak out about $35,000 Sudanese pounds missing. Joseph Lagu, as a group leader, started firing some of his die-hard aides, and Lagu as a man of principles never hesitated to discharge them in his cabinets. They returned the money; Joseph Lagu had fulfilled his promises. Even though those of late George Athor and the rest of his successors now manage to get that chance. They looked to be worse than the present one, which is why and how Kiir's failures were unbelievable to those who knew that man's principles. But all these returns to the title that "national interests and tribalism collide," and the results would be disastrous. Therefore, principles of complaints died out, so those of you who do not understand the game of our leaders may think that what they are complaining about may result in fruitful things if they get the chance of ruling. It is an empty campaign as far as I knew some of them; you better follow their tones properly before dancing, for such change is with shadows of the day. African leaders who spent much time ruling were not there because the masses liked them, but big brothers kept some for the sake of their interests. I had suspected now are symptoms of worst second degree "kokora" in the New Republic of South Sudan should one already have been approved to move the capital city to a new place called "Ramciel." When we lose sight of dialogue, the consequences or impacts are so high on innocent populations. Other countries recognize diasporas as potential assets instead of seeing them as overtakes or as traitors. The cause of the people of South Sudan had been fought on many fronts. For instance, with Ethiopians, who provided a haven for training soldiers, was a great contribution, the hero Muammar Gaddafi who gave thousands of guns, the American envoy Senator John C. Danforth with his teams, European groups, and finally IGDA groups. All these groups made credible input into the struggles of the Southern Sudanese. The majorities who fled to the Diaspora were not traitors. The real traitors were the "jihadists" Who are now collaborators with leaders or diehard advisors for president; some of us ran away not to betray the cause of South Sudanese of being subjected to become "majihadeen" against the will of Southern Sudanese. We have never been in operating rooms where the real traitors were so busy with the enemy of designing how the SPLM/SPLA should be defeated, and they are briefcase carriers of some leaders now. Perhaps, we are not against reconciliation which the President has devoted his vision to ever since; we are very much concerned about how we should come together to highlight the immediate issues concerning building the nation. If the period of the President had ended with no tangible change with regards to corruption, nepotism, employment, and tribalism, there will be no one to eliminate it.

CHAPTER TWENTY-FOUR

Pluralism and Ethnicity Conflict

Pluralism is the condition of being multiple or conditions in which numerous distinct ethnic, religious, and cultural groups are present in one country and have tolerance within society.

Meanwhile, violent conflict is caused mainly by social and political systems that lead to inequality and governance and do not offer options for the peaceful expression of differences. Most of the wars fought in Africa were not between country and country rather than within the ethnic groups in one country. Diaspora is always seen as arrogant towards their leaders, as far as the education they acquired when some decided to leave the country during the deadly civil wars; however, differences are quite categorically different from country to country. For example, on December 15, 2013, most Diaspora in South Sudan left the country after three days of killings of innocent civilians. This was termed disloyalty, in other words, cowardliness.

Otherwise, they should have participated in the killings of Nuer civilians. In fact, most of the Diaspora Kids are in the USA Army fighting now in different places in the Middle East for a legitimate cause they believe they should fight for. Even after hearing deadly divisions based on tribal lines in South Sudan, they did not relinquish and join the useless suffering war. In chapter Twenty-Three, I supported some points and disputed other opinions because the Bible said this parable: "But I tell you: Love your enemies and pray for those who persecute you, that you may be children of your Father in heaven. He makes his sun rise on the evil and goods and sends rain on the righteous and the unrighteous". (Matthew 5:44 and 45 NIV.) Both sun and rain are the bases of our survival. If one does not exist, all the living things will disappear, and therefore, Dinkaocrats should be like God, who loved both the righteous and unrighteous and made things hot and cold. There should be no retaliation to the evil descriptions because they do not know what they talked about, as Jesus said in His last hours of nailing. On May 3, 2012, President Salva Kiir wrote to over seventy-five formers and current government officials directly asking them to account for misappropriating funds. "We fought for freedom, justice, and equality," the president's letter read. "Many of our friends died to achieve the objectives. Yet, once we got to power, we forgot what we fought for and began to enrich ourselves at the expense of our people." Was this letter issued to Diaspora disloyalty to recover stolen billions of dollars from them or was it to the so-called loyalists if Dr. James Wani Igga and Michael Makuei Lueth were sound-minded questioning our Dual Citizenship? Is self-glorification suffering to our people based on ethnic causes by disloyalties Diasporas or cause by selfish leadership? When you were complaining in Rumbek Meetings Leadership that no Equatoria's were signatories to the CPA because we are making history. Therefore, each region should be represented. Did a disloyal Diaspora cause that imbalance? We, the Diaspora, are not your toilet paper to wipe yourself off after you messed up your dirty leadership, which could not acknowledge the failures while Arabs are laughing at us. Again, after issuing the recovered letter to suspects, he looked himself in the same mirror of the suspect list. He put the mirror down and said this: "I did not say the money was stolen, neither did I say four billion US dollars have been stolen. I said the money has been lost somewhere, and someone had to account for it. I have written to seventy-five formers and present government officials. This does not mean that these seventy-five officials are suspects, but they have the responsibilities. I will still write to some officials to whom I had written them and now claimed to have not received any letter from my office. I will again write to some more officials whom I did not write to earlier."- President Kiir June 13, 2012. What is not clear in this quotation is that the president is trying to cover up the suspects or deny the stolen money? Where did the money get lost, and between who and who is the question that needs to be known by the public? Why issue the list containing seventy-five names if they were not suspects? Dr. Lual Achiek and Madame Awut Deng Achuil have publicly accepted that they received the letter as the suspects. The suffering of our citizens mentioned by the president was not for portions of non Dinkaocrats alone; it was for the whole country. The president knew that they were not fighting for themselves; the sacrifices were to provide the objectives of marginalization to combat corruption and injustices in all forms. The president must restore confidence and new spirits to the public. The reputation you are trying to protect will not be easy, as you said, because they cannot maintain money and dignity. But because of your coldness and the pressuring of other generals' rebellion, let looters get away with unimaginable resources. It will be the first time in the history of the less developed countries to attempt recovering stolen money. These groups have caused much instability among the communities where the Dinka community has lost integrity, value, and dignity. Escalating violence across South Sudan was caused by lack of services, injustices, and cheating others. Four billion dollars to seventy-five people would have made significant infrastructures before the republic of South Sudan gained independence, for example, modern schools, hospitals, better beams roads, and human resources capacity building.

There are murderers, anti-development elements, antiquate, and anti-coexistence within the region. They created hatred between the southerners and assassinated Dinka respect. They also created a lack of confidence in the majority-based future hope to this party called SPLM. The president passed a lot of mines laid on by NCP to the Promised Land. The letter written by the president has put Sudan People Liberation Movement away from propaganda of zero tolerances corruption and putting the badges on their chests. The liberators backfired and caught themselves in the backyard of their won assumptions of zero-tolerance corruptions. The odd step which the president has made may have consequences if regimes are not very careful to handle it with wisdom; southern citizens will force the regime to relinquish power. The president had to restore his protest in historical reconciliations meetings between his groups and late Dr. John in Rumbek 2004. The President should not take the decision of pardoning the criminals boldly; your goal is to bring money back and leave the decision to the public to decide what should be done to culprits. The Torit faction created the corruption vacuum where few officers appeared on the surface of renting villas in Nairobi and Uganda during those years. The excessive corruptions were the cause of three reasons or retaliation. One, liberators were doubtful that the implementations of CPA were in a panic between NCP and SPLM; they should not miss the opportunity to get away with billions. Two, others feel that Dr. John's groups mistreated them, and therefore, they have a chance to enrich themselves as quickly as possible. Three, social entertainments in the houses of government officials where many were loitering, or they become burdens to any figure in government offices. The three reasons almighty God warned us to be careful how we should handle our life. It is written in this way in the Bible according to the letter of Paul to the Thessalonians people. "For you know how you ought to follow our example. We were not idle when we were with you. Nor did we eat anyone's food without paying for it. On the contrary, we worked night and day, laboring and toiling so that we would not be a burden to any of you." (2 Thessalonians 3:7 and 8) Apostle Paul's message warned His people against idleness not to provide their needs to avoid being a burden to friends or relatives holding constitutional posts. The past time without working caused a lot of spending for ministers and government officials to loans from cashiers without refunding the loans because what is regulated by law will not cover the expenses in their houses. As Deputy of commander in Chief, Kiir never rented expensive places in Nairobi or Uganda; he struggled with his soldiers in Yei and the other liberated areas. The Watergate must be viewed precisely by southern intellectuals.

Not to repeat it in the future; it will take sentry new leaders. Let me go back to my title to explain further to the audience. The pluralist belief is that such a condition is desirable or socially beneficial for coexisting. But the most frequent settings for violent conflict have not been wars between sovereign states but internal strife tied to cultural, tribal conflict, religious, and ethnic animosities. In a less developed world, groups of rulers often appeal to their supporters to eliminate people resisting the inequality and injustices in their country's political and economic systems. They also enforce themselves of being nationalistic, chauvinistic, and rejecting outside influences that challenge them or pollute their systems of rulers. Fewer developing countries are severely ill, as far as lack of having a conservative party and liberal party systems, for competition. These systems of liberalism and conservatives accommodate different views and opinions. Republicans have conservatives who have favorable traditional values and views to oppose any change. In contrast, Democrats have liberalist who prepare reform proposals, openness to new ideas for progress, and are tolerant of the ideas and behaviors of others with broad-minded. For example, in the United States of America, Republicans are well known for resisting policies that do not tolerate aggression outside their boundaries. Democrats deal with how to provide services equally, reform the economy, and allocate many opportunities for all.

Because of such competitions, both parties work hard when one is in the

White House to see that they provided the party's objectives. However, prolonged dictatorship yielded obscene corrupt systems. Therefore, the viable alternative should be rotating government seats in the forms of competitions of two to three parties rather than intimidating policies of one party, which is less to a program of any LCDs. Our constitution does not reflect democratic values, aspiration interests, and goals of common citizens of South Sudan. When leaders have no creditability or confidence in themselves, they become corrupt because they lack the creditability to serve people. Having confidence is a motivating force to dictate you to canard injustices. Since we are born naturally with weak hearts, leaders believe in oppressing their citizens. Evil spirits control their thinking to the point that they do not value human life. Westerners tried to hide that they did not have tribes, and that's why they progressed rapidly. That is not true information. In America, citizens are known through their accents, and that distinction is an indication of tribes. therefore, each nation has tribes. We should resist the malicious attempt of criticism of having tribes, as the cause of doing mistreatment deliberately is not acceptable. Having tribes shouldn't be used as a loophole for oppressing each other. Nobody will erase tribes should it not be human beings' responsibilityto confiscate their existence on earth. Where are the tribes of Israelites? They are there but being Israelites still exists ever since, and South Sudanese or Africans should look to historical facts before defaming themselves. When Dr. Martin Luther King organized the Civil Right movement, he was not defending the Negroes alone. His theme of nonviolent organized civil manner did not insult whites generally. His objectives were just rulers, and therefore, some whites stood with him why he was addressing the genuine cause for all. "The tension in this city is not between white people and Negro people. The tension is at the bottom between justice and injustice between the forces of light and the forces of darkness. And if there is a victory, it will be a victory of not merely for fifty thousand Negroes, but a victory for justice and forces of life. We are out to defeat injustice and not white persons to be unjust" (Hope Testaments, Dr. Martin Luther King). This approach had become a reality when Barak Obama was president of the United States twice. This is the philosophy South Sudanese intellectuals should adopt rather than the rhetoric of insulting words and putting themselves in box policies. Pointless definition where nothing changes an inch in our reality, instead to disarm the forces of injustices forcefully, you are trying new teeth of hatred. Addressing the root cause of devastating suffering from 1955 all away to 2005 should be a legitimate question to rulers rather than waging war and changing the name of Dinka. The truths must be spelled clearly to those who think that changing the system without involving the Dinkaocrats majority will result in much suffering because the regime will use all possible means to convince innocent's people to sacrifice themselves for them. This must be understood clearly by these generations to let them unite their own ranks rather than to be divided by the wealthiest rulers. The collateral damage we witnessed has had a pestilent effect through our masses under their brothers and sisters' leadership has been unfair.

CHAPTER TWENTY-FIVE

Current Leaders are licking their own vomits.

"You, therefore, have no excuse, you who pass judgment on someone else, for at whatever points you judge the other, you are condemning yourself because you who pass judgment do the same things. Now we know that God's judgment against those who do such things is based on truth.

So, when you, a mere man, pass judgment on them and yet do the same things. Do you think you would escape God's judgment? Or do you show contempt for the riches of his kindness, tolerance, and patience, not realizing that God's kindness leads you toward repentance" (Romans 2:1-4 NIV)? "We may blame others for undermining the CPA, but we are also undermining the CPA in our routine work" (Pres. Kiir, Juba State Governors' Meeting November 6, 2007). Some present leaders judged Garang's leadership badly by then, thinking they were cleaner than Garang. Pointing their fingers in Garang's eyes for corruption and nepotism while preparing for the worst, the Holy Ghost is rebuking you not to judge because you will be judging yourself.

Corruption is corruption, whether in your time or Dr. John's. There is no difference between the two leaders as far as gross suffering. Surrounding yourself with gangs will make no difference between the gangs of John's Garang and the gangs of Kiir. The same gangs who surrounded Garang had encircled Kiir, and that's why Kiir failed to combat corruption. I think this is revenge for what was done by Garang's boys, as many people were pointing directly to them. Other individuals complained that they were secretaries with no functions or did not know where money was deposited. Let me remind each of you who complain in the historical meeting of Rumbek regarding corruption, tribalism, nepotism, and much more. "Corruption, as a result of the lack of structures, has created a lack of accountability which has reached a proportion that will be difficult to eradicate," Kiir said. "How are these issues now under your leadership? It seems you repeat the same mistakes of the past where multiple people blame Dr. John Garang; any better structure now to eradicate the three you mentioned? I would also like to say something about rampant corruption in the Movement. Now, some members of the Movement have formed private companies, bought houses, and had huge bank accounts in foreign countries. I wonder what kind of system we will establish in South Sudan considering ourselves indulged in this respect Kiir complains or recalled." Accounts are larger now than ever before; even the international media are aware. You have choked yourself under the theme of nepotism while you complained against it, and as such, you overstepped late Garang. Your administration is promoting thieve clans to the standard, which will be difficult to be eradicated in the future among the southerners, as you said during the meetings in Rumbek because each group will come with the spirit of the same thieves. In the 3rd Session, Garang Mobil, I thank the leaders. I also want to say that the movement is in the hands of a few, and many are alienated. National resources must be shared by all, no matter how small it is. The structures are controlled by a few minority groups, which must be sorted out now in Rumbek. This minority group is the problem.

Handpicking people must stop now because it creates problems." "According to Garang Mobil, where are the national resources or cakes being shared, or are they still in handpicking as you said in the Rumbek meeting? Have you reminded the leadership how the cake is still rotating in the same picking hands you have remarked last time?" Cdr. Elias Wani said, "there is fire, so we need not burn it further." The chairman is placing his relatives in key positions, including Elijah Malok, who is too old to hold the position of Governor of the Central Bank. "There were notes that there might be a popular uprising one day, and the army will join the public." "How does Elias Wai label condition now regarding the appointments of the relatives? How many have attempted to take their life in Juba because of unemployment? All of this happened while the leaders and their relatives were laughing at those who attempted to take their miserable lives in 2007 in Juba. This is because those who have relatives took over again but with no change, as if you have not complained about those at that time" (CDR. Michael Makuei Lueth). "The distribution of powers is also necessary. The army must be organized. There is also the importance of speeding up South-South dialogue before entering the forthcoming era. The other issue is corruption. I'm saying that the leadership is not committed to fighting corruption." The former minister of Law Enforcement and Constitutional Development had tied the president's hands, and as such, his ministry was under suspicion of corruption.

He was given the authority to draft the anti-corruption laws, yet he failed to do so, and so how will the president fish out corrupters while he has no spear to hit the element of corrupters without anti-corruption laws?

Cdr. Wani, the former speaker of the National Assembly, had listed the other problems: Problem No.3: The existence of a kitchen cabinet is deplorable and creates doubts and mistrust. No. 4: The geographical imbalances found in the movement. If this is not addressed, we will never be in harmony. No. 7: The lack of implementation of resolutions and the lack of a follow-up body. Our resolutions always die on paper. No. 8: Corruption remains rampant in the Movement.

Corruption must be fought. Some years back, the chairman in a meeting informed us that Cdr. Deng Alor brought some money from Nigeria, but how that money was spent was never explained to us again. I ask the question, where is the transparency and accountability we talked about? No. 12: Nepotism. It should be fought. There are two examples to illustrate the issue of nepotism. One is the removal of Aleu Anyeny Aleu from his position and his replacement by the chairman with an officer from his village. Another is the appointment of Dr. Lual Deng as an advisor to the chairman. We all heard this in a meeting where the chairman announced Lual's appointment without any official procedures followed. When I talked about regional imbalances, all I need to say is that no Equatorians were even allowed to be a signatory of the six protocols. We are making history, and this history should involve all the people of New Sudan. The protocols are only signed by individuals from Bahr el Ghazal, Upper Nile, Nubia Mountains, and Funj." You were crying in the bush where actual bulls were not even killed. This is the time now you should raise your voice seriously. There is no difference between the late chairman and the current chairman on the matters you raised the last time and today's power imbalance. Today you are a powerful man in government if you can influence the members of the House to protect imbalances and orient them to the point where they should be answerable to their constituencies, not to the president as the case is now. They have been given a mandate by the people, not by the president, and such manipulation will result in paralytic powers in the House. There is no way where the president imposed his will on lawmakers to the point, they had kneeled downed to his will. The powers of lawmakers are more than the president because if you fail the budget, for instance, he will not be able to operate the government institutions. "In Session 5: Rumors must be treated as rumors, but there is no smoke without fire. I disagree with Cdr. Wani that the enemy created these rumors. There are people among us who are more dangerous than the enemy. I must warn the chairman that Nimeiri was made to be unpopular by his security organs. Those who are misleading you and giving you false security information about others will suffer with you together or will leave with you. The government, which you will lead, must include all. Without unity, the agreement will be a source of our disunity. We are not organized in all aspects and, as such, will be exploited by other political parties that are more organized. The lack of structure and political guidance will lead us to a severe political defeat. Mr. Chairman, you have talked about people eating the boat while we are in the middle of the river. Let me add this; the issue is not eating the boat in the middle of the river. The issue is that a few have already crossed to the other side of the river, and when the remaining ones asked them to bring a boat, they refused to return the boat. This is the problem, Kiir recalled." The moment you open your mouth to address corruption and not the favorite of our tribes or clans, it's a time rumor of an unimaginable loan of $200,000 Sterling pounds to someone in the kitchen of Gogrial. Are you telling us to let me do this to my people because I'm president? Favoritism among Dinka's has spoiled your golden chances, as well among other Dinka's, in the future. The boat has been returned so that people you were complaining about will cross to the other side of the river with millions of dollars. Also, listening to the same security who gave false information is the same as when you were complaining. Hundreds of journalists disappeared as if you didn't mention how bad it is to let others suffer for unfound. "Pres. Salva Kiir's address in the USA: "Our greater enemy. I appeal to you all to reject your tribes and unite under one tribe, the SPLM!!! Our disunity won't overcome the challenges ahead of us, and our disunity won't make us vote properly and wisely when the day of the referendum comes. You all know that our final destiny depends on our unity" ...and... "On the issue of corruption, I'd like to assure you that our government has adopted a zero-tolerance policy on corruption in July 2006. We have voted overwhelmingly for independence. We have been united under the SPLM leadership to achieve an independent purpose, yet the word zero tolerance has become a song not healing the wounded heroes, widows, and orphans. Are you not counting how many times you have been saying the so-called zero-tolerance? It was the way how Omar El Bashir and his team were making the same drama, showing many stores with huge commodities stored up, yet no one was jailed because they were preparing for the worst, so singing it will influence people more than ever before as the case in your administration. It sounds easy when you calm down people to listen, but its implementation is so hard. Flipping the coin upside down, you had put the salt into an injury of healing. (Quotes from Kirr's Speech at just concluded Governors Forum, Juba October 2, 2008). "If a few ate the money, all the rest we will go hungry, and hungry citizens are angry citizens. This is as true in the countries and states as in Juba. At a personal level, if you demand unfair benefits from your relatives in Government, that is corruption. If you are tribalistic in your employment of staff, that is corruption. If you give contracts in return for bribes, that is corruption. If you deliberately ignore the regulations and pay your staff as you choose, that also is corruption. To fight this epidemic disease in the courts, we must have the laws to do so. Until these laws exist, our hands are tied in fighting corruption while they betray our commitment to serve and provide services to our long...suffering people. I direct the minister of legal affairs to expedite the legislation related to corruption...We hope such legislation will be finalized as soon as humanly possible." Mr. President was excited when he was reading out his speeches, thinking that he was crying for the citizens, but he will come back and lick his vomit, thinking that he had fed us by saying sweet words to them. This is ridiculous and unacceptable from Kiir and his team, and we acknowledged the effort you made during wartime. Still, it doesn't mean you swallowed all the fruits of peace dividends, leaving your soldiers without shame. Kiir has become a leader of 'Kokora' because his advice is not making sense. You are the one provoking your directives. Why? because the time he was advising the regional governors' meeting, a big scandal for looting public money was underway by his own villager man. Do you think none of the Dinka's will think about your advice? You have reminded that the governors and others are blaming the CPA had been under mind, yet it was you who was undermining the principles of your address in question. In your opening speech in the Rumbek meeting, you started complaining that you are not against peace because the people of Bahr El Ghazal have suffered too much from repeated famine and the Arab militias—and for these reasons, I am the first to embrace peace to relieve them from suffering. This is how you relieve them from famine? By allowing them to be looted? Are you compensating them by harboring the gangs of thieves in your administration? Will the word Peace feed our stomachs? In Proverbs: "Where there is no guidance a nation falls, but in an abundance of counselors, there is safety" (Proverbs 11:14).

These counselors are your advisors. If they advised leaders according to their dishes, nations would fall, but if they are concerned to study the condition correctly, nations will move to prosperity. What happened in J1 twice regarding the quotation above Mr. President? Are anti- corruption laws not yet in place since that time and today, or are you condoning it deliberately? Knowing those subjecting our citizens to unbearable expectations was, frankly speaking, collaboration signs of not charging them, period.

The first leaders were not politicians; they were leaders listening to God so that they could be servants to people. Being good politicians, while you do not have the purpose of Almighty God in your own life, you will not be good politicians unless you listen to God first before you begin to serve the people. When Bill Clinton got a congratulatory message from his opponent in November 1991, the first thing he made; was to enter his room with his wife Hillary Clinton to pray because he believes that residing to God will strengthen him to fulfill his promise to the American people. He made the most incredible strides recovering the economy in American history; the American surplus was thirty-nine trillion when he left office. This is because he believed the Almighty would provide him with wisdom to meet the aspirations of the American people. Jumping into a leadership position before being inspired to have compassion, concern, and humility, you will not be a good overseer. Leaders need to reconcile opposing viewpoints without giving offense or compromising principles. At the Sudan Catholic Bishops Conference, Mr. Isaac Knogur Kenyi, Secretary of Justice and Peace Commission, "I'm calling for an end to corruption. There is real corruption in the Government of Southern Sudan. People are talking about it openly, and everybody is seeing it, and there is no shame now for this corruption. It has been condoned. The statement made by the President of Southern Sudan during the opening of the state legislative assembly on April 10, 2006, that statement declared war on corruption. We would like to see that those who are corrupt should be brought to justice." He also alleged that corruption in the GOSS ranges from ministries to the presidency. Mr. Kenyi singled out tribalism and nepotism as the worst forms of corruption (Nov. 2006). "Southerners are united when they address themselves, but it is not put into practicality. All the ministers, their relatives, and relatives of the president are warming themselves in the corruption club. It is ridiculous that all media and ordinary man and woman spoke about corruption all day and night."

"You have reminded the late Chairman that the peace agreement will be a source of our disunity. Again, the lack of political guidance will lead us to political defeat, and you will suffer from those who gave you false information about others either they will leave with you." Innocent people are being tortured now because groups of your intelligence are giving you the same false information about others as you complained. You sounded patriotic when you were out of the Gogrial circles: you represented patriotic fighters' views and concerns. Switching your ministers from ministry to ministry is not healing to their chronic allegoric rashes of mismanagements of our resources. This is my suggestion: appeal to all patriotic fighters to forgive them so that people will rest in spirit rather than hoping for singing of unbelievable recovery. What are the reasons for these quotations from person to person? This is because our leaders had the old mentality of deceiving the public opinion and themselves.

We have passed the wrong time where citizens are given the imagination to hope for nothing. We read the mind of leaders before they open their mouths to address the issues on the table. When our leaders' campaign for total change, they feel so smart that they can change things overnight. I know southerners are humble people; they will forget and forgive because both opinions are almost sick; the thieves and those who hope evils elements will vomit out their money in the nearer future. Let hearts of illusions rest like martyrs who are not in our world of confusion because big brothers will compensate that money, we are talking about without informing you. If you return money from a culprit, it will be a miracle in the history of an underdeveloped country to decompensate back money from within them. How well are we preparing to face the challenges of independence? The challenges facing the new Republic of South Sudan will not be eliminated by confrontation rather than serious dialogue between us. Putting much money because of internal insecurity cost by our backyard will not calm down the situation. Each citizen needs rest because living in fear for fifty years was enough. Therefore, why are we not ready for genuine dialogue to avoid wasting much money on our self-made insecurity? The time ahead of us is not time telling the stories of wars; it is time you should move around telling the benefits of sacrifices to those who did not make it. Because insecurity and development are enemies, both are costly to the new state that started from nothing.

CHAPTER TWENTY-SIX

Oil Shutdown of 2012

"Brave or reckless, South Sudan's decision to shut down its oil productions to protest the north has had disastrous consequences for its citizens. When the country's economy came to a jarring halt in January, it shut down oil production due to a trade dispute with Sudan." By Gabe Joseph, Voice of America July 1, 2012. Was shutting down oil pipelines a blessing or curse to the people of the new Republic? On the one hand, Kiir acknowledged that they enriched themselves. Still, in his capacity to be a president of the Republic, he informed his culprits that four billion dollars must be returned to the rightful owners. Our calculation was met with international resistance where we were denied a loan just as we pocketed four billion dollars which did not belong to us. Therefore, the only alternative to our survival as an entity is that you culprits must confess secretly to me and return the portions of the money. Also, this oil shutdown exposed the president to increase the number of thieve liberators from thirteen to seventy-five thieves, a number unbeknownst to most of the people, and all those smoking guns were blessings. On the curse side, the innocent majority were paying the ultimate prices. Shutting down the pipeline affected the small services regime, and they were cunning people. The regime era of pride is over, and the SPLM is crumbling with fires of embezzlements; they will not dash anywhere to hide. The system that cultivated lies to maintain power could abuse the supreme constitution of the country, personalize corruption, and legalize the strategies to keep the entire society away from the reality of transparency. The regime has reached a deadlock with internal communities and is losing its die-hard supporters worldwide. The President and other patriotic elements should join the assembly members to push harder for the suspension of criminals to avoid using their powers not to disenfranchise investigations. The example of the Darfur genocide should be seriously considered. Investigating the suspect while holding constitutional posts is like catching a porcupine. If they do not relinquish their posts, the president sympathizes with them rather than listening to public opinions. The MP's have thrown public confidence or mandate back to the president to choose between standing with friend suspects, relatives, and those who voted him into the office. If I were Kiir, I would have stood with my principles should you have warned them several times, but they thought the president was joking. They are in better positions unless you make another step to relieve them. They do not care about the reputations anymore; they had already prepared their pockets instead of their legacy. In the 1990s, vulnerable people were wrestling with some criminals in coordination offices in Khartoum. The person whose name I must retain for confidentiality said this. "They chose to let their pockets be happy. However, their anus will not enjoy happiness. We must feed ourselves from their anus; otherwise, they have lost personality and chose to enrich themselves." Therefore, Kiir should not waste his time to protect those who chose the wrong path for their selfish gain. "If we claim to be without sin, we deceive ourselves, and the truth is not in us. "If we confess our sins, he is faithful and just and will forgive us our sins and purify us from all unrighteousness. If we claim we have not sinned, we make him out to be a liar. His word has no place in our lives." (1 John 1:8, 9 and 10.) The suspected groups are telling us that they have not sinned against us, and they cannot confess their dark side to the president. They claim that the president is a liar. They say, "we have not robbed you," even though the president mentions their names in his letter. These are the attitudes of robbers. Always denying even when they are caught. Since those culprits refused the call of their party leader to return stolen money peacefully, they betrayed themselves. In other words, they are taking off their underwear on their own will. They have exposed their privacy to the southerners of their free will with nobody to blame but themselves. The political maneuvers between Secretary-General Pagan Amum Ockiech and Arthur Akuen Chol have failed like Makalu's play. No one was clean, as they each previously claimed. All of them were on the list of the president. The case was laughing between one tooth with another who has two teeth thinking that he's much better off than another -an Arabic proverb. Anyway, will the president rescue those who took off their underwear on their own accord to show their privacy? They should acknowledge indignation for the last six years to close their privacy not to be seen. Greediness and misreading the line between them and the international community caused a serious blow to the SPLM party. The party is collateral damage that may not be easy to repair unless the president sticks with the decision to deal with the suspect courageously for the party's survival for the next generation. Otherwise, the ruling regime will suffer in the coming election. The tough question which remains to be answered by the president is: will he pass this test? Or will he fail? Failing this corruption war will reduce the drastic change of membership of the Sudan People's Liberation Movement in the future unless members are there to enrich themselves, as the president stated in his letter to suspected groups. Corruption of the party went beyond what was imaginable; nobody was expecting such a small number to make an excessive robbing to that standard. Although some individuals declined to show themselves courageously, you, as party leaders, know who they are. It was terrible robbing even those who called themselves businessmen. It was ridiculous to become a businessman within six years, where we did not know exactly where they got their capital anyway. If they are asked how they started to become businessmen, they cannot explain the starting point to their current level. Even those who hit the jackpot could not reach what has made our businessmen prodigious now. Health business begins with difficulties to learn the holes to avoid reaching the dreams goal, but this high jump of six years right away to businessman should be observed; it might be where other smart officials are hiding under their umbrellas. Those well-known in the south are not on the surface of pride today should they know that being a businessman is a long way to reach. The so call businessmen are products of Arthur Akuen, David Deng Athorbai, and Kuol Athian. Otherwise, they wouldn't shoot up overnight quickly like that. They should now cooperate with orphans, widows, and wounded heroes and heroines rather than exalting themselves now and then the so-called businessmen. Those categories mentioned made you quick businessmen, so you better take care of them rather than exalting yourself for nothing.

Being a businessman takes thousands of years to achieve. Meanwhile, people are aware of how you were struggling to overcome numerous difficulties.

There were numerous scandals in 2008, and Arthur Akuen Chol was arrested in the same year. An unknown number of millions of dollars was stolen by Kuac and Awan's sons twice in 2013 and 2016. In 2017, the president's press secretary surprised southerners that South Sudan Bank Manger was instructed to open the Bank at night to pillaging millions of dollars. What happened in 2008 to the former minister of finance and economic planning after being arrested? Aweil Youths took the law into their hands and opened the prison by forcing them to free the suspects, and most of them were Dinka's. This was the beginning of the unlawful system. That behavior has gone without accountability and transparency, and Dinka intellectuals were and are still silent. That's hypocritical, in other words, superior behavior and overriding the country's law. In 2013 and 2015, elements within the two clans were mentioned stolen twice in J1, and no punishment as if J1's resources belonged to them! If the president was non-Jieng, what would be the position of Jieng regarding the repeated stealing of millions of dollars? He would have been forced out in the office like Arthur Akuen Chol, who was set free from prison by forces from his State. When immediate relatives and friends approached the president, he denied their releases saying.

These elements tarnished his legacy, welcomed by those concerned about Dinka's image. However, after some time, southerners were shocked by their release and appointed them in other sensitive places.

Was it a behavior of a national figure, according to EPM, for Dinka's to embezzle and the president condone it? In 2017 the president's press secretary never thought before saying that the shamed may be counted to the president. Still, he was trying to convince the public that General Paul Malong Awan may not secure public support because of scandals of opening South Sudan Bank at night. Of course, those who are tribalistic minded may appreciate what president Kiir Mayardit and his associates were doing to save the unity of the country. But that's false! It would have safe Sudan because Northerners were doing the same, as Juba leadership is repeating by enforcing the unity by force without addressing participation effectively according to the constitution. Bribing and recruiting tribally and mobilizing innocents Dinka's is the same as Dr.

Hassan Abdalla El Turabi's pretending that he is protecting Islamic ideology and Arabization. President Kiir Mayardit and his associates are not even showing Dinka's diversity, leave alone other ethnicities. EPM Dinka's must correct their backyard before assaulting other nationalist leaders of being tribalistic. We are doing worst scenarios for generalizing the Dinka name while president Kiir favors his sub-clan. What are we practicing now? Bourgeois? Hypocrisy? Do we remember when Maulana Nhial Deng Nhial and

Telar Ring Deng were airing in Motivational Radio SPLM how bourgeois targets individuals? Do we have bourgeois and hypocrite leaders or not? Do we know how many martyrs in early years 1984-1989, just they were told bourgeois was inadequate systems we are fighting it? Perhaps, President Kiir Mayardit and his so-called die- hard supporters are not comfortable hearing such words reminding him and his supporters.

CHAPTER TWENTY-SEVEN

Suffering of Self-Glorification

"Their throats are opened graves; they use their tongues to deceive. The venom of vipers is under their lips. Their mouths are full of cursing and bitterness" (Romans 3:13&14 NIV). Recklessness addressed from leaders dilapidated the country for decades because overseers must address responsibly, not jeopardizing the nation's future from his words. President and his in-laws from Jonglei got an opportunity to instigated revenge of inflecting casualties to Nuers by others not them to do it.

African Patriotism is based on impunity where the rule of governance is applied to the tribal line to pay the prices of torturing, arresting, and killing innocent people. In other words, African Patriotism is based on pillaging and sending their resources to Geneva and any other countries in Europe and America. Moreover, they failed to trust even their own African banking systems.

Furthermore, African patriotism failed to acknowledge that they were contributing too much wealth to advanced countries because money is not a receipt you had, but its circularization. In addition, African leaders have never asked themselves why European leaders and American leaders do not send money to African banks? Because they were aware that sending billions of dollars outside would shrink their banking systems. Another African patriotism or ignorance is based on the building towers, although towers are parts of the infrastructure. But successful countries are assessed by developing human capacities, consisting of quality affordable social transformation of the economic benefit of African citizens, affordable public schools, affordable health systems, and road infrastructure. As a result, towers are to complete the general picture of the country. The president initiated the suffering of self-glorification when he was visiting Lakes State on September 25, 2013. He declared war against the Nuers community in freedom square because Dr. Riek Machar Teny wanted to contest against him in 2015. The blood spill of 1991 was always used to mislead the elements against the whole Nuers, and "THORY –ACAP cattle camp confrontation between the

Agar community and Nuers was mentioned to remind them the ugliest wound to Rumbek people." On December 14, 2013, the same tone of self-glorification was the subject of National Liberation Council meetings plus hatred song, which says "we shoot anybody even if our fathers we will gun him down ."Southerners always point their fingers at Dr. Riek if he reacted, for their silencing suffering, but at the end of the day, they reap his plant seeds like separation of today and 32 states was the reaction of twenty-one states. The Torit Declaration came to the surface where Self-Determination was included in any peace dialogue with the Sudan Government, which was because of Nasir's reaction. Although the intention was not meant for tribal escalation, it turned the page of the ideology of New Sudan upside down. To those who heard what the president said in Rumbek Freedom Square and speech, he delivered those who do you blame during the National Liberation Council Meetings? Do we blame innocent soldiers defending the Dinkaocrates constitution of slaughtering Nuers? Was such language healing, or was it provocative to open healing wounds among the communities?

President and his defense minister, former Governor of North Bahr El Ghazal, who became later. Chief of General Staff exiled himself after he fell out with President Kiir while executing orders from their regime. Why are southerners not very bitter against those gunning down separatists, as they alleged in their manifesto of 1983? That the first bullets were against separatists? Do they believe the blood of separatists was not so important to their relatives? Where are we now? We are in a separated country which was the point of conflict between the ruling party and other southerners whether to separate. Which ones couldn't kill revolutionaries? The new Sudan and Separate Entity ideology also killed thousands of martyrs where their wives and children are on- street now? Nuers should not be used as scapegoats by Dinka's who were undermining the leadership position of President Kiir Mayardit because when George Athor Deng rebelled in 2010, it was unbelievable for those who wanted to join him and those opposing on the other hands. If this cold war is not ironed out in face-to-face talk between Dinka's, then the new country's people will never enjoy peace among themselves. Should the so-called smart forces and warriors' physical forces with no knowledge to run the country's affairs make compromises together, then sick souls will not rest because their eyes and hearts are on being president to rule the country. Why are other Dinka's hiding behind Nurers while they are known for their uncalculated words? When the totality of change came to the surface in 1978, it was by spearheaded by the brave, late Samuel Aru Bol, Late Ezekiel Macuei Kodi, late Dr. Toby Madut Parek, William Ajal Deng, and rest to confront Abel Alier and his groups in the daylight until he was sent home peaceful; they were not hiding behind other leaders. I mentioned this point because others besides Nuers were the cause of endangering innocent life behind closed doors. Nuers were forced into defensive for their survival; meanwhile, the real coup, attempted several times, was ignored because they were within the Dinkaocrates. The South Sudan dialogues he the president initiated early 1998 in "WoundLillet," have erased all the bitterness against each other. Yet, other elements were not convinced of peace and reconciliation. They want to let people be sick emotionally about Nuers, even though; they do not live in fear, anger, hatred, and guilt consciousness will cause untreatable diseases to those accustomed to hatred. Why are the president and his groups remembering the ugly disaster he never showed to the world Nuers survivors in Bahr el Ghazal after the disaster of 1991 to prove his cleanness? Who are the real enemies between Dinka's and other ethnic groups in South Sudan? Our enemies are poverty, chronic diseases, tribalism, socioeconomic injustices, sociopolitical injustices, and much more are equal to us all. How do we eliminate them in our society should be the focus rather than cultivating senseless suffering for our citizens? African leaders were always focusing on negative past events that they were part of disasters. Still, they should cultivate positive ideas to flush out all old differences so that they live in peace. Is political violence both self-destruction and a curse to our leaders?

Yes, it is a curse because the process of violent struggle is hugely destructive to human development. On July 24, 2013, reshuffled, the president surprised his chief of staff by surprisingly pouring in special forces (militants). If soldiers were not patient enough, it would have caused the nation heavy losses based on tribalism. On December 16, 2013, the press conference president and ruthless generals were so superior in their hearts that the attempted coup would not be like the coup of August 31, 1991.That remark was revenged genocide against Nuers. Consequently, the foreign Media carried from his mouth and minister of Defense Kuol Manyang Juck accordingly.

Some elements within the militant army had acted ignorantly. It was unbelievable that this would end quickly without asking why small David Yau Yau rebellions were not wiped off, as they think. Militant warriors were too weary of winning the war, and their generals treated fallen heroes and heroines badly, which taught them not to fight a senseless war for their sake again. Although the president displayed the utmost patience in making himself to be an example of the best president, groups of tribalistic militants were desperate to see Nuers be taught a lesson they will never forget in their life. However, they did not study the war consequences carefully, plus the fact that their militant army was not oriented to national defense causes as they were recruited on tribal lines. Southern leaders are swimming without a river to hold lies of Senseless war for their self-glorification. Nor Dinka's or Nuers will benefit should they continue with the war. The Dinkaocrat majority manufactured the escalating conflict because Nuers were used as tools of the cold war between those who term themselves smart and physical warriors without knowledge. Tribalism has become a highly contagious, outrageous disease, specifically in the continent, which created the world's civilization. To avoid being seen by regional leaders and superpowers as stupid leaders, you need to relinquish self-Glorification among our ethnic groups because that was the core of senseless war in South Sudan. A leader needs to examine his spirit before being tempted by evil to lose sight of being an overseer of the lives of their people. When a leader talks in front of the public, do not address reckless behavior because it will endanger innocent lives. Touring in Bahr el Ghazal states alone proved that the president was mobilizing his supporters for any eventuality. The little peace existing among the citizens was souring or poisoned by groups surrounding the president. The social fabrication got burned to ashes among the southerners, which will need a lot of work to restore.

CHAPTER TWENTY-EIGHT

Pride and Apostasy

"In the same way, you who are younger must accept the authority of the elders. And all of you must clothe yourselves with humility in your dealings with one another, for "God opposes the proud, but gives grace to the humble (1 Peter 5: 5.)" Pride goes and a before destruction, haughty spirit before a fall. It is better to be of a lowly spirit among the poor than divide the spoil with pride. (Proverbs 16:18 and 19). Various ethnic regimes in Africa are arrogant of insulting attitudes toward the citizens they believe they liberated. They believe that they are better, smarter, or more important than them. They have an offensive attitude of superiority, are proud in an unpleasant way, and behave as if they are nothing to them with terrible excessive pride toward other ethnic groups. In the National Anthem, Southerners asked God to bless South Sudan, but did the leaders properly examine what God needed from them to get that blessing?

God needs leaders to value the lives of innocent people. God needs each man to be in peace, liberty, and have freedom and prosperity. To peruse happiness and liberty, not kick them to one another to maintain your seat. Southerners and Eritreans swallowed their pride of living in their countries for returning them to Ethiopia and Sudan because regimes were worse than the previous enemies; they put more salt into wounds. Nevertheless, that decision to both our leaders was unpatriotic because they should die in there. After southern Sudanese got their independence, leadership never examined their souls and why there were numerous splits in the leadership since the inception of the struggle. In other words, SPLM-DC, Joseph Bangasi Bakasoro, and George Athor Deng were already navigating their ship of rebellion. The so-called political detainee was the real engine of the driving vehicle of the changing leadership. If you check their December 6, 2013, press conference, you could realize they wanted to overhaul the leadership engine while they forgot the way George A. Deng got his fate in their hands. They made self-exile for injustices George rebelled against because, by the time George Athor saw it, they could not see it. Therefore, they worked hard to eliminate him while not being aware of their turns. The intention of leadership position regarding how they should rule country had been exposed out by late Justices John Luk Jok; when he was regretting the way, he wrote the country constitution. Constitution was made to torture others by sighting them; however, almighty God brought confusion among them. He aired out the committed sin. Southerners are tearing themselves apart because of haughty hearts and pride, while the ruling party overrides others. The ruling party has never acknowledged the effort made by others before them. Even the farmers who were feeding them were the same objectives that led South Sudan to separation. They think those who died before 1983, for the cause of South Sudan, either was criminals or they were like those struck by thunder storming just they have never been to Bilpam. On the other hand, they reject any positive advice from the elders. On the other hand, they overlook anybody, which is pride. They behave as if south Sudanese struggles started with them., even those who got Massacred in the house of Chier Ryen in 1965 in Wau was the same caused which let South Sudan to be separated toady. They did not follow closely what Dr. John Garang said when he was briefing Diaspora on what protocols they signed with the government of Khartoum. He mentioned that the NIF behaves as if Sudanese people's existence started with them. To be an apostasy means a group or individual has abandoned the principles of their faith or plan of the struggle, which is exactly what happened in our country. This self- haughty and pride are destroying southerners because by overlooking the people, you are over sighting God while you are asking God to bless South Sudan. Therefore, you are prepared to make considerable catastrophes against human beings.

That arrogance and pride of preaching what they had done have become a schizophrenia disease where they expressed themselves by tribal line or regionally. This has weakened our people not to address national issues unless; they defined causes as from Great Bahr El Ghazal, Great Equatoria, and Great Upper Nile. Who will be the symbol of southerners after we regionalize ourselves? Southern citizens should not be made as obedient clients to the point they could not realize the gross violation of the rights they deserve, as the citizens who contributed to the liberation struggles. Kiir and Dr. Riek are escalating the tribalism conflict, which is baseless to the people they serve. We should not be made to turn blind eyes to the ruling party because of the eloquent remarks that they had brought independence. The eloquent speeches, propaganda, and patriotism hatred may not again convince the general opinion in the 2023 general elections. Southerners must use conventional wisdom to change the condition on the grounds for their unity; otherwise, we have been patient enough to give the ruling party a long rope to let them hang themselves forever. Our Independence was the collective's works from all southerners, and regional countries and superpowers alike, which were supportive of our separation. However, the reality is the Arab parable, which says, "let your dog starved to follow you." This is precisely why our citizens have been engaged in tribal conflict and clan's feud; we are made to be so starved and kick one another for our welfare. Late Chief Mangar Maciek was the first individual who discovered the unacceptable moral grossing eating. Chief Manager said, "I quote why some individuals are distinguishable in being fat as if they were not in liberation struggle"? The answer goes with the ugly word, "which says birds are flying by tribes or clans, whereas nobody was commanding clan's troops." In the Republic of South Sudan, when qualified citizens are applying for employment, they are told government does not have a budget for employment. Still, the government does have funds for their ministers and other officials to transfer them into private accounts. In this case, the president needs to decree dismissals of officials or bring them back like the case in his office of 2013. Ruling parties have corrupted everything, especially in the Agar area, where expensive marriages were the cause of clashes because stealing cows among themselves was the order of the day to marry expensively. Organize forces were tribalistic when sent to prevent clashes; they took sides among their communities. Such a system had never existed even during the colonialism era when the Arab and Britain were controlling us administratively; rules and orders were in place.

Untrained communities are armed to defend their properties against external aggression, but before the intended enemy comes, they begin to murder themselves. Will kitchen cabinets clean these killings of innocent Nuers and bring the culprits to justice? Time will tell us. Dr. Riek Machar Teny and his groups failed to examine the cause of chronic headaches of their leadership since the inception of the Movement. Claiming federalism without knowing each statehouse's whole income taxes will be another financial disaster to the national government. Southerners are attracted to any new terms they hear because the federal system funded 90% grant by the central government will be absolutely liabilities states. Shifting from transformational and loss of party vision into creating more federal states was unjustifiable to their claims of reforming the rotten party. The reformation should separate the twin's name, that's to say Sudan people liberation Army from Sudan people liberation movement because it's no longer representing the national army. There is no way to use the Sudan name; unless you used the South Sudan army, South Sudan currency, or flag of South Sudan. Separating these two, therefore, the army will protect south Sudanese generally rather than protecting individuals. Is negotiating yourself to be first vice president and other so-called political detainees was the whole issue of slaughtering and displacing almost 2.5 million people? Will southerners, widows, orphans, wounded heroes, andgenerations to come learn a lesson from these leaders. Three generations from 1983, 1991, and December 15, 2013, tragedy among the South Sudanese has gone just for self-Glorification and excessive pride, for nothing more than a corrupting system.

CHAPTER TWENTY-NINE

1991, Song of Circumcision Agar Parable!

During the SPLM split of 1991, there were clashes between the Dinka and Nuer Ethnic Groups. Unfortunately, history repeated itself in 2013 when the same conflicts arose between both ethnic groups over the same political reasons.

First and foremost, I'm not undermining the pain of those who lost their loved ones in 1991 and 2013. In those years, no one was expecting to lose her husband, son, and other relatives.

However, I will be focusing on what false similarities the Dinkaocrats tried to show between the 1991 and 2013 ethnic conflicts. The 1991 Ethnic Conflict was a mutiny led by Dr. Riek Machar and Dr. Lam Ajawin. Both leaders gathered the Nuer and Shilluk soldiers and incited a coup to overthrow The Oppressive Dinka regime leading the liberation movement.

During the Second Civil War against North Sudan, John Garang and the Dinka Elite that surrounded him would not allow the opinions of anyone that wasn't Dinka. The inability of the Dinka elite to operate equally and harmoniously with leaders of other Ethnic backgrounds led to a split in the SPLM faction. During this mutiny, Nuer and Shilluk soldiers, led by Dr. Riek and Dr. Lam Akol, massacred Dinka soldiers and innocent Dinka civilians. Similarly, but not the same, the 2013 conflict between the Dinka and Nuers saw the same, but in reverse, the massacre of Nuer soldiers and innocent Nuer civilians.

The difference between the two events is this: the 1991 coup by Dr.Riek and Dr. Lam Akol was an explicit offensive to overthrow the Dinka Elite of the Liberation Movement over violation of Human Rights and a total disagreement on the future of South Sudanese people in Sudan at that time. John Garang wanted to keep Sudan as one country and liberate and create an equitable society for all Sudanese. However, Dr. Riek, Dr. Lam Akol, and other Dinka Elites around Dr. John Garang did not favor Sudan's unity. However, in 2013, Dr. Riek and others did not come forward aggressively. Instead, they came forward as whistleblowers about the corruption of the Dinka elites and the need for Reformation in the Party.

What the Dinka Elites did in 2013 was use revisionist propaganda to rally Dinka soldiers and civilians behind the government to kill innocent

Nuer civilians and soldiers. The propaganda spread by Kiir and his supporters saw Dr. Riek as an aggressor instead of a leader concerned about the direction of the Party and Country. Kiir and his Dinka Elite use the 1991 Massacre as a tool of political survival and mobilizing individual Dinka's to oppress others, even their own.

They use this to distract the Dinka people while they still fail to provide necessities of daily life, only arming civilians with weapons to kill each other and themselves.

For instance, there is no conducive, secure atmosphere for the people across the country. In addition, school fees are too expensive for vulnerable widows and orphans, and there is no affordable health care for the wounded heroes. As a result, the inability to propel the country forward is constantly blamed on the false comparison of the 1991 and the 2013 conflict. The failure of South Sudan's progress is because of the corruption and tribalism of Kiir and the Dinka and Nuer Elite. Dinka and Nuer leaders used tribalism as political life support when they were under critical scrutiny by the public for gross corruption.

Circumcision was once controversial and taboo in Agar's culture. The idea of circumcising boys was so contentious that it used to cause conflicts among people by just the mere accusation that someone's son was circumcised. If a boy were insulted as being "circumcised," fighting would erupt immediately between the families of the accuser and the accused. After some time, circumcision became less controversial and normal in Agars society. Thus, the Agars people then termed hurling of this insult "The Song of Circumcision" and agreed to no longer fight as the procedure became normalized in society. The hurling of this insult and the response that resulted is like when Dinkaocrats constantly bring up The Massacre of 1991. In both situations, the events are brought up as a dog whistle- almost a call to arms for both opposing sides to ultimately fight over something archaic.

Reviving the 1991 massacre repeatedly will not improve the failures of SPLM leadership. We are still killing ourselves and using it to intimidate Nuer leaders, even when they address genuine suffering. It may be disintegrating our people and the country.

Another "song of circumcision" is the Israeli and Palestinian conflict, where the Arabs quickly come for support morally, financially, and physically as soon as they hear Israelites assaulting or vice versa. Israelites determined their fate in 1948 by capturing its capital Tel Aviv. The defeated events did not convince the Arabs, and they had to reorganize themselves and try again in 1967. Those who were participants in the Six-Day war were Egyptians, Jordanians, Syrians, and Sudanese, which resulted in a significant victory by Israel against all of them in Six Days. The Egyptians were not yet satisfied by the Israelites' success! They retreated and made another surprised storming attempt in the Yom Kippur war of October 6, 1973. Israelites hit back seriously, capturing border areas, and crossing the Suez Canal. President Anwar Sadat had to accept a peaceful solution between Egyptians and Jews. He flew to Jerusalem by himself for peace, without meditators, due to many casualties in both men and military equipment. Peace and reconciliation came either way! You are defeated or not. You must pay in deaths in any case.

During the 1991 Massacre, the Nuer came to Rumbek and attacked the Agars community. The Nuer came three times, storming the cattle camps surprisingly early morning! Agar youths jumped over bodies facing the enemy. In other words, they hit back vigorously so that the enemy felt the hottest payback. Consequently, peace and reconciliation were viable between the Nuer and the Dinka Agars because the Agar's fought until the Nuer felt that peace was a more sustainable solution.

Those nurturing the dangerous slogan of building the Dinka Kingdom or that Dinka's have been targeted are digging a hole. You will be crushed like Dr. Hassan Abdallah al-Turabi.

Dr. Hassan Abdallah al-Turabi spearheaded the Arabization and Islamization of Sudan. But unfortunately, this backfired when Darfurians faced genocide and rape by the same Kingdom he devoted all his youth towards building and strengthening.

Another "Song of circumcision" was "Sectarianism" and "Bourgeois." In the early years of the Sudan People Liberation Movement, and immediately when the motivational Radio was on the air, those two words above were buzzwords always presented by Nhial Deng Nhial and late Ambassador Telar Ring Deng. During the early days of the liberation movement, the marginalized groups of Sudan condemned sectarianism and the bourgeoise. Are the leaders of today who were mobilizing southerners using sectarianism and bourgeois deliberately, or have they forgotten now after achieving what they were campaigning against those words in their manifesto? Do these leaders now not realize that they have become the same bourgeoise they fighting against it during the liberation movement?

Many southerners blindly believe that what is blocking the unity of our people is Dr. Riek Machar and his supporters. But then, if you critically review the problems, it becomes clear that.

75 percent of the issues stem from Dinka leaders based on how SPLM Leadership was composed at the beginning of the SPLM.

In 2004, rumors came out within Dinka's, which almost was an atomic disaster within ethnicity regions themselves if it was not faced by Agar community wisdom! It Would have thrown CAP into chaotic situations. These groups who were left by the unfortunate death of Dr. John Garang de Mabior have never been satisfied with Kiir Leadership and his groups. The Yei palace of Kiirdit and Nairobi caused 2013 moved by Dr. John Garang groups using Dr. Riek as their alternative shields. Kiir and individuals in Jonglei got an opportunity to revive president Kiir & JEC to renew 1991 as repeating itself based on assumptions that Nuers were the majority in Army and therefore, we must coin up something to deal with Nuers. President touring in Bahr El Ghazal states after the dissolution of entire cabinets and appointing new cabinets was the mobilization of his supporters! Meanwhile, Dr. Riek Machar never toured Upper Nile for those who ignorantly blamed Dr. Riek Machar for the 2013 crisis. Recently, in 2019 president repeatedly toured BG. Regions made rallies when he was inspecting Highway from Juba to all BG. States. "He said this" I believed the Highway connected Juba and BG. States were bad, and I will bring Chinese to do it to rescue me in Juba if something happens?

Rescuing the president from what happening? Are Highways were made for battling each other? Or delivering services to the entire nation! Then, of course, the president's seditious behavior again, like his 2013 remarks.

Peace and reconciliation were in processing when Dr. Riek Machar apologized to Jongeli Community in the house of late Dr. John Garang in 2012. he started looking for resources for reconciliation; indeed, groups approached the president to take the initiative of reconciliation from Dr. Riek and gave it to someone else, not Dr. Riek. He hands over initiating initiatives to Archbishop Deng Bull! Where was that peaceful initiative? Almighty God, president Kiir, and his ill groups know it, and that was before the 2013 crisis. The coup attempt Dinka's were trying to sell was found empty because there were no single documents to justify their claims of a coup, apart from violating the constitution of frying two elected governors before the ending period according to the constitution. President Kiirdit is above the Law, and his supporting individuals are not abiding by the country's Law! Reconciliation and peace had to start within Dinka's themselves now. Otherwise, there will be no meaningful reconciliation and peace should peace, and reconciliation are not bought by money as the case president is thinking and his advisors.

With its unworkable delusional approaches, many Sudanese regimes tried many years and couldn't work out real peace and reconciliation previously and now in Sudan. So, president Kiirdit should disregard the attitude of reconciling people through buying individuals rather than addressing their grievances.

Widows, orphans, and wounded heroes; you have been given a bare bone of 1991& 2013. However, country resources are looted in daylight, and you are suffering daily, specifically Dinka's and Nuers. You had to disregard the 1991 song of circumcision like what Agar has done previously and beyond otherwise. If you counted those killed by the Agar community themselves, Apuk and Aguk clashes were more than those killed in 1991, but then beings brainwashed; you do not realize that facts. When I was in Rumbek in 2013, and the sectionalism feud had engulfed the whole Lakes State by then, I asked some groups of intellectuals why should we not make disarmament? Their answer was pointing fingers at Dr. Riek Machar's spill of 1991 as the consequence of many guns in citizens' hands. Why not disarm all people across South Sudan after Dr. Riek Machar becomes a part of the system in Juba? They just laid their back on chairs with no satisfactory answer.

CHAPTER THIRTY

Wrong Tools of Regime Survival

Any regime could use the wrong tools for survival, like changing the regime. Dinka's are the target, Sudanese indigenous were using religion and Arabization, and President Donald Trump wants to Make America Great Again! Furthermore, JCE stands for Jieng Council of Elders protecting Dinka's interests. All those and others are tools of manipulating people behind the regime, whereas; the facts of the matters remain the same; neither one will come into reality.

Arabization and the Islamic system are being confronted now by no Christians in Sudan, and making America Great Again was facing challenges of building promised wall became impossible. However, Jieng was running the following institutions, the President of the Republic of South Sudan, the Ministry of defense, and the Chief Justices. General Chief of Staff of South Sudan People Defense Forces changing hands, Police general Inspector, Ministry of finance changing hands Ministry of Foreign Affairs and in International Cooperation was held by Jieng, and the failure to protect them so-called interests of Jieng? How would it be possible for JCE to protect that interest known to them? What about the other ethnicities who would protect their interests? If not, how would the country's unity survive according to JCE's paranoid thinking? Was paying $3.7million for campaigning justices and reconciliation, which was meant by Pope, or denying justices? In revitalizing peace agreements, justice, and punishment for those who killed innocent civilians on both sides should be concurrently punishable during the implementation of revitalization peace agreements because there will be no reconciliation while justices are absent. What are the interests JCE is defending if the president denies justices? Who are original Dinka's ins and fake as many supporters of the president comments always on social media? Preventing the High-bird court is denying justice to both who were killed by government forces and rebels who killed innocent civilians in Bor, Belit, and Bentiu.

My target question to those agitating fear Dinka's may be in danger because of regime change? What nasty have you infected to other Nationalities in South Sudan? Instead you are lecturing about being liberator apart from Dr. James Wani Igga, Gen. James Hoth Mai, Gen. Mobeto Mommer Mete, and Gen. Oyei Deng Ajak, and none Dinka's were doing? Yes, the tremendous contribution of manpower and resources for sustainable struggle is undeniable. However, it does not mean the country belongs to Jieng or oppressed those who contribute a small number of participants of both resources and manpower. Those individuals should be courageous enough to tell the public about their fears so that everybody should be careful about their neighbors, even within Diasporas. When the so-called Arabs were using those tools above, they were precise to Sharia and Arabization, which connected them with the Arabs World; if no Muslims ruled the country, its identity might change! Do you think Nurer, Bari speakers, Chollo run the country, we may not be speaking Dinka Language? Do you think the identity of the country may change? I know why many Dinka's were concerned that it was 1991 catastrophic. However, who was safe in Bahr EL Ghazal Regions among Nurers in 1991 except those under the leadership of Dr. John Garang in Torit? As an out boxes politician-minded, John Garang couldn't allow the killings of innocent officers and soldiers of Nurers in Torit. He has perverted and tarnished Nasir leaders and save the life of the soldiers and officers under his command.

Moreover, remembering the ugliness days of 1991 will not bring meaningful unity and healing among South Sudanese should be cowards will always be influential Dinka's behind them. We are not frankly saying truths of being feared; you may be labeled as a shying Dinka. Not being Dinka is delusional thinking. Saying realities do not make you half Dinka; instead, rallying people behind you because of manufacturing hatred of unknown fears is dangerous to the unity of our country! If this country disintegrated those, who say they liberated it would be losers, as far as you were liberating this country to be peaceful and prosperous. Let me highlight facts points why President Kiir failed to minimize corruption, nepotism, tribalism, and managing diversity; he executed his complaints against Dr. John Garang in 2004 in Rumbek Meetings reconciliation. After the split of 1991, main streams or Torit Faction was divided into Zonal Commanders! Other Commanders under Leadership of Dr. John Garang and others under his Deputy Salva Kiir

Mayordit, those who were with John Garang consisted of Gen. Oyei Deng Ajak, Gen. Deng Alor Kuol, Gen. Pagan Amum Okieck, Gen. Gier Chuong Aloung, Gen. Kuol Manyang Juuk, and the rest. These groups acquired wealth before the CPA, fitting by dressing in all forms of military uniforms and military equipment. They were renting villas in Uganda and Nairobi for their families, and this was where corruption became an epidemic in the Movement not to be eradicated.

Kiirdit, accordingly to those who know him, believed that he was not a corrupted guy. But I may add my view due to the Yei crisis. If Salva Kiir Mayardit were practicing corruption or participating in that dirty game of renting outside Yei, he would have been arrested in Yirol. So, being none amongst corrupters safe his life.

Secondly, leaders of SPLM denied that there were no supporters of Dr. John and that those behind Salva Kiir Mayordit were/are deceiving the southerners, and themselves should corruption became difficult to stamp down now by President Kiir because he gave his die-hard an opportunity after taking over leadership in 2005, review back his first personalities in Khartoum and Juba were purely Yei Palace supporters.

Thirdly, our brothers in Jonglei have become exploiters! Continuously when the Civil War erupted! They just joined and sneaked away when it's become hard and go for studies. After the war was over, they came back with their Degrees and claimed the leadership based on papers. From the 1955 war to 1972, Addis Ababa Accord; Jonglei participants in the civil war contrasted with Rumbek citizens, which consisted of Tonj, all to Yirol were having sizable numbers in rebellious, and yet Abel Alier Kuai became President of High Executive Council. During the first Civil War, John Garang sneaked for studies and Majak de Agoot in second civil war and the rest within Jonglei sneaked again for studies. Does such an attitude need critical thinking from those left to face the enemy? I said categorically always the problem which is overwhelming the country in all forms are not other.

Nationalities who are causing insecurity, corruption, taking Laws into their hands are Jieng. If we deny it is not addressed correctly, the country may never be in peace.

In the earlier years after Sudanese got independence and before Civil War, they erupted in Torit on August 18, 1955. Sudanese were using tools of

213

blaming the British for were problems of the Civil War in Sudan consequently, and the actuals fact were brushed aside, which was the federal system and identity of the country. According to Farouk Gatkuoth! The identity of the country was conscious; defined during the process of independence before other Sudanese were consulate to make an input, that negligent caused extremely bleeding in Sudan and particularly the Southern part of the country. Did SPLM and Dinka's define the country's identity before consulting others? Now ruling party have adopted the same going around and not addressing the realities facing governing systems in all forms of corruption, tribalistic slogans, and even clannism practiced in employment.

Blaming the British couldn't prevent southerners not to struggling for their rights and other marginalized areas. In addition, these negligent and blaming tribes were a very radical approach. We should have zipped our mouths or avoided such pointing fingers regionally and tribally should it endanger the unity of the country and its citizens. If the leadership failed to observe the past experiences of struggles, then we had to search our souls before pointing fingers at others. Also, using the wrong tools to change the government or defend it is another dead-end fact to prevail or maintain unity. Am shying away as Dinka? Not at all, but I don't want to be among both who are blinded spiritually and physically. Putting salt into an injury of injustice is ignorance and shying away from principles of struggle. The absence of conscience and fairness has consequences of applying impunity based on ethnicity and is likely to destroy co-existence and pluralism.

Kiir supporters, mark my word for the future! Enforcing unity and threatening of killings of Michael Makuei Lueth may not serve the interests of South Sudanese from now and many decades to come, believe me or not. I rest my case take it or ignore it, you will be eyewitnesses like late Sadig El Mahdi, who witnessed the division of Sudan while he was prime minister twice and Sudan was itself waring.

CHAPTER THIRTY-ONE

Lakes Province Before 1983

Who were Rumbek people before 1983?

Rumbek society is composed of Tonjdit, Yirol, Cueibet, and Wulu people. All these different ethnicities were under one district since the surface of colonization and after Sudan got independent in 1956. They were living forcefully and friendly sharing everyday things socially and politically among themselves! Protecting each other during the colonization period though most youths were not yet enrolled in schools those days until the earliest of 1900. Before the war of Any-Anya, the first civil war, which started on August 18, 1955, historical Rumbek Secondary School was built seven years before the Civil war. It is crucial to mention the war of Any-Anya began in 1955 before Sudan got independent! Those who joined the civil war in four districts stated early had a sizable number based on the absorption of forces in the Sudanese Army and other organized forces of South Sudan. Rumbek absorbers were exceptional in numbers compared with other regional autonomous South Sudan districts after the Addis Ababa Accord of 1972. Gordon Mourtat Mayen was the second to command the Movement of Any-Anya one civil war in the earliest 1967 and was the first individual who raised the flag of South Sudan as an idea of having an independent country (called Nile Provincial Government). When sort of power struggles emerged between him, Aggrey Jaden Ladu & Joseph Lagu, he relinquished power for the struggle not to divide people based on ethnicities. Now, the current leadership of SPLM is grabbing the history of southerners by the fishtail, which may not fit totally; nullifying or scrapping other previous leaders before you were self-glorification and inefficient of how struggle started. In the earliest 1940, the idea of building a Secondary School in South Sudan came up, and each governor within three Districts of South Sudan was asked to give a recommendation where Senior Secondary schools should be based on people's behaviors and environmental climate.

Bahr El Ghazal's Governor's recommendation won Senior Secondary School; as a result, his recommendation was excellent regarding the people's behaviors of Rumbek, resources, the main center of South Sudan, and the environmental climate. All those above made Rumbek the best choice for Senior Secondary School 1948. On the other hand, Agar's integrity, dignity, honesty, and behaviors differed until the second civil war, which started in 1983 and ended on January 9, 2005.

When other Dinkas heard Dinganyai Dhal, Professor K, and Monica Yom Kon! They may make a mockery of us; hence, don't judge Agar my current situation, which was caused by failed leadership of the central government in Juba. In other words, call your memories back during the Liberation and beyond for those who might have attended Rumbek Secondary School! In September 1987, in Wau, when Fertit Militia's came into , they surfaced and killed Pabek Makur Awan, a son! Brigadier Gabriel Chol Makueinbet, colonel Kothea Kedit Mourtat, and Lieutenant Colonel Dominic Madol Alawya called a military parade and hit back at the enemy hard, which co-incided with word of Mathon Mathon who "said if Agar gets killed," serious confrontation will happen. In 2004, a group of Gangs was almost to arrest Salva Kiir Mayardit in Yirol and kill him. Possible Agar Community intervened and convinced Salva Kiir Mayardit to come to Rumbek to find grievances Meeting and save his life. In the elder's Meetings of security with Abu-Guron, Abdalla Abu-Guron, Commander of Sudan Army Forces in Wau, met Ramiz Monyping Chier, Samuel Mabor Malek, Alfred Mawut Mayen, and Alfred Deng Aluk where there, and Abu-Guron smells them. How do they mockery on us? During the Liberation, which county mobilized tremendous resources like the Leadership of Paul Mayom Akec to the war front around Juba in South Sudan? Which county had been liberated by their sons and daughters except for Rumbek on May 1,1997? Enemy forces have never overrun Agar during the split of 1991 and beyond. Yes, Agar is the belly of South Sudan geographically. The way we addressed social injustices of ethnicity made us exceptional, Peter Awuol Alijok was an MP from Rumbek ticket in 1982 as testimony. The causes of southerners' struggle were denial of their call for the federal system as a form of participation and governance system. I may not be dwelling tremendously to explain many reasons that led to the civil war twice should they be closely connected with what Southerners face now in Juba. Controlling substances or lucrative ministries and departments by one ethnic group was equivalent likes denying southerners for holding the so-call supreme ministries and chief Justices, for example, in Sudan by then.

Before the second Civil war started, there was an underground called NAM, which means Nationalistic Action Movement; this was initiated by intellectuals secretly behind closed meetings among Southerners! And it was composed predominately of Bahr El Ghazal citizens and particularly Rumbek or Agar intellectuals, and they were as follows: Eng. Joseph Malwal Dong Riak, Eli Magok Manyol, Eng. Marko Chol Maciec, George Maker Benjamin, Bol Makueng Yuol, late Sir Ani Keueljang, late Charles Julio, who was State National Security in Rumbek, Edward Lino Wur Abyei, Dr. Amon Wantok chairman of the groups, and other various universities students, NCO's, Army officers including Dr. John Garang de Mabior. These intellectuals risked their lives because of the freedom others are enjoying today. At the same time, those who wake up and cultivate an idea have been denied not to participate effectively in their invention. The concept of NAM started as leftist, and it was so complicated across the region to be accepted readily. On June 14, 1983, Its Lieutenant Abednego Majak Barkuei and NCOs made mutiny in Malou headquarters of Rumbek Army, which has never been on the surface among the contributors in the same caused during famous Radio of the SPLM. How were the recognition criteria of those who rebelled in Bor and Ayod based, left alone those who joined without frying bullets to the enemy like Salva Kiir Mayardit? In July 1984, PSC Lieutenant Colonel Martin Makur Aleyou Mathiang was intercepted between Tonj and Wau by the recruiters coming from Bahr El Ghazal heading to Ethiopia.

He went with them, and he was sent back with the Rhino battalion under his command to recruit soldiers in Bahr El Ghazal. After the mission of recruitments! Other ill leaders within Bahr El Ghazal sent unfounded accusations against him, and he was arrested with those of Dr. Amon Wantok and Malath Joseph Lueth. He and Malath Joseph Lueth and Martin Majier Gai where their lynchings were announced over BBC on August 2, 1992. Immediately due to his military capability and Malath as a man who couldn't tolerate injustices and being Agars with such capabilities as a threat to others. Agar people are like Axe used for specific purposes. After mission accomplishment, they were through away and recalled back for the next seasons of needs; Agar defamed themselves for appreciating other leaders while they were capable more than them; thinking that someone may acknowledge their silence. So, supporting others has become an automatic of using us; nevertheless, Agar Community was set up secretly during Liberation Movement. I don't know whether they were aware because many soldiers and officers got killed by the instructions of Kuol Manyang Juuk. Those soldiers and officers deployed under Kuol's command were denied permission to see their wives or parents! One example was "Makur Awur Polic" from the currently Eastern County of Rumbek. Keeping silent has been exploited as stupidity to the point we don't glance back to protect our welfare. In addition, Mujahideen were prisoners of war in Yei 1997 while they were already condemned to death by Dr. Hassan Abdalla Al Turabi and former president Omer Hassan Al Bashier. Yet, our Rumbek Citizens were slaughtered on May 1, 1997, the same year. We never figured out the facts behind the killings of innocent people, and thousands of Mujahideen were prisoners of war. Our obstinate position always to the cause of South Sudanese has become our weakness and exploitation by current leaders and previously in the Liberation Movement. We have supported William Deng Nhial; Samuel Aru Bol turned down Joseph Lagu Yonga. Rumbek Veterans who contributed to the cause of South Sudan's independence were more than any other.

When INF OR NCP Revolutionary assumed power in Sudan, they were joined by the General of police George Kongor Arop. The massive mess of forced retirement was declared mainly against Rumbek citizens. That was done deliberately to frustrate us to join and support the Jihadist government to betray the cause of struggles like others surrounding president Kiir Mayardit. Taking advantage of our silencing may not be suitable if we are forced to address the Pretension of Nationalism, who were stomach loyalists they were cultivating at our expense. Rumbek people were and are in central of loyalty for struggles of Southerners since the beginning of 1955 and after, we were there in front whether in talking and military confrontational. We were always there with our resources and manpower capacity. Our forces have never left their colleagues on the front line, joined universities worldwide, and came back and claimed leadership positions. Our few officers surviving from Liberation were by luck; after they had been confronting many battles! Their capabilities elevated them into the position they are in now without favoritism. Agar's survival is based on liberalism and conservative politics, morals, equality, and respect. It promotes individual rights because of its rigidness of not relinquishing values like opposing Sudanese dinars and using cows for cultivation were a few examples. Agar should reverse negative attitude toward each other which others took advantages of subduing them directly or indirectly because of aggressive to ones another for nothing.

.

CHAPTER THIRTY-TWO

Unwavering Support

Unwavering support is defined as unshakable supporting, continuing supporting, persistent loyalty, and unfaltering support. Whereas wavering supporting is moving in a quivering way, faltering, weakening, and hesitating between twice possibilities of supporting and not supporting. If Agar community countdown roughly, the actual numbers of precious lives we lost within us clashes were more apparent than those killed by Nuers in 1994,1995&1997. Yet, we are not acknowledging that fact. Moreover, overlooking what kinks of leadership we are dedicated to should be an issue, which we should examine carefully who is supposed to quell the sectional feud that denigrated us. Those supporting Dr. Riek Machar were frustrated with no tangible disarmament agenda and a lack of clear direction on where our country was heading. Perhaps, we are aware that they are the same birds flying in the same direction of nepotism. As a result, we try to push the regime to change her attitudes. Agar which consists of five sections was not quickly visiting each other like before the pandemic virus of killing ourselves, and that's the events concerning us so much. Was it because those supporting different camps apart from the Mainstream party created that gap? Perhaps, neither within us lacks regime precise strategic planning toward the coexistence of our citizens across the country. Lakes State citizens are not spoilers of south Sudanese interests if they support none to their ethnicity or political affiliation, which is the basis of support, not progressive ideas, and Joseph Lagu and Joseph James Tombara were our witnesses when we were brought up in Africa and particularly Jieng Dinka styles of childhoods! Children, both boys, and girls of four years and above, are cautioned on how to sit correctly and not abuse their private parts or pooped explosive sounds in the middle of Elders are regarded as disrespect to self and prohibited. That advisable should be a role model in the political arena should kneeling downed to support a person like you to the point you opened your private to him, or she is tremendously an insult to us perhaps if politics is a dirty game, interest in prostitution! Why make unwavering support to the point of forgetting that you may be having political clashes of some issues differences at any time? In South Sudan, those killing innocent civilians protecting president Kiir Mayardit are today his opponents. Gossipers penetrate between the president and his die-hard because of a power struggle! Seriously, who was aware General Paul Malong Awan would have been rewarded with unsympathetic feelings from president Kiir Mayardit to the point he couldn't see his daughter's body, who died in Nairobi? But should unwaveringly support result in such consequences, which should be a lesson to generations that politics has no permanent friends and enemies. Therefore, we should support with conscientiousness reservation not to show the private part, which is our dignity. All clips of those supporting Salva Kiir Mayardit regarding thirty tow states are being displayed on social media to let them evaluate themselves for praising support and what direction they are in today. African leaders always exchanged supporters within ethnic lines and clans! They are leaving citizens of states in clashes while they are running their business affairs comfortably. Supporting one party unanimously because the security of the ruling party crushes other parties has significant consequences, and that's why Africa had instability in the political arena and no progress socially and economically. Competitive competition should be a role model of focusing on delivering services rather than controlling resources in pockets should leadership not fear other parties may be doable next competition. Perhaps, our politicians are not reminded of what political maneuvers they were saying previously, and none are delivering services now. Being cautious in politics promotes a democratic system in the western world; however, our leaders are wearing two uniforms simultaneously. Juntas were wearing military uniforms during the elections and another day wearing suits after rigging elections. Sometimes, they concocted that he is elected president while expressing an opinion, criticizing the types of democracy are subjected to arresting, torturing, and disappearing. Expressing opinion and criticism are potential keys like a mirror where leaders see themselves whether they are progressing or not because using a mirror in the dressing room is how you look gently or else you may change the styles you were wearing.

So, throwing unwavering support to the undemocratic government where decrees do things is uncertain. Perhaps you will be laughing stocks if he changes his mind, like in the case of thirty- two unconstitutional states in

South Sudan. Unanimously, reserving ten states indicated that the majority secretly opposed thirty tow states. If the presidency were within the decision of declaration of thirty tow states, the president would fail in reserving to ten states and therefore, the unilateral decree was Jieng Elders Council influences base on Oil Lands. Sometimes we see president Kiir Mayardit as ignorant. Unfortunately, he will decree without consulting his unwavering supporters for the sake of peace and unity of our country. One of Rumbek's citizens "Abel Akec Gum, said," it's the first time Jieng Dinka got an undescribed person in history; if you say Salva Kiir, Mayordit is useless! You may not narrates how useless he is? Then how best he is also indescribable. If you are not very cautious of your political future while working with president Kiir Mayardit may turn you into laughing stocks of southerners.

"Journalists seek clarifications on Federalism in South Sudanese new paper on Monday, June 30, 2014, say security officials have told the Media not to debate switching to federal systems of government. Briefing from Ateny Wek, Ateny said the president's priority is to restore peace in South Sudan, not debate what system of governance the country should have. Once South Sudan is at peace again, Ateny said Mr. President would support a referendum to decide what the rights system of governance should be, end the remark." That was an opinion of the president, and the majority of Dinka's were not favoring federalism when it was discussed at a table at the Equatorians conference in 2012. Again, the proposal of Dr. Riek Machar's delegation, which proposed 21 States, was also rejected by the president's delegation in Addis Ababa. So, when did federalism become the popular demand of Dinka's apart from Equatorians and Dr. Riek Machar? Suppose we read Ateny Wek's briefing carefully. How did president Kiir Mayardit become champions of federalism while instructing his spokesman to be informed the public not to debate federalism in public? President committed political Adultery to the girl who was engaged by Equatorians and Dr. Riek Machar, in other words plagiarizing the opinion of others and failing to acknowledge and cite them.

President Kiir and most Dinka's elites were not with the federal system because of the devolution of powers and equitable resources! What pushed the president was the identification of Oil Land, which they think was probably problematic for Dr. Riek Machar and Nurers followers. Now, viewing his defending thinking because he is not independent in his decision, the ministry of petroleum was given to Dr. Riek according to power-sharing; meanwhile, they were thinking of denying him that Oil is Dinka's resource, not a National one. Was it not contradicting policies or illusional thinking that almost disintegrated the country? In a sovereign state, national resources and other minerals that do not belong to communities should contract, and the conditions or communities do not determine prices. Its demand of the world consumers fixed costs, and the owners have no right to argue with buyers.

President Kiir Mayardit applied the same virus of North Sudanese thinkers where allocations of the portfolio of substances departments and lucrative were given to the Northerners like posting Ambassadors in riches countries, and critical ministerial positions were given to all so-called legitimate sons and daughters. So, who are fair sons and daughters and not honest within Southerners?

The same mentality of Northerners, which spilled Sudan into this condition, is being transferred directly or indirectly due to no inclusivity of the national Agenda except SPLM Oyee no more or less. Although resources were scarce during the Addis Ababa Accord, education and universal health care services were free during those days. Now, promises of Liberation are gone without questioning leadership, nor do they come up and explain the consequences of no free social services to our citizens.

Why? Most of the illiteracy and tribalism has become an opportunity of not knowing their right, so they get away unquestionable. If your question, you might be asked where he is coming from? Or you might be called a betrayal of the Dinkaocracy Government.

CHAPTER THIRTY-THREE

Fundamental Principles

"The SPLM a forum in which citizens shall have the right to ask their government representative where are the hospitals, the school buildings, and the road you promise to construct? The SPLM is a forum in which citizens have to report a member of the SPLA to face justices in the court of law if he has committed a crime against civilians Dr. John Garang de Mabior."

Is SPLM a forum where Southerners ask what was promised to them by their leaders during the struggle? Since they had been divided along with ethnicity, sectionalism, regionalism, and as such is a forum of many names, SPLMIG, SPLMIO, SPLMDC, and Real SPLM; all those names were causing many deaths, corruption, sectional feuds within the states, and resulted into hating one another.

What were the fundamental principles that connected revolutionaries with Martyr? are they revolutionaries if the principles of revolution are not implemented by the living ones or executed basic principles like the quotation above from Dr. John Garang? If there were not in place, then martyrs would have gone with basic principles, and current leadership betrayed those who left, and that's what we are entertaining now in South Sudan. Nothing connects Dr. John Garang's speeches with current leaders, except oyee, which they are using, as fundamental principles attracting literate majority and tribalistic associates while doing the opposite. Was Dr. John Garang lecturing something else and treating his supporters differently apart from his appropriate words to attract revolutionaries? After he was sworn as first vice president in Sudanese history of our struggle, he appointed governors placing each person differently in each state across South Sudan. After his unfortunate death, Salva Kiir Mayardit took over and changed the fundamental principles of appointees. Were they in the opposite direction in revolution principles? If not, why change those logical principles, which might have prevented too much mismanagement of resources and building a society where regions distinguish citizens not being South Sudanese?

What combined southerners were fighting Arabs with different principles not to follow if the leader gone, otherwise; why hostile to his speeches like sun and moon? And therefore, there were secretly differences in ideas. I explained thoroughly how the Movement ran parallelly after the split regarding the comfortability and vulnerability of Kiirdit supporters in Yei.

Furthermore, see more details where I quoted Garang Mabil that others were alienated in small or significant resources should be divided equally. These are facts. Those still around the president from Dr. John Garang's camp are gossipers not of being loyalists previously to Salva Kiir Mayardit. But they are surviving of gossiping of the colliding president with his real loyalist to him, like those who stood beside him in Rumbek meetings restoration 2004. When I spelled out such realities, I'm not encouraging divisions. Still, these are undeniable situations we are living in today in South Sudan, and that's why the president failed to meet his complaints against Dr. John Garang and his loyalist for whatever repeating itself, being corruption and nepotistic employment. President and his new associates died because they were trying to create a new ideology and Agenda besides what Dr. John Garang was pursuing.

On May 16, 2020, president Kiir Mayardit read this and quoted: "The SPLM/SPLA was not formed to fight for the rights of a few to positions of power and wealth." The president is not minimizing corruption within SPLM leadership because this word is called, we brought independence, or we liberated you. Despite the undeniable fact that it was collective work, it shouldn't be a license of betrayal, as the president highlighted now and then.

I was reading the Autobiography Book of Ariel Sharon while he was visiting Kenya, Uganda. I ended in the Central Africa Republic, where he met a powerful General who was fighting in 1948, 1967 &1973 for the historic independence of the Israel state. That General was implicated in embezzlements or misappropriation of funds after he realized he was likely to be punished severely! According to Ariel Sharon, he ran away, living in a miserable situation. However, that's what you are supposed to do; if you think that we suffered in the liberation struggle, as some of the footage justifies officers and soldiers bravely, consequently; you should forgive them, then there is no need to mention being ashamed. You know what you are doing. As a result, many may cease opposing you and join the club of increasing the suffering of our citizen's period.

Leaders whose common Agenda reminds citizens in his dressing occasion, quoting one word from their leader at least, as showing solidarity and sympathize, however; using the slogan of Oyee is an insult if there is nothing tangible reflecting what leader was devoting his life for.

"We don't want to repeat the experience of other countries where they use the Oil money to build a consumer society." Dr. John Garang

What are we experiencing now for the last fifteen years? As our leader didn't highlight it early yesterday, are we a consumer society? Why because they had brought independent and collided citizens across the country so that they remain vulnerable while pocketing oil money. Don't tell Dr. Riek Machar has interrupted as usually closeted! Just narrated the program of economy, universal social services, social justice, and foreign policy, to name a few that the president was having before December 15, 2013. Dr. John Garang left us with thousands of sufficient words; as a leader and real revolution committed to ideas, if there were followed at least, we wouldn't have been in this mess of suffering and setting up a regional competition and ethnicity entity that was not fundamental principles of revolutionaries. Salva Kiir Mayardit and his new associates never questioned him why all his speeches were no single one in their place? If they were supporting revolutionaries, not financial beneficiaries? Instead, friends, relatives, and lobbyists are the ones who make recommendations for reliving officials and appointments. The political Bureau is just used informally to let others believe they are in the major decision. One, for example, was dividing the country into 32 states was living testimony, rescinded back to ten states was another indication confirming that organization name is rendered in another word paralysis. Those who asked such quotation above are either marginalized within or split away using many names above for survival, otherwise, creating party name differently; citizens may think that you are crazy, as a result; you come around and maintained SPLM something.

Dr. John Garang spoke concerning weak government! Weak citizens are not productive. He asked the revolutionaries who an old man called government was. He explained the meaning of weak citizens' weak institutions should they not produce to the degree they had a surplus for exportation. It would reflect government has no sufficient funds to deliver social services. Our citizens are weak due to no peace on the ground since Salva Kiir Mayardit assumed power in 2005. South Sudanese were inter-communal clashes, should they disarm and weapons regaining back from unknown and no question where weapons were flowing into the hands of our citizens. Security personnel should know where guns are flowing. If security doesn't have control in borders, for example, then either we have not had trained personnel Security, or they are the ones rearming them back after collections.

South Sudanese intellectuals expressed warm approval to leaders who lived more than those who lost life inaction of Liberation. Still, every citizen was patriotic like farmers cultivating for purposes to feed freedom fighters for decades were not salve. What did Dr. John Gaang say regarding being a guerrilla fighter and relationship with citizens, "he said, you are like fish in the water; when water drain up eagle may pick fish up should there is no water to protect it. You are in the same conditions; you must respect them to protect you and provide you with whatever they have". Today citizens who were shields of freedom fighters are wrestling and fighting each other in Lake's state, Warrap state, and Jonglei state or have no universal health care and free education for their children as promised.

Mismanagement of diversity creates a lack of social justice, and equilibrium of distributing resources for the welfare of the whole ethnicities was the problem that led southerners to wage struggle. Failure to start from the beginning disqualified SPLM leaders, not only those of today, but since they didn't consider in the early stage, all generations would follow the same shoes that were under minding the revolutionary principles. Even if southerners were supporting SPLM leadership apart from whatever tribally, regionally, and fundamental principles of struggle are not in place, selectively corruption would have still caused suffering of our people like before the division of many names.

This country where citizens are allowed to nurture tribalism, envy toward others, deceitful toward ethnicity, and hateful speeches may surprise our uncertain future, should maximum precautions be not put in place in early stage by generations now. If you are ignoring those signs deliberately, you will be a witness to an unexpected eventuality situation!

Don't tell me we are powerful to crush those who are not submitting to Arabs would have scored victory; if it was so easy, like what some believe. Defending lies is too costive to human being life and the resources of the country. Should you ask northerners how many casualties they encounter in both men and resources for defending lies. Regime leadership divided southerners into three groups: those in government control areas, Diasporas, combined areas controlled by Movement, and refugees camp as units treating them differently. Meanwhile, those notorious for liberation struggle within government are their friends plus picking individuals within the respective states, while those who were loyalists and not notorious are their new enemies.

CHAPTER THIRTY-FOUR

President Salva Kiir, Taban Deng, and Dr. Riek

Before I deliberate on three of them, it allowed me to utter suspicion from two Paramount Chiefs of Kok sections of Rumbek East County,i.e., "Magondhoor" Majak Malok and "Yiekngekede" Mangar Maciek, during Liberation and after CPA. Their observation of the leadership of SPLM became an undeniable and educative reality. Thus, Chief Manager Maciek said early in the struggle was true conscious, tangible, and visible, which doesn't need further explanation. In the early days when southerners were almost for the referendum, the government sent intellectuals for the enlightenment of their citizens to each state to let them vote for separation. Chief Majak Malok Akot listened attentively to both lecturers and those who jumped in for comments, whereas his observation and opinion were different from commentaries of others. He deliberated his factuality and questioned the lecturers whether there is another way left behind to govern ourselves? Because SPLM leadership didn't demonstrate credible styles of leadership. Examining his points, someone may categorically misunderstand his great question. Still, he was crowned in 1953 to be the native chief before Sudan got independent, and his asking was not just a simple question. He worked with governments of colonialism, Arabs, "Anya-Anya one," and SPLM. His concern was sectionals Feud, lawlessness, and corruption. Without a positive response, consequently, we may vote for the sake of South Sudan to be a country, not because of the leaders to govern us. Mangondhoor believed that losing values of not addressing coexistence, poor leadership with corruption, and lawlessness were alarming remarks to liberation leaders.

Was Magondhoor right based on his observational folks? Our learning reading and writing are to connect us with social contextualization existing because his observational to leadership was completely irrelevant contrasted to two governments and "Anya-Anya one leaders." His consciousness questioning leadership was credible, and one of the toughest which valueless SPLM leaders do not tell me they brought independence, as usual, phenomena; if you have a country and resources are pillaged by few without rendering services, and insecurity enclosed the whole country, then you have independent with suffering citizens.

Politics has several dirties definitions that are known to us, so I may not dwell on each one for an explanation. The fascinating points might be what combined Taban and President Kiir Mayardit during the elections in 2010. Meanwhile, Mrs. Angelina Teny parallelly ran against Taban; hence, her husband was the running mate of President Kiir Mayardit. Of course, if elections were creditable, Taban would have suffered from being defeated by her. Still, her opponent won the result due to the lack of transparency and fraud in African elections. After Taban won elections with a lack of originality where he came from! The family of Monytuil never slept, whispering in the president ears to let him be removed from Governorship through its violation of the constitution to fire the elected official before the time of the defined constitutionally period. But then, the Monytuil family succeeded. Taban Deng Gai got fired, and the man changed, shifting his allegiances to his first enemy, Angelina Teny's husband. It was one of the political definitions I avoided its explanatory. That's how and where the genesis of the crisis started in our country, interestingly; the president and his associates failed to define what brought the former governor of Unity state together with Dr. Riek Machar!

Was it Nuerism or ideology where he pledged his loyalty to President Kiir Mayardit during the elections of 2010? Taban moved the so-called Garang Boys, Chol Tong Maya, and convinced Ezekiel Lol Gatkuoth from political detainees and emerged with them. He was the one who created July 8, 2016, dogs fighting in J1 to chase Dr. Riek away or kill him if it was possible. He was one selling Dr. Riek that he is a tribalist. If Taban was a nationalist, why did he intercept the former minister of petroleum to rejoin Nuerism? Again, if Taban Deng Gai was a nationalist figure, why did he apologize to the former president of Sudan that he made a mistake in the Heigeli war confrontation in 2012, blaming Dinka leadership? President Kiir has never been Baptist again to believe him and his associates, as new reborn Christians for their thinking and action. After all those confusions, he pledged his allegiance again to his first enemy, who fired him from the governorship. Taban Deng Gai sold Dr. Riek at the lowest prices of ethnicity that Riek opposed Dr. John Garang in 1991 and president Kiir Mayardit in 2013. All those catastrophic, he was with Machar. If he was not opportunistic, plus his dirty background, why was he following the wrong man twice? President created enemies within his political party.

They joined Dr. Riek and repurchased them by appointing them, for example, Himself Taban, Dr. Dhieu Mathok, Chol Tong Maya, Dau Aturjong, and others were switching with highly hope they may get their share.

However, this time around may not be easy to repurchase rivals because of the systems where appointments and governing our resources by ethnic groups and clannism had destroyed the image of our country. Those who opted for the SPLM party are not opportunistic and are looking for green pastures, as always from Kiir associates. Meanwhile, the president is not giving them the poison of being supporters. Three of them are on the same page regarding erratic behaviors. In 2004 Salva Kiir Mayardit staged a coup against Dr. John Garang for the following reasons, tribalism, nepotism, and difficult corruption to be eradicated. The same now in his administration even MPs are in the president's pocket rather than answerable to their constituency problems.

What is new now in his fifteen years in the office to the above? He degenerated his die-hard supporters that they were consumers, not severing leaders, and yet appointed them in rotating manners from ministry to ministry. He promised southerners during the difficulties of CPA implementation that I may not back you again into a refugee camp. However, he promised southerners that he might not return them to refugee's life, yet he dishonest his words by coining unfounded documents to prove the coup allegations. These obnoxious attitudes were/are destroying social fabrication because of using ethnic violence against each southerner for survival leadership and party. Hence, he disregarded his word and provoked the situation by touring Bahr el Ghazal states after dissolving cabinets entirely and installed in new cabinets mobilizing his supporters for 2013, and lying there was a coup. Likewise, Taban Deng Gai follows Dr. Riek Machar in horrific disastrous twice meanwhile trying to distance himself from him. He said over the BBC in 2014 that dictator President Salva Kiir Mayardit in an opening prison guards South Sudanese. Still, he is around a dictator now, milking resources with a dictator.

With the same equation and notion, Dr. Riek Machar complained the leadership had lost vision because of corruption, nepotism, and tribalism.

Again, his formation of current cabinets proved his allegation that he was lying to his supporters. Southerners should remain vigilant because we shouldn't be feeling SPLM leaders have won citizens like prisoners of war, country, and resources like equipment captured in operations zone to the point they killed who and left who for their mercy. When I came across those who said they support President on social media, I wondered what do they support his personality or system? A system where ethnicity and sectional groups were guarding resources and others were alienated, and the president is for all? Even if Salva Kiir Mayardit appointed Jesus Christ to take care of our resources, and the law of misappropriation of funds is not applied orderly, leave alone appointing the foreigners there. Would be nothing unless the country's sovereign law is belligerently and appropriately used against corrupted individuals.

Furthermore, since the president had five vices and recently the government was a coalition, he should involve parties in a revitalized peace agreement to design and pass a formula resolution to the August House for deliberation. This August House body will incorporate the law in an article related to severe punishment for those who may not comply with the law passed by the August House. But making decrees for collecting fire army failed several times because of lack of technical knowledge of doing it, using it as something you are getting prestigious met many catastrophic, and you are part of arming other section against section. Salva Kiir Mayardit is a security personality trained to inflict severe pain and suffering and manufacture lies like lying.

There was a coup without a single paper caught. That made the wall supporting the SPLM Party many cracks. Leaving and coming back are signals of something wrong within the leadership.

CHAPTER THIRTY-FIVE

Leaders by Coincidence

Indescribable leaders came accidentally into power in developed nations and less developed countries. Donald Trump and Salva Kiir Mayardit coincidentally fried two influential leaders in one day; James Comey, the director of the FBI, and Paul Malong Awan, General Chief of Staff in South Sudan Army Forces, on May 9, 2017, and repeating simultaneously reckless addresses which cause insidious in Capitol Hill on January 6, 2021, and another sending signal of brutality within South Sudanese in Jonglei state peace conference January 23, 2021. But the only differences were that; what happened in America was condemned by GOP, whereas the ruling party in South Sudan was enjoying as if paranoid leader said precisely as they wished. White supremacist ideologies were the same as ethnicity identification policies in Africa, what Americans witnessed in the Trump era, and what Africans endured for thousands of decades. The incitement addressed, followed by brutality in Capitol Hill, was finally nailing the democratic system and free licensing to the dictators of the developing countries. While I was contrasting two's Principals, American politics domestically and internationally may not be the same again because what we witnessed shocked the world community looking for democracy.

The sentiment of the liberation struggle brought southerners together twice. However, policies of ethnicity identity disintegrated them twice also because of the failure not to address ethnicity identification which destroyed Regional Autonomous in 1983. Though the Khartoum regime was used merely as a point of dishonoring the Addis Ababa Accord, ethnicity policies were the primary cause for dismantling the Accord. What brought southerners again to fight back against the common enemy, as southerners not based on ethnicities, but then; it seemed divisive, or ethnicity identity was repeating itself among the SPLM leadership. Southerners or SPLM leaders failed to address what made them to struggles for decades, the reasons for polarizing the regional Autonomous, and how we overcame grievances to fight Khartoum elites back. After finding the root causes, the country's constitution should be based on previous polarizations between southerners and

Khartoum elites and how we destroyed the High Executive Council not to surface again. Southerners are easy to unite for everyday purposes and quickly slide back practices of identity majority policies. The brutality of Anya-Anya tow caused by the ideology of separation and unity, in other words, hijacking of power from them, and fueled again by spilt of the Nasir faction! Since then, southerners had never witnessed peaceful coexistences.

Belligerent and distinguishing policies of Upper Nile minority ethnic may be repeating the Addis Ababa scenario of the South Sudan state collapsing if it is not addressed correctly. Elements within Upper Nile may dispute my point, but the history of your behaviors justifies my objective point. If cancer is in one part of the body is likely to poison the whole body quickly, but you may say Lake's state and Warrap are on the same foot of killing each other, which is undeniable. But then, we have not reached the point of rejecting appointed government officials like yours.

Moreover, no section calls the government to intervene to help the other side, which is different between ours and yours. This game between ethnicity elements within Bahr El Ghazal and Upper Nile elements politicizing solvable issues by Chiefs and Elders across the country is derision because generally, Bahr El Ghazala's are not bringing up their kids for sacrificing them over grievances of Upper Nile people's game.

We had sacrificed our recruits from Bahr El Ghazal because of the problems created by Dr. John Garang, who didn't want to be under somebody. Meanwhile, Anya-Anya two were in Bush for ten years, and most of them were from Upper Nile waiting to sacrifice Bahr el Ghazal citizens. Its Upper Nile ethnicity groups created the 2013 genesis crisis, pushing Nurers into door-to-door killings. Upper Nile has an intimidating and threatening information minister who's too arrogant to sacrifice Bahr El Ghazal youths more than them if you deny political neighborhood with Chollo and other ethnicities. At the same time, you are not sure who may be wearing Salva Kiir's Mayordit shoe after he may be political suicide. How do you miss the formula of Abel Alier Kuai's peaceful neighborhood among upper Nile citizens? Dr. John Garang, and currently Mabior John Garang, is trying his political margin closeness of its neighboring citizens of Upper Nile, which gave them an opportunity to dominate the High Executive Council twice previously and SPLM during the Liberation? When was Salva serving in Upper Nile as a security officer for specific years? Was he aware Pandang and their neighbors were misunderstandings who belongs to Malakal Town and its borders and who doesn't? If not? Why are Padang and other ethnicities subjecting themselves to the hottest miscalculation of their political future? You should have been reviewing the previous political survival of the Upper Nile with their neighbors before the president interfered in solving grievances peacefully like Ismail Al-Azhari, Sudan's President, who created many problems and left them unresolved till South Sudan broke away. If Ismail Al-Azhari is coming back now, and he wouldn't believe how badly the foundation of his administration disintegrated Sudan. Padang Leaders and their youths failed not to question the president's administration for the suffering of their citizens in Oil areas because of inadequate environmental safety, which should be the main reason for their concern, instead of creating mistrust within their neighborhoods. Consolidating a community of peaceful coexistences should be the best option within your regions before you trust the outlying area of a president who failed to reduce peace within his region. Previous Sudanese leadership Behaviors should be a lesson to southerners not to tear themselves apart unless we don't understand the consequences of their leadership. Southerners shouldn't create delusional assumptions like the so call Arabs who made disastrous to their absent generations when former president Omer El Bashier took overpower and declared suicidal Jihad, which resulted in untold casualties for both resources and men without prevailing victory against marginalized people except surprisingly witnessing releasing thousands of Mujahideen prisoners of war by SPLM. But then, those born while El Bashier was president overthrew his government, because of concocted lies for decades, couldn't convince the present generations. We shouldn't create many issues for unborn generations to confront each other for unfound lies. These people of the Upper Nile had been coexistence for thousands of years before president Kiir Mayardit became mischievous about his political survival. Because of President Kiir, Padang of Upper Nile should not spoil their relationship with neighbors, whether Chollo or Nuers. Even if we rewind his age to continue ruling, he will still be unsympathetic to you for long, like Paul Malong Awan. This is a tip to those who have ambitions to be president and competitive competition with other regions; if you disregard it, forget about sitting in J1.

Accepting the truths is difficult for generations born outside South Sudan, nor studies the genesis of Sudan conflicts believed everything should be resolved through the threatening of their father, Michael Makuei Lueth. His name never surfaced among the famous commanders in operations during struggles. Their youths are so desperate to strip naked Mading Aweil citizens where Mathiang Anyoor came to rescue them, and yet brushing aside funeral clips of president Kiir to them. However, they are toxic of create many enemies. Again, remember where is General Paul Malong Awan now? Is negotiating with the government he was defending vigorously for four years how they fooled apart with president Kiir Mayardit. Nobody is sure what may happen in other centuries after president Kiir Mayardit if present grievances are not satisfactorily resolved across the country! Remember Yugoslav ethnic conflicts and the Soviet Union led to the collapsing of both empires because of mismanagement of diversity where leadership collaborated with other ethnic and undermined the values of coexistence. The geographical structure of South Sudan should be alarming for southerners to let them remain harmonious because of the Nile and ethnic grievances conflicts could quickly disintegrate our country. If SPLM Leadership doesn't overhaul the attitude of no transparency, accountability, and justice for all are not addressed professionally, the future of our country may be in jeopardy. Ultimately, nurturing and demanding Administrative Areas in every area in Upper Nile are symptoms of declining South Sudan statehoods. Specific southerners will be responsible for South Sudan collapsing like a regional autonomous because those administrative and many states without equitable distribution of wealth and devolution of powers stated clearly by the constitution are dead-ending and delusional demands which could lead to the collapsing of the Country instantly.

CONCLUSIONS AND REMARKS

When other people who do not follow their cultural foundation properly from their ancestors present one and are proud of them, they cut short and conclude that their ancestors' cultures, norms, and dignities are backward. Therefore, they adopted the westerner's environments. But Dr. Francis Mading Deng and I could not believe in an environment where we denied Dinka rich cultures and prepared Western ones. Dr. Francis elaborated a fantastic point, which Dinka's believe. "Immortality through posterity is one of the foundations of Dinka cultural continuity. The better the dead are remembered and represented, the more conditions remain as they left them, and vice versa. For to abundant tradition would mean denying the ancestors' existence and their contributions to the culture of their progeny. But, while the Dinka believe that the dead ceases to exist organically (making some allowance for the bones), they seem to believe in some form of spiritual existence. The dead continues to communicate demands to the living through dreams or divination. If these are not met, they may punish the living to death. In addition, to communicate supposedly initiated by the dead, the Dinka pray to their dead to beg God, lesser deities, or other dead to forgive their wrongs and stop being whimsical against man." (Dr.

Francis Mading Deng: The Dinka of the Sudan page 11.) "God also said to Moses. Thus you shall say to the Israelites, "The Lord, the God of your ancestors, God of Abraham, the God of Isaac, and the God of Jacob, has sent me to you: This is my name forever, and this my title for all generations" (Exodus 3:15) These illustration made by the author to Dinka have no different to the verse above which Almighty God told Moses to convinced the Israelites that it is God of their ancestors who sent him. Dinka glorified God in the form of their ancestor's God, whereas Dengdit or Garangdit (stands for Christ or Jesus) is called for healing and prosperity for living people. But to oversight (Dengdit or, Garangdit), Dinka terminology (to Jesus Christ) is betraying their ancestor's beliefs. However, connecting dots of glorifying Him are the same; no one is superior to other. God is neutral to the ways of worshipping; He is not very specific to the one glorification should His ears are opened to all languages of human beings around the globe. We tried to joke about Isaiah's prophecy about us, but there was no evidence to defend our original connection; our minds were manipulated with false teaching and where the Bible originated. However, look at the two rivers watering the Garden of Eden that pass through (The land of Kuc) present Sudan. I touch on social similarities based on Biblically facts between Nilotic and the Israelites, specifically the Dinka's of the Republic of South Sudan. Do spiritual leaders jump to the conclusion of paradise and hell to those who question Western evangelists?

Why they should not believe in our way, God will judge us according to our relationship with Him, others may be committed Christian fleshly or false, but nobody knows their hearts, except God himself; he's a lamp of the spirit in you me.

After God created human beings, He gave Adam the responsibility for whatever was in the Garden of Eden to use for his benefit. He named them according to the way we knew them, and this is where other individuals like me differ from evolutionists because their findings had no better conclusion of who had named each thing. Another important issue is the question of segregation, where others think they have the lion's share with God, whereas others are not an important element to God was an illusion. Questions of why we differ in races have been defined in a way that has nothing justified Biblically; Not only that, but an attempt had also been made during the Second World War, where ill elements tried to reject the blood of black men as it should not be given to the white men. However, there was no proof of any differences. Also, wealth is from God, who provides the ability to use it for the welfare of others. Still, we will pay the price if we use it arrogantly, like prostituting ourselves with girls or engaging with someone's wife without reasonable cause. The evil spirit is not separated from us; it is an act in our daily life. The moment we act maliciously that is an act of evil within us; you can reference back to see how Eve acts (Genesis Chapter three). Her spirit tempted her and answered her spirit because the fruits pleased her eyes, and her desire accepted to act by eating the Fruit of Knowledge of Good and Evil. When one tries to adjust to the Creator's way, those adjustments have tangible stories in the Bible, such as his first Dictator, Nimrod, who turned the people away from God, which had consequences for Africans. Otherwise,

Africans would not be behind now in terms of industrialism, technology, etc. Check Isaiah (Chapter forty-three) and think about why God had paid the African descendants as a ransom for the sake of the Israelites. Again, those who inhabited Sodom and Gomorrah were destroyed because some individuals felt that having sexual relationships with three angles guys would make them happy, like how we are entertaining one another now in western societies. So readjusting norms and cultural life under the theme of freedom have consequences because if the Creator allowed you to become world police and use the power arrogantly, you would pay the price in any time frame. The facts of these statements are clearly stated like this: "Therefore, thus says the Lord concerning the king of Assyria: he shall not come into this city, shoot an arrow there, come before it with a shield, or cast up a siege ramp against it. He shall return by the way he came; he shall not come into this city, says the Lord. For I will defend this city to save it for my own sake and the sake of my servant David." (2kings 19, 32, 33, and 34) Think deeply, why have archeologists always gone to Africa and South Asia for verification evidence of previous centuries, while their descendants are not able to do that? It is because those living in those areas have mishandled the power at that time, and God eliminated certain generations. "That very night, the angel of the Lord set out and struck down one hundred eighty-five thousand in the camp of the Assyrians; when morning dawned, they were all dead bodies." The seven nations were powerful to the point everyone had feared them, but the Almighty God had rooted them out. Although some remnants are still here and there, they are powerless. Those who require much knowledge and advanced technology should not think like that, and they can readjust the social norms of legalizing nasty things.

Amongst the Third World leaders, power is recycling. Open your heart to receive it; it is time we should kneel to repent so that He will glance at us. Power and wealth are tests of any selected nation by God. If one feels much pride, one will receive the opposite in different forms.

Something good does not come quickly; it needs patience and a humble heart. To those spiritual leaders who sympathize with Westerners because of money, you may be accepting legalizing abortion the same-sex marriages under the theme of freedom that the pastor will be accountable to his soul. We do not want to be on any other mistake like what Nimrod did previously, where our grandparents had created the most visibly important things until today with great loss because of pride. For those of you who think that they are poor, we are not poor, but what affected us was singing it with their leaders, especially in churches where most Christian believe that they are poor, and yet they do not know that they have agreed with the enemy to take advantage of them. Underrating our abilities, both enemies—evil spirits and colonizers—have inflected serious defeat to us because we have already given up not determining the ability we have. Nobody should take advantage with regards to the Bible because those who assumed that the text belonged to them had failed the principal tests of the Bible. The text has nothing to do with colors; it is about who obeys the principles, in other words; to fear the existence of Him. Of course, building churches was the main goal of the rainmakers. I think they were so blessed, but after confusion between the traditional ways and Christianity, our population failed in a confusing situation where they remained vulnerable to each other. Neither has been served properly by so-called Christianity nor continues with their previous life mentioned by archeologists as a sense of their worshipping. There was no contradiction between them and the archeologists finding what Christian's practice today. What they were practicing never made the Creator angry with them, like the attempt in Sodom and Gomorrah, which brought them to total elimination. Also, readjusting marriages into same-sex marriages was not practiced by idol worshippers but rather by those who believed in resurrection and paradise. Those who got their fate in Sodom and Gomorrah were not a polygamist. However, they were committing the crime of today's society in the Western world. If having more than one wife puts people to hell, then those of Moses, Abraham, and the rest had already gone to hell because of having more than one wife. But I believe they are in paradise; otherwise, the blessings we are proud of today are not a blessing to someone in hell. If Westerners disagree with me that those of Sodom and Gomorrah did not go to hell because of what they had done, then the Bible will not make sense in our life. In the Good News (November-December 2009), Melvin Rhodes wrote these: "Darwin's theory did not just alter political thinking, contributing to fascism, communism, and two world wars. It also changed the thinking of huge numbers of people within Western societies. Values based on centuries of Judeo-Christian teaching on the sanctity of marriage and human life, in general, began to erode. Darwin's theory did not just provide an alternative explanation to the biblical account of creation. It effectively led to doubts about everything in the Bible, including the moral laws. Today, many in the West view marriage as a quaint but outdated custom. At the same time, the idea of fidelity and sexual commitment to one partner for life is held by only a small minority. In the minds of many, sex is solely for pleasure, and children are an inconvenience.

Without realizing it, one of the inevitable consequences of Darwinism is a genuine threat to the very existence of the western European peoples who have embraced his teaching." The indigenous peoples of the seven nations paid their ultimate price when they introduced their gods rather than obeying the real God. Now, it is turned to our brothers who had introduced the styles of denying the existence of God and recognized same-sex marriages. But they may be safe because some individuals were conscious to dismisses the theories of evolution discussed above. What I'm trying to explain here is not because I'm defending polygon at this time to be legalized, but it should not be condemned as sins, whereas the actual sins are not condemned. Harboring sins among you and attacking innocent polygamists because they are practicing the legitimacy law of God will not yield the real resurrection and paradise within the Western society because Creator had known the fact beyond our imagination and thinking. Let us advise the interest groups to make sure that they can render the best services to their spouses because we have challenges where the number of girls is too much than boys. If the girl agreed to share husbands, that's much better than being a client to anybody looking for a warm night. The Babylonian state, Assyrian state, and Egyptian Pharaoh's state lost power and wealth because many words were the order of the day, like what our brothers and sisters are doing nowadays in the Western world. When social intercourse loses the creditable logic of using it according to the well-known procedures of producing human beings, another essential climate will harm people because of missing proper directions (De Ciek, Creator Madhuol). All those above were my conscious predictions before I got clues about who wrote the Bible! Thanks to indigenous African Nana Banchie Darkwah Ph.D. for his tremendous revelation and surprise to Jewish and Europeans Scholars.

Copyrights References': New Revised Standard Version Bible 1989, Holy Bible King James Version 2003 by Thomas Nelson, and the Teen Devotional Bible, New International Bible 1973, 1984 by International Bible Society, Other sources were first Fruits, God's Plan for Your success by Dr. James C. Hash, Sr, and Spiritual Leadership: Principles of Excellence for Every Bel, therefore ever by J. Oswald Sanders. The Dinka of the Sudan by Dr. Francis Mading Deng Majok, and finally African Economic Development, Edited by Emmanuel Nnadoize.

Nirmod picture the son pf Cush (kuc in Dinka Agar) is available online, also Hagar who is spelled Agar in Latin is online.

The Africans Who Wrote the Bible: Ancient Secrets Africa and Christianity have never Told.

NANA BANCHIE DARKWAH, Ph.D.